Us, Against Fate

by

Cathrine Goldstein

Us, Against Fate

Contact Information: info@thewildrosepress.com

Cover Art by *The Wild Rose Press, Inc.*

The Wild Rose Press, Inc.
PO Box 708
Adams Basin, NY 14410-0708
Visit us at www.thewildrosepress.com

Publishing History
First Edition, 2025
Trade Paperback ISBN 978-1-5092-5794-2
Digital ISBN 978-1-5092-5795-9

Published in the United States of America

Dedication

As always, for Jay, Penelope, and Pickle. I love you.

We are all born with a unique destiny.
A "blueprint" of our lives.
The lucky ones are those who are ignorant of their fate,
and spend their lives chasing the unknown inevitable.
The unlucky ones are the two who are marked.
One as masculine.
One as feminine.
For they alone can save the world.

–Joshua Cadman

Prologue

Josh

"Turn here." I direct Dad to take a turn down a streetlight-less, long, winding road on the outskirts of yet another small town in the middle of nowhere. It's creeping into the dead hours of night just before early morning, but we're not tired. We tell each other it's because we've taken turns driving and both gotten a good amount of sleep on this track from the South northward, but who's shitting whom? Neither one of us has slept a wink, and rolling into a new town makes our nerves on edge.

Especially this town. Especially now.

The cold, wet, late-March air sits heavily over the town, isolating it and making it look like a scene straight out of a horror movie. I sigh as the sleepy little downtown, complete with a discount food store and a Shakes 'n' Slaw, fades away, far behind us. It's all the same. Over and over.

Another new town. Another almost new beginning.

Another step closer to the end.

"This one?" Dad raises his eyebrows doubtfully but yanks hard on the steering wheel of Ol' Sally and takes the turn anyway.

There's a thud behind us, and we both start. It's ridiculous, of course, but we're anxious, and whenever we relocate, even though I'm eighteen years old and a grown man, he has some kind of "fatherly paranoia" kick into high gear. It'll eventually cool a week or two after we arrive, but while it's here, and he's flying his freak flag, I get caught up in it. I glimpse his fists tight on the wheel.

Turning, I check the flatbed, but everything—the bags and boxes that hold all our worldly possessions condensed and crammed into the back of our old pickup and our dining table I insist on taking everywhere we go—looks okay. I turn back, pushing up the sleeves of my army jacket, and place fingers on my temples. I rub away the dull pain collecting just above my cheekbones and radiating behind my eyes.

"Headache?" Dad turns to me, and his dark eyes flash with concern.

"Nope." As promised, the headaches are becoming more frequent and are getting worse, but I try not to show it. Violent, shooting pains crash through my head like my very own internal and unrelenting lightning storm, and my vision is altered—sometimes to the point of blindness. But this headache isn't one of them. I can tell because it isn't sitting in my gut, making my stomach tighten like a damned vise. One of my spiritual guides once told us that these smaller, *nuisance headaches,* as he called them, were because I was conflicted. I didn't fully accept who I was. Well, hell, no. I don't fully accept it. I don't even fully *understand* it. How the hell do I accept something I don't get?

"You got a feeling it's this way, huh?" Dad shifts his weight behind the wheel, sitting taller. As we travel down the deserted road, the overgrowth of the trees smacks against the windshield and sides of the truck. It's like being in a medieval torture chamber that doubles as a carwash.

I hold up my phone. "No feeling. Using an app."

Dad chuckles, and I smirk. We've been on the move my whole life, following my instincts, chasing my destiny; we have to find humor in everything we can.

A branch falls across the hood of the truck. "Damn it," Dad mutters. "Damn, damn, damn it all. That's all we need now. Damn it." The branch isn't big enough to elicit this response, and we can restore the dent with no problem, but that's not the point. He's venting.

We drive a few more feet, and the darkness and overgrowth lead to a gravel driveway that reveals a picturesque, a word I've recently picked up, little house we've just purchased. Buy and sell houses. That's another thing we do that makes no sense. We should just rent and move on, but I press to buy the houses because I want every place we go to be the right one.

And at the same time, I don't.

I wince and rub my temples again as another sharp pain shoots behind my right eye. The one with the slightly drooping eyelid. I take a deep breath, and the pain passes. Oh well, the houses we buy always end up making us a few bucks. We move so often we don't bother unpacking some of the few possessions we own, like Mom's papers from college and her collection of colorful wigs that Dad refuses to part with. Even though she's been gone for eighteen years.

Normal, we're not. We both know our life would be considered absurd to most people and yet, ironically, people are the sole reason I exist.

The very people who would shun me are the ones I'm here to save.

Supposedly.

But I can't do it alone. I need my other half. And that's why we're here. I've been wrong before, but there's something nagging in my gut that's telling me this time is for real. She's here. I'm certain of it. I have to be.

I just hope she's ready.

Chapter One

Gracie

Pushing through the sea of kids, I clutch my books to my chest, making my way to my locker. I just about choke on the musty smell of last-semester-senior-year-in-high-school: too much cheap cologne and not enough soap. But I'm not one to talk. Showers have become a definite luxury. Between last night's shift of grilling cheap make-believe-beef dogs and cleaning up Mom's puke—I reek. I passed out on our uncomfortable couch around three a.m. and could barely force my eyes open when the alarm went off at seven. All I had time for was to make Mom her dried toast and plain tea and to kiss her turbaned head before I dashed out the door. I turn the corner toward Senior Hallway and—

"Watch it!"

One of the boys from the rugby team bumps into me, and my worn-out blue binder, the one I've carried since freshman year, lands with a thud. Loose papers glide off everywhere.

FML.

"Pull it together, Gracie…" Mumbling, I squat down to gather my things. First bell rings as I grab my papers and jam them into one wrinkled mess. Standing again, I hold my papers to my chest. I can't bear to assess the damage, but I can't be late for bio again, either. Gibbons hates me, and I need his class to graduate. That means I have to show up. There's no way I've come all this way to drop out now. The last time I was late, Gibbons threatened an afterschool detention, although he, as well as every other teacher in this school, knows I can't possibly be detained after school. Ever.

Second bell rings, and a wave of kids passes right by me. This time, someone just brushes against me, but I still lose my balance.

"Hey!" I glare at him.

"Oh, uh, sorry." He's short with glasses and skinny jeans, and he seems shocked that I'm here. In this school. Even though we've been in class together since preschool. But he, like everyone else, keeps going.

Crap. There are more papers scattered across the hallway. I'm being careless because I'm exhausted, and my mind is still on last night. Who was that guy in the old army green jacket sitting on the bench outside the Shakes 'n' Slaw for half my shift yesterday? Yeah, from a distance, he was cute with the vintage jacket and longish locs…but so are lots of serial killers—cute, that is.

With my back to my locker, I squat down again and start to pick up the rest of my papers from the floor. A few kids pass by, but no one bothers to help me. No one even asks, "Hey, Gracie. How's it going?"

It's not like I expect them to really care or anything. It would just be nice to hear it once in a while. Standing up, I run a hand through my dirty-blonde hair—adjectives that once described its color now describe its condition.

"Get it together, Gracie…" I mumble like it's my mantra. Around me, kids disappear as quickly as they came, which means I've only got a couple of minutes to make it to class. *If* I go to class. As I stand there debating, I spot more of my papers wedged under the lockers. Is that…? *Shit*. My bio paper. Reaching out with the toe of my filthy black high top, I slide the paper to me and then scoop it up, trying to smooth the wrinkles.

Why the hell am I bothering? The freaking paper has a giant coffee stain smack in the middle of the title page. I glance at it. That coffee stain, it's the color of the dark circles under Mom's eyes this morning. They weren't just dark. They were also kind of bumpy—like turtle skin. I've got to remember to look that up later to see if turtle skin under-eyes are a normal side effect of chemo. But what's normal when you're seventeen and dealing with chemo and breast cancer all alone?

The last of the doors to the classrooms slam with a dull thud, and I peer up and down the empty hallway that leads to biology. The hallway would be dark if it wasn't for the blinding yellowness of the lockers. Dead ahead, at the end of the long corridor, are the red doors leading to the courtyard with the single broken lunch bench…and…freedom. My legs start tingling, no, more like zapping—as if someone has a voodoo doll of me they're stabbing with pins and needles. I shake my head. Voodoo doll. Ludicrous. For someone to have a voodoo doll of me, it would mean someone, somewhere, would have to know I exist.

My legs are feeling antsy. They want to run, and so does the rest of me. Do I really need to deal with Gibbons today or hear anything more about the human body? The things I could tell him—about medicine and side effects and what they do to the inner organs, drug interactions, and how tumors can literally burst through the skin before your very eyes—well, it's all too real for him.

The last seconds of my two-minute grace period are ticking by. Screw it. Who needs it? I can afford an absence. I'm skeeved out just thinking of Gibbons and the way he looks at me with that stupid smug expression on his face—the way he lifts his clean-shaven chin to glance down his skinny nose. He doesn't buy me or my life. There's no way one stupid kid could do everything I claim to do—work a full-time job as the manager at the Shakes 'n' Slaw while caring for my sick mother, running a household, and finishing school. It's impossible.

Some days, when I'm home with Mom, I expect Gibbons to come peer in the window, trying to catch me having sex and smoking weed with my boyfriend or something. Well, joke's on you, Gibbons. I don't have a boyfriend, I don't plan on ever having sex again, and the smell of pot from the medicinal weed Mom smoked about a year ago when she could still stomach it turned me off drugs forever. To me, weed equals death.

That's it. I need a break, which means I need to get the hell out of here. Bending down to grab a lone pencil off the floor, I shift my weight from one knee to the other and—crap! My frayed jeans rip clear across the knee.

"Oh, come on," I mutter to myself. Could anything else go wrong today?

Suddenly, the glare of the neon lights dulls, and I'm in a shadow.

"Hey, baby."

I tilt my head upward and then drop it down fast, shoving a few more stray papers into a haphazard pile. Shit. It's the gang of bougie assholes who torments our school. They hardly ever get caught, and on those rare occasions they do, their parents—who are still pissed off about their mini-mansions getting rezoned and their sons getting bussed to our crappy school—make a stink and buy a shitload of new athletic equipment to make it all go away.

I close my eyes. *Please go away. Please go away.* I open them again and will my shaking hands to stop trembling.

"I know you." The lead boy squats down next to me.

I know them, too. They call each other by color. Their rep says the color corresponds to the number of times they've gotten laid—by force. This one—the redhead with horrible skin—is Black. Like a black belt. The other members of his group are Brown, Red, Green, and Yellow, in order of relevance and ranking. My shaking intensifies, and everything from my thighs to my jaw quivers.

Black reaches forward and places a hand on my shoulder. I flinch, yanking my shoulder away, daring a glimpse upward. Shit. The whole group of them is standing there, chuckling. Black cranes his head like an ostrich, so we're face to face. He's wearing a dopey grin.

"You hang with Janette and those girls from the track team."

Track team? I shake my head. Obviously, he's remembering me from Shakes 'n' Slaw, but I'm sure as hell not going to remind him of that.

"No track team?" He taps his middle finger to his chin like he's pondering world peace, licking his lips as he does.

I gaze from boy to boy. My thighs burn from holding this position, but I'm too terrified to stand.

"What, are you mute, too?" He leans forward, resting on his knee, making ridiculous hand gestures as he speaks slowly and loudly. "Or only fucking deaf?"

I glance down at my papers and back to him, fighting to keep the fear from my eyes. With five of them it would only take a minute for them to haul me into the boys' bathroom and…

He laughs, turning his head to look up at his friends. The way he looks at them makes my gut ache—like I've eaten whole peach pits that are ricocheting off the lining of my intestines.

"Let's see if the scummy, deaf-mute can understand." He takes his forefinger and slides it in and out of his fisted opposite hand. He repeats the action, grunting as he does. Sweat rolls down my back.

Shaking my head, I crawl backward. This can't happen. I don't have time to be a victim. I clutch at my throat. It's too tight to scream. Maybe if I can force my mouth open and eke out something, someone will hear.

"I—"

THUD.

A beaten-up black motorcycle boot appears in my line of vision. I glance up quickly, shielding my eyes from the glare of the overhead fluorescent lights to see the boot is attached to a boy.

"Leave her alone." His voice is deep and authoritative.

"Hey, asshole, get your own girl." Black scowls and then looks at me. He reaches out and takes a lock of my hair. He twists it around his finger. "This one's mine." He tugs. Hard.

"Ow!"

Flailing, I try to get away, but Black grabs my wrist and pulls me until I'm mere inches from him. We're face to face, so close, I can see the whiteheads on his pimples.

His breath smells like day-old salami.

"I said, leave her alone." The boy's large hand comes down on Black's shoulder and grasps his denim jacket. Black looks stunned as he releases my wrist and is pulled to his feet.

I stare up at them, too terrified to move.

"Mind your own fucking business." Black breaks free and pushes the boy's shoulder, but he might as well be trying to move a mountain. The guy's tall—taller than me, with wide shoulders, dark skin, and locs. Even the guys on our wrestling team aren't built like this. Still, no matter how big this boy is, it would be one on five. There's no way he can win this.

Black drops his chin and snarls at the new guy. "I don't think you understand the rules around here. We do whatever the fuck we want, and *whoever* the fuck we want, and no one says shit about it. Got it?"

He pokes the new guy with his finger, but New Guy doesn't flinch. He repeats the action, and New Guy still doesn't move.

Black looks over his shoulder at his gang and back to New Guy. "What? You too scared to fight back?" He laughs, and his gang laughs with him.

"I'm not scared of you. Not in the least."

New Guy takes a step closer to Black, and my already fast heartbeat takes off in a sprint.

"What I want," New Guy continues, "is for you to let her go and to stay the hell away from her."

"Not gonna happen." Black licks his liver lips and raises an orange-colored eyebrow that's covered in white flakes.

"Yes, it will." New Guy crosses his strong arms in front of his chest. "Just walk away."

"Or what?" Black is in New Guy's space now, craning his neck like a rooster about to crow just so he can look New Guy in the eye. "Why should I?"

"Because it's the right thing to do."

Black lets out a blood-chilling laugh. "You think I give a fuck about the right thing to do?"

I want to crawl away, but I can't leave this poor guy here. Not after he came to help me.

"I think you should," New Guy tells Black.

"And I think you should mind your own fucking business."

Black punches New Guy in the gut. He's so fast, I don't even see it happen, but I piece it together when New Guy doubles over at the waist.

"Now you gonna think about minding your own fucking business?" Black snarls.

He punches him again, and New Guy falls to one knee. New Guy grimaces, and his shoulders rise up and down.

Black chuckles. "Look how easy it is to make a mountain fall!" He howls as the other boys descend on New Guy, pushing him down onto his back.

They take turns kicking and punching him mercilessly, but New Guy doesn't fight back. He simply covers his face and turns to his side. Crawling backward, I press myself against a locker, frozen. I should run and get help, but my legs won't obey.

"No." My word's a squeak so no one hears me. "No!" I say louder, but the beating continues. My gut aches with every punch he takes for me.

Then he turns toward me and tries to open a swollen eye. "Run."

I shake my head.

“Run!” he says, using what must be the last ounce of his strength.

I nod and force myself to my feet. Taking off down the hall, I sprint as fast as I can toward Gibbons’ class and burst through the door. “Fight!” I scream, panting.

Everyone in class turns to look at me, and Gibbons glares. A couple of the girls giggle behind laptops. They’re probably laughing at my hot mess of filthy hair, stained clothes, and rumpled books and papers.

“There’s a fight.” I clutch my binder tight to my chest, wishing I could shrink into myself. But no. I stand taller as my books shake in my trembling arms. I have to help this poor guy who rescued me from… God knows what. I thumb the hallway behind me. “Y—you have to help. Please.” I’m shaking so hard my words come out like yelps.

Gibbons leaves the smartboard and walks to the closet way too slowly.

“You have to hurry, please.”

He turns to me sharply. “I don’t have to do anything, Ms. Jackson.” He wrinkles his nose like he’s just tasted bad cheese.

“But they’re hurting him.”

“Who?”

“Black and his gang. They’re…they’re hurting some new guy in the hallway.”

Gibbons opens the door to the closet and reaches in. It feels like hours are ticking by. Finally, he pulls out an aluminum bat.

“Please, hurry.” I stand by the door, ready to follow him out.

Gibbons steps into the hallway, and I pass him, rushing ahead.

I wave him on. “They’re over here. Senior hallway. I was at my locker.” A couple of the kids carrying phones follow Gibbons, probably to catch the fight on video, but thankfully, most stay back in the classroom. “They’re he—” I turn the corner to the hallway, but they’re gone. Spinning in a circle, I look for any proof that there was a vicious fight that took place here just a few minutes ago. I find nothing. No blood, no sweat, no tears. “They, they were just here,” I mumble.

Closing my eyes, I take a deep breath. Am I so sleep-deprived that I imagined it all? No. No way. I was here, and I saw it. “They must be gone.”

Tucking the bat under one arm, Gibbons crosses his arms before his chest. He looks down his nose at me. “Yes, they must.” He uncrosses his arms. “Ms. Jackson, I would appreciate it if next time you keep your little fantasies to yourself. The rest of your classmates are planning to graduate at the end of the semester and need to complete their work.”

Shooting pains radiate in my gut, and I place my hand on my abdomen, rubbing. “I plan to graduate, Mr. Gibbons.”

He sneers. “Unless your paper is brilliant, at this rate, you’ll need an ‘A’ on your final exam to pass my class.”

“I’ll do it,” I say in a tone that doesn’t convince either one of us.

“We’ll see. Now”—he turns to the few students standing by—“I would suggest everyone here head back to the classroom. There’s a pop quiz on last night’s reading.”

Last night’s reading. Damn. I didn’t exactly get to last night’s reading. I clutch the books I’m still holding.

Gibbons raises an eyebrow.

"Um, I think I'd better go to the nurse," I mumble. Rolling my shoulders in on myself to make myself as small as I can, I turn and then race down the hallway and away from class.

Chapter Two

Gracie

"Hi, Gracie."

I look up from resetting the soft serve machine. It's him. New Guy. In a black T-shirt. "Oh, hey." The high pitch of my voice surprises me. "Um." I clear my throat. "How do you know my name?"

He points to my chest. "Nametag."

"Oh, right." It's not bad enough that we have to wear these ridiculous uniforms, but we have nametags as well. It's an invitation for every drunk idiot who stops by late at night.

I flip the switch on the ice cream, but nothing happens. Damn. Last time this happened, the machine was out for two weeks. As nonchalantly as I can, I steal a peek at New Guy's face. His eye's nearly swollen shut, and he's got a gash across his top lip, but it's definitely better than it was earlier. He must be a crazy fast healer. And even with all that, he's incredibly handsome. His eye that's fully open is a warm, chocolate color, and thankfully, his strong cheekbones appear unharmed. And his skin color…it's a beautiful deep brown.

I drop my gaze to the machine and take a deep breath. I catch a whiff of him, not because he reeks or anything, but because he smells good. Really good. Like fresh air. Between work and keeping the house tight for Mom, I don't get to smell fresh air very often. Since I'm on one side of the opened window and he's on the other, I close my eyes and take one more long breath.

When I open them, he's staring at me.

"Uh." I grab a rag off the counter. "Can I get you some ice cream?" I bang on the side of the machine, hoping it'll respond to brute force like the ice maker does. No light. Nothing.

"Nah, thanks, though."

"Good, 'cause I don't think it's going to work right now."

"What's wrong with it?"

"Got me. I usually unplug it and then plug it back in when it stalls, but this time it's not working."

"Maybe the motor's overheated?"

"Maybe." I nod and then force myself to cool *my* motor, calm my nerves, stand still, and make eye contact through the open sliding glass window. "Anyway, I'd like to get you something. As a thank you for today." I start rambling again. "But I wouldn't recommend the hotdogs. We use some pressed meat substitute or something. Smells nasty and tastes worse, but people seem to like them." I shrug.

"No thank you necessary. I'm just glad you're okay."

"Thanks to you."

He nods stiffly.

"No, really. Thank you."

"Sure." He looks down at the ground.

"How about some ice for your eye or something?"

He chuckles, looking up at me again. "Does it look that bad?"

Dear Lord, nothing on you looks bad. "Looks like it hurts."

"It's fine."

I nod. "Well, I'm really sorry about today."

"It wasn't your fault."

"Maybe not. But I still feel responsible. You took a beating for me. Most guys would have just run."

"I'm sorry to hear that."

This time, it's my turn to glance at the ground. I take a deep breath and then make eye contact again. "So, um, are you okay?" Stupid question. A piece of my hair falls from my messy bun. I grabbed a quick shower after school when I went home to check on Mom, but I still haven't had time to wash my hair. I wipe my brow with my forearm, pushing the loose hair off my face. Then I catch a whiff of my scent and drop my arm. Quickly.

"Yeah, I'm okay." He smiles.

I start wringing the rag I'm holding with both hands, and little droplets of water spray my old white work shoes.

"How come…" I look down at the ground and then back up to him. "How come you didn't fight back?"

"How come you didn't run until I told you to?"

Huh. Dropping the dirty rag into a bucket under the sink, I heat the grill that's tucked off in the corner. I still have a clear view of the window from here. "I don't know." Moving away, I dig for the hotdogs in the refrigerated bin behind me. My asinine uniform rides up as I reach down, so I yank at the sides to keep it in place. *Why didn't I run sooner?* If New Guy hadn't come along just at that moment… I replay the scene in my mind, shivering.

"You cold?"

I turn around with a large box of hotdogs and shake my head, mortified by this stupid yellow flouncy uniform I'm wearing. "No. I just was thinking that if you hadn't come along…"

"They ever bother you before?"

"It was a one-time thing because I was stupid enough to be in the hallway alone."

"It wasn't your fault. You should be able to be in the hallways alone."

"I know. But they've never even noticed me before. I doubt they will again."

"I'm sure they've noticed you." He smiles in a straight line like he's a thirty-five-year-old man in a boardroom answering a question about why his company's stock just tanked.

I look into his dark eyes. His good eye has a slightly droopy lid—but droopy in a really cool way—like an aging Hollywood action hero who hasn't gone to get an eye job. It's not even noticeable unless you're really looking. Which, I guess I am. I turn away, trying to get a hold of myself. My heart is racing almost as fast as it did this morning but in a totally different way.

He runs a hand over his incredible mane of locs, and I draw a sharp breath. Then, it dawns on me…

"I know you." Using a long tong, I place dog after dog on the spinning grill. As they brown, I flip the switch on and off the ice cream machine again and then walk closer to the counter. There's no one in line behind him, and I'm fairly caught up on work, so I take a moment and lean one hip against the counter to rest. Jerry, my boss, isn't here yet, so I've got some time to talk.

"I mean, not just from school. I've definitely seen you somewhere else—Crap!" I back away, slamming myself against the ice cream vat. "Oh, come on. Are you a stalker?" Shaking my head, I grab my phone off the metal counter behind me. I thumb the screen open and glance down, holding my finger over the "emergency" button. I face him and hold it out to show him.

"Excuse me?"

I've moved back so far he needs to lean down to make eye contact through the window.

"You were at school today, and yesterday you were here, at Shakes 'n' Slaw, weren't you? And now you're back? Wait." It dawns on me. "How do you even know where I work?" Anger rushes through me. Enough with these f-ed-up boys. I have enough drama without them. "Listen, I don't care what you did for me today, I don't have time for crazy."

He starts.

"Go find some other girl to stalk."

"I'm not a stalker."

"Then why were you at my school?" Still clutching my phone, I cross my arms before me, standing to my full five feet ten inches. It's nearly impossible to tell through the window, but I think he's much taller than me. The smell of the fake hotdog meat permeates the air. "My boss is in the back room," I lie. "All I have to do is call, and he'll come running."

"Wait, wait. You don't need to call your boss. I was at school because I go there. Just transferred." He reaches behind him and lets an old faded brown backpack slide off his shoulder and onto the ground. Digging in and rummaging around for a moment, he smiles and then pulls out a bio book, shaking it.

I place my phone down and go to the counter window to get a better look. Resting my forearms on the ledge, I take in the lines on his forehead and crinkles around the corners of his eyes. "You're a senior? How old are you?"

He smiles a crooked smile, exposing nicely imperfect teeth. "I'm uh, eighteen."

Lifting a hand high, he places it flat against the window frame and leans down, smiling. It is the most freaking masculine move I've ever seen in real life, and it hits me deep in my core. Smirking, I bite the side of my lip and glance up at him.

He grins. Damn. He is sexy.

Way too soon, he lets his hand slide down and drop to his side. "I know I look older. Everyone tells me that."

"Everyone?" *Like your longtime girlfriend and her mother?*

"My dad and I move around often, so I start over a lot. I'm hoping this place is my last, though. I'm planning to graduate in a couple months."

He reaches up and knocks on the side of his head with his fist like he's knocking wood. Considering all the other bruises, I hope it doesn't hurt.

"With you, right?"

His smile nudges my tight shoulders down from my ears.

"I hope so. Wait." I don't care what he looks like and how nice he seems; I'm not getting suckered into this. "That doesn't cover it. Shakes 'n' Slaw? Why were you here last night?" I ignore my sweaty palms.

This time, he rests his forearms on the counter and leans forward so it's like we're on opposite ends of a small table at some romantic bistro, about to hold hands. He drops his chin and raises it again. His smile is filled with humor and timidity. His cheeks flush a light red. "I came here to grab something to eat, and I saw you."

"You were here for hours."

"Like I said, I saw you."

My cheeks burn. "And today?"

"After what happened at school today, I just wanted to come back and make sure you were okay."

I make eye contact, and he lifts one shoulder, shrugging.

"That was really nice of you to check on me, but shouldn't I be the one checking on you?"

"I'm fine. It was nothing."

He leans forward so he's hovering even closer to the open window, and I swear, it's like he has his own damned gravitational pull. I feel my body rocking toward his like he's the moon and I'm the sea. It's surreal.

"So." He smiles and holds out one hand to shake. "Friends?"

Sliding my hand into his, I nod. "Friends."

"Good." He moves our hands up and down and holds on just a little too long.

"Well, I, uh…" I think of the cameras Jerry has recording everything and take my hand away from his. Standing up, I pull my ponytail forward and let it drape down the front of my chick-yellow uniform that's cut way-too-low and way-too-short. It's been so long since I cared about my appearance. I'm not sure I remember how.

"Why don't you try the soft serve machine again?" he asks.

"The…" I'm barely lucid. "Yeah, sure. You in the mood for ice cream?" I tease.

"I'm pretty good at fixing things. Maybe I could take a look if it's still not working."

"Um…"

"I promise I'm not a stalker," he assures me. "I'm

just a guy who's new here. And I don't know anything or anyone."

"I wish I could help you out," I mumble. "But I don't know anyone either. If you're looking to meet people, you should hang with the girls on the track team. They're super popular. Or how about the cheerleaders?" I allow my gaze to dash up and down his body just once. "All guys like cheerleaders."

"I like you."

His smile goes straight to my gut.

"I, um, people are probably going to be coming soon. Let me just try the machine. Maybe I'll get lucky." I chew at my bottom lip as I flip the switch on the ice cream vat. Sure enough, the light comes on. "Hey, it works." I turn to him and smile. "That's weird. Why would it just turn back on? Do you have magic powers or something?"

"Me?" He chuckles. "You're the one who made it work." He stays close to the open window, and even though there's a glass partition between us, he's literally in my space—as close as two strangers can get. "So, uh, Gracie. I'd really like to see you sometime outside of work. But…since I'm sure you have a boyfriend, I probably need to back off."

He smiles, and the waves in my ocean crash against his shore. Hard. I smile back.

"That means yes?" He stoops down and speaks through the window again, cocooning me in this incredibly intimate…*aura*.

"No. I mean, what?" I glance down at the filthy floor that I'll have to clean in a few hours when my shift is over. But right now, I don't care. I close my eyes for a second, willing my breathing to slow. I'm not entirely sure what's going on here. I mean, aside from work, I haven't really spoken to a boy in, well, ever.

"So…do you have a boyfriend?" His words have a slow, sexy rhythm.

Sweat drips down my back and collects in my armpits. I'm going to reek, but I don't care. It feels so good to be this close. It's like I'm on a way-overdue mini-vacation that may only last a couple of minutes, but I'll take it. I pull at the polyester material at my waist, trying to cool off.

"Uh, no. No boyfriend."

His eyes flash with something, but it doesn't look like happiness. But then again, I'm not exactly a pro at reading signals from boys—that is until he flat-out grimaces. *WTF?*

"Okkkkaaaayyyy…" I shrug. "You know, you asked me."

"Sorry. I just, uh, I didn't really expect you to say you were free."

I scoff. "I'm hardly free, but I don't have a boyfriend." I make one more dive into the freezer, and this time my skirt rides high, probably exposing that stupid birthmark I have crawling up the back of my left thigh. Of all the things Mom could have given me—her gorgeous mane of red curly hair, her perfect straight nose—she had to give me her birthmark.

I wheel around to see him standing there, frozen.

Once, when I was little, Mom hit a deer with our car. Just before we struck, I made eye contact with it, and I could tell that that deer knew it was about to die. That's what New Guy looks like right now.

He looks like a man who's just witnessed his own death.

Shaking it off, I grab the coleslaw makings out of the walk-in fridge behind me and take a silver bowl down from a high shelf. The bowl's probably big enough to bathe a set of triplets, but that's something I'll never know. I cut open the bag of slivered cabbage and dump it into the bowl. Then, I open the mayonnaise.

I can feel New Guy staring. Over the past couple of minutes, this situation has gone from fun and sexy to downright creepy. I glance at him and then go right back to work. "So?" I ask. "You know my name. What's yours?"

"Josh," he ekes out. "Joshua Cadman."

The energy between us has changed drastically. It's like those moments before a storm.

"Hi, Josh Cadman, I'm Gracie Jackson." I scoop in mayo, add vinegar, and toss the slaw with two giant spoons. "I don't know why we make so much slaw. Hardly anyone eats it." I raise one shoulder and drop it. "But since we're Shakes 'n' Slaw, I'd better have some ready." I glance at him.

Now, he's scowling.

"Yeah, well, uh, that makes sense," he mutters. "I'm sorry, but I just remembered there's someplace I have to be." He looks left and right and then forces himself to make eye contact with me. "Uh, see you around, Gracie."

Reaching down, he grabs the backpack off the ground and slides it over one shoulder. Then he takes off toward the parking lot.

He leaves so fast a breeze blows through the open window, making me shudder. I stare after him, dumbfounded. What the hell just happened?

Whatever it is, good riddance. I don't have the time for it.

"Crazy," I mutter as I finish tossing the giant vat of coleslaw. "Cra. Zy."

Chapter Three

Gracie

Why the hell is ice cream so sticky and hard to clean? Using all my strength, I reach lower into the vat, scrubbing and—

"Hey, Gracie."

Startled, I pop up to see Josh at my window. This time, he's wearing a thin black leather jacket, and his eye is significantly less puffy. He must have been icing it. And he has…wait… I squint to see better. Oh, damn. He has the tiniest little gold hoop through his left nostril. I turn away and scrub harder.

"Gracie? What did you mean earlier when you said you didn't have a boyfriend, but you were 'hardly free'?"

"Really?" I raise my hand, holding the sponge. It's dripping with chemicals that burn my skin. We're out of size small gloves. Again. I need to remember to tell Jerry. The larger sizes let the chemicals drip in, roll down my forearms, and pool at my fingers, which is even worse than not wearing gloves at all. I gesture to the ice cream machine, vats of hotdogs, and coleslaw before getting back to work.

He nods. "I'm sorry if I sounded…well, a little nuts, earlier."

I glance up at him. "Yeah, that's kind of exactly what I'm worried about."

Just then, Jerry materializes from the backroom and

glances at Josh. "Everything cool, Gracie?"

"Um, yeah. Thanks." I move on, wiping the handles and outlet valves of the ice cream machine. I'm working on a crusted glob of soft serve while I simultaneously try to keep my ass and that stupid birthmark covered. I yank on my tutu skirt. F this uniform.

Jerry is still staring at me.

"He's, uh, a kid from school." I peek at Josh out of the corner of my eye. There's nothing that says "kid" about him. I stop for a moment and speak to Josh. "So? Can I get you something?"

"Oh, uh, yeah. Chocolate milkshake, please."

I abandon my scrubbing and smile at Jerry. His brow is furrowed. He's clearly worried about me. Jerry's always been cool. Poor guy lost his wife to breast cancer three years ago and does all he can to help me out with Mom—giving me extra shifts, sending food home, and always padding my Christmas check.

Reaching into a case behind me, I scoop hard chocolate ice cream into an industrial-sized blender container. When I turn around, Josh is eyeing Jerry. Now Josh is the one with the troubled look on his face. Men are so weird.

I put the container onto the base and add chocolate syrup and milk while the men continue to stare at one another. It's so bizarre. I can't turn the blender on fast enough. As the loud whirling starts, I consciously drop my shoulders and take a deep breath. Thank heavens for noise.

All too soon it's ready, and I busy myself by pouring the thick shake into a blue-and-yellow milkshake cup. I add a lid and stuff in an environmentally unfriendly straw.

Josh takes the shake from me and smiles, giving me a five in exchange. I go through the motions of handing him his change as the two men just keep staring. It's like I'm the star in a really boring play, and they're just waiting for someone to pick up a gun and shoot me.

Josh takes a long draw of his shake and stoops down a bit, peering in through the opened sliding glass window. "Gracie, how 'bout I wait for you and walk you to your car?" He speaks more to Jerry than to me.

I glance over at Jerry and then back to Josh. I'm getting a definite protective vibe from him. But why?

The phone rings in the back, startling me. Whew. Saved by the bell.

I nod to Jerry. "You getting that, or you want me to?"

Jerry pulls his focus off Josh and gives me his attention. "No, no. I've got it." He leaves slower than he should to answer a ringing phone, looking over his shoulder one last time at Josh.

Jerry disappears into the back, and I return to wiping the hardened ice cream from the sides of the machine. I speak while I work.

"Walk me to my car, huh? Are you actually going to stick around this time?" Even though I'm totally not into games or any of that passive-aggressive crap, I don't look at Josh when I ask. I guess I'm more pissed than I realize.

"I'll be on the bench. With my milkshake."

I nod without looking up.

****

When the machines are cleaned and the floor's mopped, I haul my exhausted ass toward the breakroom to grab my recycled supermarket tote bag with my rumpled mess of clothes stashed inside. I push the door open and nearly jump out of my skin.

"Crap. Jerry." I place a hand to my racing heart. "I didn't know you were still here."

Jerry sits at a desk in the far corner, pushing some papers back and forth. He taps a pen nervously against the desk that's so small it looks like it was made for elementary school kids. He doesn't speak.

"Didn't expect you to be in the breakroom," I continue. "Didn't you give yourself a fancy office across the hall since we made this the women's changing area?" Walking in, I grab my bag and my plaid shirt off a hook on the far wall. I feel exposed in my skimpy uniform, so I slide into my shirt and pull it tight around me. I glance at my watch. "Why are you still here?"

He shrugs. "No reason to go home."

I nod. That's true. There is no reason for him to go home except he always goes home by seven to watch a gameshow he likes, and it's eight-twenty now. Wait, is this…? No, it isn't the anniversary of his wife's death or her birthday, so why is he still here? An uneasy feeling washes over me, and although he's a stranger and might be nuts, I'm grateful Josh is waiting outside. If, in fact, he is. I scratch an itch on my arm. I'm desperate to go.

"Well, uh, don't work too late." I force a smile, moving as quickly as I can to the door of the breakroom and toward the back exit. With Jerry sitting there, there's no place for me to change, and frankly, I wouldn't even if I could. Right now, I can't get out fast enough. Tonight, for some reason, being alone with Jerry feels "off."

I make it to the back exit and reach for the door handle—

"Gracie."

"Crap!" I turn quickly, and Jerry is there, behind me.

I'm face to face with him, staring into his shifty eyes. His greasy skin glistens, and he pushes his glasses up higher onto the bridge of his nose. They slide down again. Still facing Jerry, I reach behind me and wiggle my fingers until I find the door handle. The cold of the metal door shocks my exposed legs as I press back against it.

"Who's this guy?" Jerry nods over his shoulder and toward the front of the restaurant. Obviously, he means Josh, who may or may not be waiting outside.

"Just a kid from school." I repeat what I said earlier. Maybe this time Jerry will believe it.

"School?" He turns, glancing behind him, probably trying to see if Josh is still at his post.

"Yeah. We're in biology together." Why do I need to justify this to Jerry?

"Oh." He runs a hand through his limp hair, and his glasses drop even lower on his nose.

My gaze travels over Jerry's face. His cheeks are swollen like a leprechaun, and his lips are puffy. He's probably a drinker, although I'd never ask. I'm nowhere near old enough to buy him a bottle of anything, so what does it matter? He's not, in the least, attractive. But who cares? He's always been a nice guy.

"I thought you were going to tell me he's your boyfriend." He inches closer to me.

"Josh? No." I laugh it off, trying to end this conversation. "He's just waiting because, you know, with my crazy schedule, I need to get schoolwork done later in the evenings. We're working on a project together." I try to calm my racing heart. Something's not right. Why should it matter to Jerry if I have a boyfriend? "He's got a girlfriend, from what I hear. Some college girl."

"Oh." Jerry nods, exhaling audibly.

I point to the door over my shoulder. "If you don't mind…paper is due tomorrow."

Jerry squints at me. "I thought you said project?" He's standing way too close.

Oh crap. "Yeah. But it's got a paper due, too. Got to tell them what we're doing, and then do it. You know, bullshit school rules. And I still have to figure out what the hell we're doing. That's why he's waiting. We're discussing it for a few minutes after my shift."

"Aren't you going to change?"

Shit. Jerry has a "No uniforms in public" rule, but tonight, I don't want to take the time to change. I just want out.

"As a manager, you've got to set a precedent." He raises his eyebrows like I imagine a disapproving father would.

I shuffle from worn-out foot to worn-out foot as I gesture to the women's changing area. "I couldn't while you were in the breakroom. Jerry, I don't wanna go back to change. I'm tired. Just tonight, please. There's no one here but us, and I've already got such a long night ahead of me. I'm just going home. Promise." I place my hand on his forearm, solidifying our relationship. Somewhere deep inside, I know this is what's going to let me out of here. It feels wrong, but it works.

"Oh, yeah, yeah." He steps aside. "Of course. Well, uh, just take care of yourself, Gracie."

"Thanks, Jerry. I think you're not working again until Saturday?" I spin on my heels, not waiting for his response. "See you then!" I rush out the door.

As soon as I'm free, I take a gulp of the chilly night air. It's April, but it still gets dark so early. The cold air feels wet against my bare legs, and I just can't shake the feeling that something bad is going to happen. I know it's my overactive imagination, but still, my spine tingles and my hands tremble. Tonight, I just want to get away from Jerry and get to Josh.

I dash around the side of the building to find him, but the bench where he was sitting is empty. Again? He left me again? What the hell is his problem?

Storming back toward the parking lot, I give myself a new mantra: *No more crazies*. If another boy ever comes near me, I'll ask for letters of recommendation before I even have a conversation with him. And why not? Employers do it all the time when they're hiring, and that's just so they can stand to be in the building with someone. It only makes sense to background check someone I may potentially kiss.

Asshole.

I walk faster and faster toward my car, but it feels like I'm barely moving. Like I'm trapped in a nightmare where I run and run but can't move forward. And crap—I glance at the chain fence attached to our parking lot—where is Old Man Perkins' damned Pitbull? That dog scares the crap out of me. He looks nice enough, with his brown and white fur, but then he snaps and snarls. Most nights, I throw him a few scraps of food, thinking Perkins may be starving the dog for fights or something, but still, the dog growls at me.

I'd hate the parking lot even if Perkins' dog wasn't there. It's especially terrifying alone at night, but thankfully, Jerry put in extra lighting so we can get to our cars safely after closing.

Glancing at the gate leading to Perkins' lawn, a jolt of sadness passes over me. I feel like I've been plunged into ice water. As awful as that dog was, I hope nothing bad has happened to him. I don't think he's evil, just misunderstood. I slow my stride. Huh. Maybe I'm misunderstanding. Maybe I misread everything that just happened. Jerry's always been wonderful to me and Mom. Maybe he's just being protective?

"Hey." Josh walks up to me.

"Crap!" I jump, placing a hand on my heart. "Why are you lurking in the shadows?" My heartbeat races so fast and so hard I feel it in my ears and throat. What's with these men tonight?

"I'm not. You said I could walk you to your car."

"I thought you said you'd meet me on the bench."

He shrugs. "Thought I'd save you a trip."

Okay, so that makes sense. In the dim light of the parking lot, his eyes are even more intense. I glance past him and to the back of Shakes 'n' Slaw, where I spot the outline of Jerry. He's in the window, watching.

I look at Josh again. "Listen." I drop the volume of my voice, standing as still as I can. I clutch my shirt tightly at my throat, covering this ludicrous uniform that makes me look like I'm the star in some really bad porn. "Something's up with my boss tonight." I glance at the building again, feeling uncomfortable in my own skin. "He's acting weird. I think maybe he's just being paternal, but I kinda told a little lie. Would you mind backing me up?" The cold night air sends a shiver, like an electric current, up my spine.

Josh turns his head to look at the back door of the restaurant. "What lie?"

"I told him you were waiting for me because we're doing a biology project together, and we needed to decide on the topic for a paper that's due tomorrow."

He looks at me again.

"I'm really sorry to drag you into anything. He just seemed… I don't know."

"You do know." He presses me. "He seemed what?"

I shake my head. "Look, I have no experience with this so I'm sure I'm misreading it, but it kind of seems like he's…jealous."

"Jealous?"

He stands up taller, and I catch a whiff of expensive leather and fresh laundry detergent.

"I know." I force a chuckle. "It's ludicrous. He's probably just being fatherly. I have no experience with that either."

"No?"

"Just me and my mom. No dad."

He nods. "Just me and my dad. No mom."

An image of the two of us as characters in some depressing anime pops into my brain. It's sad that we're both without a parent, but my perpetually frozen core warms. It's nice to be near someone who understands.

He glances back at the building and pushes up the sleeves of his jacket, exposing thick forearms.

"So, uh, would you mind backing me up?" I consciously skip the lie about Josh dating some college girl. I'm clearheaded enough to know that's not right. I shouldn't have to lie to my boss about my dating life.

"Of course, I don't mind. But your boss shouldn't be jealous. Maybe it's time to get another job?"

I frown, shivering. "Can't. I've got health insurance with this job, and I need the income. He's made me a manager because he understands my situation."

Josh raises his eyebrows. "Situation?"

I look away, pressing my lips together, and turn back to him. What the hell? It's not like it's a secret. Everyone at school knows. Seems my mini-vacation is over. "My mom's sick. Stage 4 breast cancer. I need the income to support us." I look at my feet, kicking a pebble with the worn sole of my sneaker. I make eye contact again. "You know what? It was a late night last night. She had a rough reaction to this new chemo they're trying. I'm just tired. Exhausted really. I'm sure I misinterpreted."

He nods, but I can tell by his expression that he doesn't agree with me.

"Anything I can do?" he asks. "To help with your mom?"

I step back like I've been slapped in the face. "Uh, no. Thank you. My mom's pretty private about the whole thing. When she's feeling better, it'll be different."

He nods. "Of course."

I swallow a lump in my throat. No one has ever asked me if they could help. Together, we stroll toward my car. We stop when I'm standing next to the driver's door. "Anyway, I'm sure we've been talking long enough to make my story believable. Thanks, Josh. I really appreciate it." I turn, insert my key in the lock, and then look back at him. "And thanks for walking me to my car. I'm always a little uneasy when it's dark out. This was a nice break, thanks."

He steps closer. "I could do it again. Wait for you, that is. Make sure you get to your car okay."

I smile. *I'd love that, Josh. Really love that.* "Thanks, but that's probably not such a great idea. I really can't afford to piss off my boss. Guys hanging around shifts—even just friends—is against the rules." I shrug. "Tonight was a one-time thing."

He nods. "Got it. So maybe I could walk you to your car some other time? After school or on the way to school or something?" The left side of his mouth turns upward in this sexy, lopsided grin.

I sigh.

"That would be great, Josh, really, but uh, I think I may be a little too busy right now." I remove the keys from the lock and open my car door. "Maybe once my mom is feeling better."

He nods. "Yeah. Sure."

He stands next to my door as I climb in. Stepping closer, he blocks the door with his body, one hand on the doorframe and one on the car. I swear, warmth radiates off him, and just being here like this…feels…so…good.

I squirm in my seat, hoping he can't smell the layers of grease on me. His jacket is opened widely, and I catch a glimpse of his muscles underneath his plain black T-shirt. There's a gold chain around his neck, and whatever medallion is attached to it is tucked away behind his shirt, against his chest.

Lucky, lucky medallion.

"Drive safely, Gracie."

"Thanks, Josh." I pull my door closed, although it's the very last thing I want to do. But what I want to do doesn't matter. I have responsibilities—real, adult, overwhelming responsibilities, and I have to honor them. Maybe someday I'll have some fun, but right now, there's work to be done.

I put the car in *drive*, and it rolls forward. Looking in my rearview, I see Josh.

He raises his hand and waves, watching me as I drive away.

Chapter Four

Gracie

I pull into our gravel driveway that's only the length of two cars, glance in my rearview, and…

There's Josh. Behind me. At my house.

I grip the steering wheel while my racing heart settles in my chest. I should be freaked—really, really freaked—but I'm not. Truthfully, it's nice to see him here. Yeah, he lost it earlier at Shakes 'n' Slaw for some weird reason, but before that, the man took a beating to save me. He *can't* be a bad guy. And besides, I like that he's not perfect. I couldn't handle perfect.

This time, when I glance in the rearview, he catches my gaze and nods to me. Crap, crap, crap. Now my heart is pounding all over again, and the butterflies in my stomach are racing. I reach across my body and shimmy the seatbelt to get it to unlock, grab the broken door handle, and, holding it in just the right way so it won't break off, I push the door open. Climbing out, I close the door quietly.

I shield my eyes from the glare of his lights, and he cuts his engine and hops out of his car. He stands tall next to his opened door, resting his arm on the doorframe. Damn if he doesn't look good.

I yank my shirt around me until it nearly wraps around me twice, covering my stupid uniform as best I can. I walk toward him. "You followed me home."

"It wasn't easy." He chuckles. "You've got a lead foot." He closes his car door carefully like I did. It clicks with his touch.

"I have to check on Mom. She's been alone for almost five hours." I shake my head, trying to clear the horrid possibilities from my brain. "Why'd you follow me?"

The gravel crunches beneath my feet as I walk toward the house. He follows, and his footsteps make an even louder crunching sound.

"What if your boss drives by? We have to make our story believable."

I pause before the concrete steps and peek through the screen door. I lift onto my tiptoes, trying to see through the window of the front door of our little ranch. "Uh, we need to keep our voices down, please. My mom, I'm sure she's sleeping."

"Sorry." He nods. "You don't want her to hear anything about your boss, do you?"

"No." I raise one shoulder to my ear and then let it drop. "She doesn't need to worry about anything else."

"I get it."

"Besides." I ignore the burning feeling in my gut. "I'm sure there's nothing up with Jerry. Like I said, I'm just being oversensitive tonight. Probably from being so tired."

"Oh, uh, should I go?" He thumbs his car.

I shake my head. "No. I mean, not if you don't want to."

"I don't want to." He smiles.

"I really have to check on my mom." I climb the steps and open the screen door. "If she's asleep, I have a few minutes. Then I have to get going on some bio homework I'm behind on. Want to sit here?" I motion to the steps. "Have a drink?"

"Drink?" He raises his eyebrows.

"Yeah, I have tap water and oh, seltzer. I love seltzer. You?" I slide the key into the lock.

"Sure." He chuckles. "Seltzer would be great."

"Great." I turn away and roll my eyes. Can I be this bad at conversation? I glance at him over my shoulder as I push the front door open. "Have a seat." I point to the steps I just climbed. "Sorry, I don't have chairs," I whisper.

"It's cool. I like the front steps."

"Okay. I'll, uh, be back in a moment."

Ducking inside, I hold the door behind me with both hands and then ease my arms forward, allowing the door to glide shut quietly. I take a deep breath. Our house doesn't smell like a house should, like homemade cookies or fresh laundry. It smells like sweet antiseptic and thick medicine. It's the aroma of an old doctor's office in a strip mall in the middle of nowhere. I scrunch up my nose, but the heavy smell lingers in my nostrils.

I glance around for Mom.

She's not on our old brown couch where she should be, and the wingback chair has a pile of hand-knit blankets neither of us has touched in months. I step around the couch and—

"Oh!" I trip on the stiff office rug with the dizzying polka dot pattern that serves to keep Mom's feet warm as she paddles back and forth from the bathroom to the couch. Thankfully, I catch myself before I fall or make any real noise. Damn, that's not safe for her. I make a mental note to fix it later when Josh leaves.

But, more importantly, where is she?

Sweat drips down my spine as I glance into the kitchen—nothing. The too-large round table and mismatched chairs are exactly as I left them, and the worn-out cabinetry hasn't been touched. The same warped doors hang in the same way they did right after school. The handprint towel I made for Mother's Day when I was in first grade is draped over the oven handle.

I spin in a circle. She's been sleeping on the couch lately, so where the heck?

With my heart racing like a mom whose teenager is out way past curfew, I stride through the living room and rush down our tiny hallway toward our one very pink bathroom and both bedrooms.

I stall outside her door and place my hand on the fake wood, resting my head against the door. I don't want to disturb her, but we really don't have the luxury of privacy right now.

Keeping one hand on the doorknob, I raise the other and tap gently on the door. No answer. I force my breathing to slow and repeat my knock, louder this time. Still nothing.

"Mom?"

With my heart in my throat, I turn the handle and push open the door.

She's there. In bed. And there's a gentle rise and fall of her blankets with her easy breath. Oh, thank God. I squat down by the opened door, collecting myself. She's okay. I breathe deeply, exhaling through my mouth as I place a shaking hand to my chest. Thank God she's able to breathe, and the fluid in her lungs isn't suffocating her. Thank God she's resting. Thank God she's alive.

Shaking off my terror, I stand and slip out of her bedroom. Checking on Mom isn't foreign to me, but it never gets any easier.

The relief of seeing Mom there, alive, allows all of the stress I've been carrying to morph into excitement—like bubbly water running through my veins. As long as Mom's okay and asleep, I have bonus time I wasn't anticipating.

And I know exactly what I'd like to do with it.

Not bothering to change out of my stupid uniform, I rush to the fridge—quietly—and grab two small bottles of seltzer. I glance at the labels: "Mandarin." Hope he's an orange guy.

"Hey." I emerge from the door of my house carrying the two bottles, my bio book, and an old composition notebook.

"Hey."

From his seat on the step, he turns toward me, and I can't help but smile. I hand him a bottle of seltzer, keep one for myself, and then plop down next to him on the small step. His leg bumps mine accidentally, I think, and it's like electricity shoots through my body, zapping me with sparks. He uses a strong hand to open his bottle and gives it to me. Then he takes mine, opening it for himself, and drinks.

"Hope orange is okay." OMG. Could my conversation skills be any worse?

"It's great, thanks." He cocks his head toward me, dropping it slightly, and looks at me over one strong shoulder. "So, Gracie. What's your story?"

I take a sip of the bubbly water, and it burns my nose. "My story? You're seeing it. This has been my life for as long as I can remember."

He looks away, resting his forearms on his thighs. The bottle dangles from one hand, hanging low between his legs. “How old were you when your mom got sick?”

“Fourteen.” I shrug.

“She’s been sick for four years?”

“Almost. All through high school. At the beginning, it wasn’t bad. But the last two years…” I shake my head, looking off. “It’s been tough.”

“Do you ever have time for you? For anything fun?”

“I uh…” I glance at the driveway and back and then hold up my bio book. “I’m kind of all full right now. But I’ll get there. Once she’s feeling better. What about you, Josh? What’s your story?”

He chuckles, dropping his head back, revealing an exposed Adam’s apple. When he rights his head, he’s smiling, but it’s not his warm smile. It’s his boardroom smile again. “There’s not much to say.”

“Well, how’d you get here?”

“My dad and I travel a lot for business.”

“What does he do?”

“He makes high-end cabinetry. Incredibly beautiful. He’s an artist, really.”

Every answer he gives me feels final, like it’s punctuated with a boulder-sized period. I don’t care. I press on. He’s the one who followed me here. The least he can do is tell me something about himself and let me know he’s not certifiable. “Do you work with him?”

He nods. “Yeah, but I do the books and the website. I have no skills as far as carpentry goes.”

I frown. “I’ll bet you’re wrong. If your dad has such a gift, I’ll bet you have it, too.”

He shakes his head, taking another long drag from the bottle. “I can whittle a little. But that’s it.”

“Still. That’s something. I have no artistic talents whatsoever. As in zero. Frankly, thinking about it, I really have no talents at all." As soon as I say it, I feel the words sit heavily between us. Why do I have to be such a downer?

He turns to me. "No. No way. I've only just met you, and even I know that's not true."

"I wish," I mutter. This is getting way too intense. "So, uh, Josh, what do you do for fun?"

"This." He raises his bottle to me.

"You sit on the front steps of unsuspecting young women everywhere drinking orange seltzer with them?"

"Nah. Usually I drink lime flavored."

He nudges me with his shoulder, and his entire body shifts closer to mine. This time, when the denim of his pant leg brushes against my bare leg, neither of us pulls away. My stomach is on fire.

"Cute. But, really. What do you do for fun?" I wring the seltzer bottle in my hand.

The smallest sigh escapes his lips, and he looks away, but his leg presses tighter against mine. I close my eyes, committing every detail of this moment to memory.

"My dad and I restore classic cars," he says, finally.

"Wow." I point to his car. "I'm sorry, but I don't have the car gene. Is that some amazing classic car I should *ooh* and *aah* over?"

He shakes his head. "Nah. That's just something I like."

"I like it, too."

"Yeah?" He raises his eyebrows, turning to me.

"Sure." I nod. "I've never seen a car like that before. But I like it."

"Well, good." He smiles, his body swaying toward mine. "Because I like you."

I smirk, keeping the side of my body tight to his as

we sit together, sipping from our bottles, staring out into the nothingness that lies before us.

Chapter Five

Josh

I stop the car on the street right before the turn into the driveway. Dammit. The lights are still on in the garage. I take a deep breath and let out a long, exaggerated sigh, the kind I reserve for times like these—when I'm alone, gripping the steering wheel of my vintage orange sports car. He hasn't done this—stay up too late because he's worried about me—in years. Thinking about it, the last time he stayed up because he was worried about me, I was just a kid with a fever. I shift in my seat. Yeah, I really should have told him I'd be out late, but sometimes I've got so many other things on my mind I just forget. And tonight, well, hell yeah. Tonight, I had a whole shitload on my mind.

Digging my cell out of my leather jacket, I press the screen to unlock and scroll through my texts. Most of them are business, well, correction, Dad's business that I run for him, but thankfully, he didn't text me. Which is good because that means I didn't miss it. I've got to give it to him. The man's got incredible restraint. It has to be so hard for him when he doesn't know where I am or who I'm with. Maybe it's just as hard if he does know. Jesus, just being my dad has got to be impossible.

I shift the car into gear and roll forward, all the way up to my parking spot in the driveway, right next to Ol' Sally, his big, red '63 pickup. Turning the key, I kill the engine but don't move. I'm stalling. I know he's in there waiting for me, but I need to process this for a minute. A minute. Yeah, right. Processing is all I've been doing since I left Gracie's side a couple of hours ago, and still, I've come up with nothing.

She's the one. I know it. It's as clear as that birthmark on her beautiful leg.

And now? What the hell do I do? Am I really going to do this to a girl who hasn't even begun to live?

Fuck.

I glance at the house again. It's time for me to stop being a coward. About everything. The least the man deserves is to know I'm all right.

Shaking my head, I lean back against the smooth leather seat. Out of the corner of my eye, I spy his silhouette in one of the two tiny windows of the garage. I check my phone again. Just after midnight. Now I'm just being rude.

Jamming my cell into my leather jacket pocket, I step out of the car and stretch myself to my full six feet two inches. I reach my hands overhead, and they tingle in the cool night air. Dropping my hands, I amble toward the garage door, running a hand across the scruff on my chin. With a deep breath, I climb up the few steps and push the door open. Immediately, the scent of warm wood and strong glue hits me, relaxing me the tiniest bit. This is the smell of Dad's garage. None of that oil-gas-mustiness of a normal garage here.

"Hey, Dad."

"Hey." He keeps busy, using an awl and hand planer as he sets in a new row of dovetailing on the cabinet he's creating. His plain black T-shirt is decorated with sweat stains—one large on the lower back and two round circles under his armpits that become visible when he pushes his arms forward to plane.

I stroll closer, admiring his handiwork. He is incredibly gifted. “I like the two-tone dovetailing. Those are going to be some cabinets.” I nod.

“Thanks.” He runs the planer over the newly set wood, smoothing it until it shines.

“That kind of detail work has to keep you busy.”

“Uh-huh.” He crouches down next to the cabinet drawer he’s working on, eye level. He closes one eye and looks down the dovetailing with the other. He runs an experienced hand over the top and then stands and resumes planing.

“Dad. You didn’t have to wait up, you know. I’m eighteen years old.”

He stops and looks up at me, letting his hand with the planer lay at his side. A drop of sweat falls from his short black hair onto his cheek, and he wipes it away. “I am well aware of how old you are, Josh.”

I nod.

“Believe me. No one is more acutely aware of your age than me.” He turns back to his work. His arms move back and forth feverishly, and sweat drips from his forehead.

“Yeah.” Guilt washes over me. This isn’t how I wanted to start this conversation. Maybe change the subject? “So, I was wondering, there’s enough work around here?”

He stops again and stands tall, facing me. He’s an inch shorter than I am, but the way he carries himself makes him seem like the taller, stronger one of us. He smiles the way a father smiles at his child who’s just skinned his knee. “I’m plenty busy, Josh. You’ve got to stop worrying. Every time we move, you think I won't be able to find work."

I raise one shoulder in a shrug. "It's just, this is a small town. Is there enough interest in high-end custom cabinets?"

"Columbus is not so far. A lot of business there."

Exhausted, I drag my hand across my locs and flop down onto our garage couch, which is really the backseat of a car. "Columbus is nearly three hours away. I didn't mean to make you have to travel so far—"

He puts up his hand, stopping me. I gaze at it. It's all full of nicks and cuts but so powerful and so steady. Always.

"Josh. You set me up with a website that works magic. The truth is, I have more work than I can handle. I only travel for measurements and installation, and I don't mind the ride. I get Ol' Sally over there"—he points out the window and to the pickup—"and we make a day of it."

"The damned truck doesn't even have air conditioning."

"Ah," he waves me off. "Being cool is highly overrated." He sits next to me and clamps his warm hand on my forearm. His touch feels right. "Josh, the moving." He smiles through closed lips. "This is where you needed to be, so this is where we needed to come."

I nod. What I really want to ask is, is this the place for him? After?

But I don't. Instead, I stare into his dark, soulful eyes until it becomes too much, and then search his face. He looks tired but incredibly handsome, and despite the fact that we're dressed similarly—well-worn jeans, faded black T-shirts—we look nothing alike. He's fifty-three with skin much darker than mine, wide cheekbones and a short, graying beard. His hair is black and cut short. But it's his smile that really sets him apart. He has a wide, warm, welcoming smile with perfectly straight white teeth. It's friendly and easy-going, and when he smiles at you, you can't help but get drawn in. Ask any woman in the grocery store, the car wash, the PTA, or on any job he takes.

The thing is, the feeling is never reciprocated. He is a one-man woman. Always was and probably always will be. It's too bad she's been gone for nearly twenty years. And it's not just grown women who are all over him; I can't count the number of girls in my high schools who have crushed on him. I chuckle.

"What are you laughing about?"

He leans back, stretching his arms long across the back of the couch and immediately I'm enveloped by the faint smell of cumin, turpentine, and wood shavings that's completely him. I smile.

"Just thinking about how many girls I've known who've thought you were hot." I spare him—and me—the embarrassment of calling him a DILF.

He laughs. "Yeah, well, who could blame them?" He sits forward, reaching toward the small fridge we keep next to the bench. He opens it, grabs two bottles of domestic beer, and then pushes the door shut. He pops the tops and hands one to me. We clink bottles and both sit back, relaxing as much as we're able. He takes a long drag of his beer, resting the icy cold bottle against his forehead.

I spin the beer slowly between both hands, leaving a thick residue of cold wetness behind. The label starts to loosen, and little bits of logo speckle my palm. This time together, it's a scenario we know well. It's father and son bonding time, but usually it happens because I was wrong about my instinct, and it's time to move on.

But tonight, it's because I was *right*. Only he doesn't know it yet. But he should. I rub at the burning sensation settled in my esophagus.

"Josh, the times we've followed your instincts traveling from place to place, it doesn't mean you were wrong. It means you needed to be at that place at that time for some reason. You know that."

I smile. "You're starting to sound more and more like Mom."

I never knew her. She died during childbirth, but the stories Dad's told me—no matter how much I didn't want to hear them at the time—make me love her more and more each day. I also have no idea what she looked like, not really, anyway. I know she was blonde and fair-skinned, so I get my lighter skin color from her, but the only pictures I've seen of her are from far away. When I was little, I used to lay awake and imagine her face before me. Every few months, it would change. Her cheekbones would be wider, her lips maybe fuller, but one thing always remained the same—her smile. She'd always be smiling at me, and corny as it was, in that smile, I knew how much she loved me.

I take a long drag of the ice-cold beer and glance at Dad out of the corner of my eye. There's no way there's enough beer in that fridge tonight.

"I wish I sounded like Celia." He sighs, and that glazed-over, wistful look comes into his smart eyes.

"Tell me more about her."

He turns his body toward me, squaring his shoulders and bending his knee in a way that allows his long shin to rest on the couch. He drapes one arm across the back of the couch, and the beer dangles from his nimble fingers. "You don't usually like to talk about her." He swings the bottle gently as he talks.

I shrug, drinking.

He nods. "Okay. She was a fighter. Fierce. That's what she was. Everything about her was fierce. Fiercely smart, and driven, and beautiful. She had this *mane* of long blonde hair. By the time I'd met her, she had marched in a rally for every cause I'd ever heard of and so many I hadn't. Women's rights. Equality. LGBTQ+ rights. Protect the oceans, the forests…" He chuckles. "You name it, she fought for it."

He sighs again. I know this is hard for him. He's been living with only her memory for the past eighteen years.

"And all she ever wore were T-shirts with one cause or another plastered across the chest hanging over these loose hippie pants"—he mimes bell-bottoms with his free hand—"or long skirts, or too-tight jeans." He shakes his head, smiling. "And those awful flip-flops. Would've worn those damned things in winter if I didn't nag her to change." His eyes light up. He's happy at the memory of being needed. "Her feet were always dirty." He chuckles. "Permanently darker than the rest of her body."

He raises his bottle, draining it, and sits so his back is once again flush with the couch. Then he reaches for another beer and grabs one for me, too. He hands me the bottle, and I finish my first, stacking it on the floor by the couch like he does before I start on my second. He turns his wrist splotched with hair and glances at the time on his watch. "It's after midnight. You going to school in the morning?"

I nod. Hell yes.

"Well, maybe we should—" He sits forward, obviously about to stand, but I stop him by grasping his forearm. He looks down at my hand.

"How'd you know?" My words are soft.

He leans back on the couch and scrubs his face with his hand. His gaze is filled with pain. He's tired. "How did I know what?"

I tilt my head at him, and he raises his eyebrows.

"Really?"

"Yes. It's her."

He stares at me blankly.

"She's marked."

"Jesus, Josh!" He stands abruptly and tosses his beer across the garage. It lands with a smash, breaking against the far wall. Beer bubbles dance on broken glass in the corner.

He turns to me, and his shoulders rise up and down in time with his fuming breath. "Marked? Really? After all this time?"

I stare at him, and he looks away.

"I'm sorry," he mumbles. "Who is she?"

"A girl at school. Works at the Shakes 'n' Slaw after. Takes care of her sick mother."

"How sick?"

"Stage 4 breast cancer."

He squats down, leans against his workbench, and buries his head in his hands. "Josh." He shakes his head, dropping it low.

"I know."

"Do you?"

He mumbles his question, but it's rhetorical, so I don't bother answering. Instead, I walk over to him and lean down, placing my hand on his shoulder. He glances up at me, and I stand straighter.

"Have you two…?" He raises his eyebrows.

"Of course not. We just met. She has a lot going on. All I did was sit with her on her front steps for a bit. Drank orange seltzer." I scrunch up my nose at the memory.

"You hate seltzer. Told me it's like drinking battery acid."

I shrug. "Maybe it's not as bad as I thought."

"I see." He runs a hand through his hair, and then he nods and stands stiffly. "Well." He forces a smile, clearing his throat. "We should get some sleep. It's late. I'll, uh, I'll clean that up in the morning."

He walks across the garage and toward the door leading to the house.

"Dad?"

He stops without turning back. "Yes?"

There are so many things I want to ask him. So much we have to say. And as of right now, we have so little time to say it.

"Good night."

"Good night, Josh." He walks through the doorway, knocking on the frame for luck as he goes.

Chapter Six

Gracie

"Are you going to prom?" Mom rolls onto her side, her grimace thinly disguised by her smile. "Oh, ow." She's quiet in her agony.

"Are you in pain?" What a stupid question, but sometimes stupid questions just happen. "I'm sorry. I mean, more than usual."

"I know what you mean." She smiles again and slowly slides her frail body tight to the inside of the couch, closer to the chair I'm sitting in, and then pats the cushion beside her. "The pain is better today."

She's lying. I know it. I can see it in the way she tucks her left arm toward her ribcage, holding her left forearm with her right hand. She's guarding. She's in excruciating pain, pain I can't even fathom, but she'll never tell me. We lie most often to the ones we love the best—that's what love is, isn't it? A series of fables we tell one another to get us through the day. Sure, you look great… No, my pain's not so bad… Yes, school is wonderful… Of course I'll be here for your wedding day.

Fuck you, cancer.

I stop flipping through my notebook and look at her. The lines around her eyes cascade down her cheeks and meet the grooves along the sides of her mouth. Those lines weren't there even a year ago. Feeling my eyebrows knit together, I consciously relax them and look into her eyes. She has beautiful, bright blue eyes that, for the past few years, have been camouflaged by pain. But tonight, they're brighter. Somewhere in there, she's happy.

"So?"

She pats the couch again, and I drop my English Lit notebook. I remove the hand-knit brightly colored blanket from my lap and drape it on her, from her feet to her lower ribs, covering her. I sit next to her, careful not to shimmy the couch, and tuck the blanket as high as I dare, not wanting to put even an ounce of extra weight on her chest.

"Mmm…" She snuggles down, closing her eyes, and then opens them again slowly.

I swallow hard. When I was a child, before this devil came to live with us, she would cover me with this blanket in almost the same way. She'd stand over my bed, give the blanket one good shake, and allow it to float down over me as the cool breeze it created blew gently against my skin. Then she'd lean over me, tucking the blanket high under my chin, insisting it would protect me from any monsters in my room. The fuzz of the yarn tickled my neck, but I didn't care. Even though it was only ever the two of us, we were okay. Together.

"Gracie Jean," she would whisper as she stood up tall, hands on her slim hips. "You have nothing to be afraid of. No monsters can ever touch you. You, Gracie, are destined for great things."

And stupidly, childishly, I believed her.

Guess what, Mom? You were wrong. The monster is here now. And he's fucking terrifying.

"Prom?" She blinks quickly. Her light-colored lashes that refuse to give over to the chemo are batting up and down. "Are you going?"

"To prom?" I shake my head, pushing away my sorrow as I always do. I've gotten so good at burying my feelings, I think my body must have been hollow once. Now, it's filled to the brim with unexpressed fear and anger. "Mom, where would you get an idea like that?"

"Oh, I don't know." She rolls carefully onto her back. "You're a senior; it's spring."

She coughs, placing a hand on her chest as she fights to sit up. I slip my arm under her back, helping her. She's so skinny I can feel every bone of her vertebra and ribs. As she coughs, something in her chest rattles, and she wheezes. Damn, this isn't good. We've fought off fluid in the lungs once before, but it was a freak thing. Lungs filling with fluid shouldn't be a symptom of breast cancer. No—if you have to get cancer, get breast cancer. It's the one you want. The one you can beat. Breast cancer should be fightable. It shouldn't fill your lungs with light amber-colored fluid that makes it impossible to breathe. Unless you're in Stage 4. And they find the cancer in your lungs.

In case it didn't hear me the first time, *Fuck You, Cancer.*

She finishes coughing and nods in appreciation. I exhale when her breathing returns to normal. I reach over to fetch her water that's balanced on the low wood coffee table near the couch. The water's placed next to a stack of out-of-date magazines and unread romance novels I get her at the library every week. I know she never reads them, but my plan is to keep her mind busy while I'm at school. Although…truthfully, I don't know how much longer I can leave her while I go to school and work. I'm away too many hours. Something's got to give—but only one can.

When I lift the blue plastic water cup from the table, the condensation has left behind a ring on the cheap veneer. Who cares? Once upon a time, Mom would have cared. Back then, she cared about everything, from her appearance—using a coconut oil masque on her long curly strawberry-blonde hair—to me having an education and a future. But now, since nearly all hope is lost for both of us, what does old damaged furniture matter? What does anything matter?

"Mom."

She finishes drinking, so I place the cup back on the table and look at her. Her head is resting against the couch pillow, and her neck looks strained.

"Are you comfortable? You want a bed pillow?"

She rolls her eyes. "What I want is for you to stop fussing over me and to have a life of your own."

"Excuse me?" I sit back.

She reaches out with her right hand, placing it on mine. She's cold, and her fingers are bony, but still, her touch calms me. I close my eyes, drawing in a moment's peace.

"I saw you outside last night." She grins, her eyes happier than I've seen them in years. "With a boy. A handsome boy."

"You saw us?" My cheeks flush, and a tiny smile starts at one corner of my mouth. I press my lips together. "If I had known you were awake…"

"You would have abandoned that cute boy to come in and fluff my pillow." She raises her hand and lets it drop in exasperation. "Enough fussing over me, Gracie. Tell me about him. Is he your boyfriend?"

I shake my head. "No. No. I just met him, really. He and his dad move around a lot. He's finishing the last couple of months of school here." I shrug. "We met yesterday. He..." I stop abruptly. I can't tell her what really happened. How he took a beating to save me from who knows what. "I was late and dropped my books, and he stopped to help me pick them up."

"Handsome and chivalrous." She smiles.

"Yeah. Then he came to work yesterday and ordered a milkshake. Stayed outside for hours. Walked me to my car after my shift."

"And then he just ended up on the front steps?"

My smile is becoming harder and harder to fight. "He followed me home just to make sure I got here okay." I omit everything about Jerry acting strangely. "So I asked him to have a drink with me on the front steps. He likes seltzer water, like me."

"Uh-huh." She places her good hand over her mouth, fighting her smile.

"What?" I pull her hand away carefully.

"What?" She chuckles, rolling her head away and back again. "*What* is he likes you!"

"I don't know about that."

"He walked you to your car, followed you home, and pretended to like seltzer water?"

"He does like—"

She puts up her hand, stopping me. "No man likes seltzer water, Gracie. They drink it for us. No man likes sitting outside Shakes 'n' Slaw through your entire shift, either."

"I think he's just nice." My stomach races with butterflies. "That's all."

"Hopefully so. But I think he's extra nice to you because he likes you."

She tilts her head to one side, placing her cold hand

on my cheek. She strokes my cheek lovingly, and although her skin is so dry it's like sandpaper, her touch is magic, sending a direct current of peace to my heart.

"Gracie. I know what you do in a day, and honestly, I don't know how you do it all. Between school and work—and everything you do for me." Tears flood her eyes. "I didn't want this to be your life, Gracie," she whispers, nearly choking on her words.

She coughs, and I help her change position again.

"Mom. This is just for now. You know that. Just until we beat this thing. Then, I'll be in college and have all the time in the world to be a normal college kid—pulling all-nighters and being late for class or whatever college girls do."

She nods sheepishly but doesn't smile. Seems neither of us believes this pep talk we give each other lately.

"Gracie, you always ask what you can do for me, so I'm telling you now. Have a life. Go out with this boy. Let him take you to prom."

"I have plenty of time for all of that."

"I don't." She holds my hands with hers.

"Mom. Don't say that." My throat constricts around my words.

"Oh, Gracie, we have fought the good fight, haven't we?"

"Mom." I shake my head. My throat aches, but I push away my sorrow.

"Gracie, you know better than anyone that I'm not getting better. You know that. I'm sorry, baby, but you have to be ready. And I'd really like it if, when the time comes, you weren't alone."

"I'm not alone." I clear my throat. "I have you."

My eyes meet hers, and she tilts her head.

"I want everything for you. I've robbed you of enough life."

"You haven't robbed me of anything. I wanted to be here. We're a team."

"I know." She nods, and just like that, we fall back into our traditional roles, she as the caretaker and me as the child. "But a parent and child, Gracie, they're not really a team. You need to be part of a couple. Spend your life with someone. Do something with your Amazing. Find out what you're destined to become."

"I will, Mom. I will have all that."

She rolls onto her back, staring at the ceiling. "They say at the end you let go of ego and you concentrate on those who matter most. But for me, Gracie, I find I've grown incredibly selfish."

"What are you talking about?"

"I want to see your life. I want to see you be happy. We both know I won't make it to your wedding or even your college graduation, but I can make it to your prom. I promise you that. Go to your prom with that handsome boy. What's his name?"

"Josh." I pull at the collar of my faded New York T-shirt.

"Ah, Josh." She nods, reaching out with her hand to pat mine. "Nice name. Gracie, go to the prom with Josh. Let me know you've been happy at least once in your life."

"Mom, even if I wanted to, prom is soon, and I don't have anything to wear."

Her eyes sparkle again. "That's where you're wrong."

"What do you mean?"

“Go to the closet.” She nods toward our entranceway.

Sliding off the couch, I make my way the few steps to the closet, place my hand on the handle, and stall. I can’t shake the feeling that I’m starring in a horror movie, and everyone but me knows I shouldn’t open this door.

But hell, it’s scripted, so I’m going to.

Taking a deep breath, I pull the door open.

“What?” Laying in the overstuffed, messy row of winter jackets, raincoats, and never-used tennis rackets is a dark blue dress hanging on a wire hanger in a plastic dry-cleaning bag. I grab the dress and hold it away from me so I can take it all in—the deep navy color, the thin spaghetti straps, the molded cups and fitted waist, and the simple cascade of blue silk. It’s beautiful.

“Do you like it?” Mom has contorted herself over the back of the couch, watching me. “I found it in the back of the storage closet.”

Her smile is so wide I don’t ask why she would do something as dangerous as dig through our storage closet—that’s shaped like a long piece of elbow macaroni—all alone. She would have had to duck to step in and then shimmy herself around to find anything. Frankly, it’s a miracle she was able to. But there’s no way she’d ask for help.

Now I have to pray she doesn’t get some chemo-nesting urge and decide to go digging through my closet. I can’t take that risk. Tomorrow, I’ll put a lock on it.

“Gracie?”

“I—” I hold the dress to my body and cram my emotions down. Focusing on the dress, I imagine what it would look like on.

"Go to the mirror," she instructs.

Mom points to the three-quarter-length mirror hanging on the wall at the far end of the room, and I move toward it, careful not to trip on the flowing plastic as I walk. Peeking into the mirror, I hold the dress higher in front of me, aligning the straps to my shoulders. Wow. Even for a kid who dresses in jeans and plaid shirts every day, wow.

"It's—"

"Seems Cinderella wasn't a complete fantasy, huh?" She raises her eyebrows, teasing me. "I'm sorry the fashions were so bad in the early two-thousands." It's like she has a sudden burst of adrenaline as she moves herself around, getting a better angle to watch me. "But as the fashions of the time go, that one's not so horrible."

"It was your prom dress?" I'm finally lucid enough to make sense of it all.

She nods. "I went with your father, Nathaniel. Our senior prom."

I drop the dress to my waist and turn to her. "You went to the prom with my father?"

She nods. "Of course. We were high school sweethearts. One of the best memories I have. We danced and danced, and I gazed up into his eyes, so dark they were almost liquid." She inhales deeply. "He held me so tight whenever they played a slow song." She closes her eyes and wraps her arms around herself. Thankfully, this time, she's not guarding from pain but reliving the magic. "It was an underwater theme, and he told me I looked like a beautiful mermaid." She laughs. "How corny. But he was sweet."

"I never knew." I plop down on the couch, holding the dress in my lap, careful not to wrinkle it. I smooth the plastic. "How did I not know?"

She draws her feet up toward her body. "Growing up without a father was hard on you, Gracie."

"No, it wasn't. I never knew any different, so I couldn't miss him. It wasn't like he was a part of my life, and then—" I stop short, shaking my head.

She cocks hers. "I guess I should have told you more about him. He came to my school my senior year, just like Josh, I suppose." She smiles again.

"Did he really die in a car wreck?"

She nods somberly. "I was in school in Pennsylvania, and he was in school in Upstate New York." She points to my T-shirt. "That's where you get your love of New York teams, I think. Anyway, he had picked me up for spring break."

"Wait. You went to college?" I sit up, my heart racing.

"Yes. Never finished, though."

"You've always said you never went," I protest.

"I said I never graduated."

"I…" My words fall away.

"It was our anniversary celebration. Two years." She smiles, looking ten years younger. "I was going to tell him the exciting news."

"What exciting news?"

"You." She nods to me.

"What?" I shake my head. "He never knew about me?" I stand, unable to control my racing thoughts and shaking body.

"He did. I hadn't told him yet, but somehow, instinctively, he knew."

"How do you know?"

"Because when they salvaged his bag from the

wreck, there was an anniversary card inside. In the card, he wrote, *Even though it's no longer just the two of us, it will always be you and me. Will you marry me?*"

"How did he…?"

"That's Nathaniel. That's your dad." She shrugs, wincing and covering what would have been her left breast with her arm. "Then the car toppled on that damned ledge, and we rolled over and over down that embankment." She closes her eyes, drawing a deep breath.

"I knew you were in a car accident. I didn't know it was with him." I drop down onto the couch again.

"And you. Growing inside me. The fact that you and I survived all that crushed metal and broken glass—how we survived the airbag…" She shakes her head. "Nearly an hour we were balanced on edge on that hill. Your father died on impact, but we somehow survived. It was a real miracle. And that's when I knew."

"Knew what?"

"You were destined for greatness."

I chuckle uncomfortably. Does greatness wear a porno star's outfit at Shakes 'n' Slaw? "Mom."

"Just watch, Gracie. Give yourself a chance." She smiles. "My time is done. I raised you as best I could. Now it's your time."

"No." I repeat my word and shimmy in my seat, scratching an itch on my arm. My skin feels like a million little bugs are crawling over it. I hate it when she grows morose. I need to change the subject. "Where were you going? When he picked you up?"

"To the beach." She smiles. "Jones Beach. Long Island. Just us."

"The beach." I sit back against the couch. "I've

always wanted to see the beach."

"I know." With the help of couch pillows, she sits up and squeezes my hand. "And you've been stuck here in this landlocked town in the middle of Ohio your entire life." She shakes her head. "Gracie, promise me that you'll go away for college. Get away from here."

"Mom." I fiddle with the plastic from the dry-cleaning bag. "I can't take off. We're a team." I remember her words. We're not a team. Not really. "I'm not leaving you."

She shakes her head. "You won't be leaving me, Gracie. I'll be long gone by then." Her eyes glass over.

"Stop saying that." My words are guttural.

"Gracie, honey. It's time we talk."

"I don't want to." I shake my head, looking away.

"But you have to understand, I'm not getting better. This cough—there's fluid in my lungs again. I know it. So do you."

"We'll get them drained again."

"Gracie."

"Mom." I place my hand on hers, looking deeply into her eyes. "I don't want to have this conversation. Not tonight. Please."

"Fine."

She sits back, conceding, and my shoulders drop. I sigh heavily, releasing a thousand pounds of stress. As long as she's willing to wait to have this conversation, it means she believes there's still some hope.

"So college?"

"It's last semester senior year. I have to make sure I'm even graduating from high school."

"What?" She shimmies herself up slightly, and a look of concern colors her face.

Crap. I've said too much. "You know what I mean. Don't want to count my chickens or any of that." There's no way I'm going to stress her with my worries about failing bio. "And it's not like I can just pick a college and go."

"You can if it's a community college. Pick one in a place you want to live and work your way to a four-year school. You can do it, Gracie. If anyone can, it's you."

I glance up at her and then back down at the frayed carpet.

"I never wanted this to be your life, you know."

"I have a good life, Mom."

"No, you don't." Her face clouds over, but this time, it's not from pain. It's from sadness.

"Yes, I do." I force a smile. "I have school and friends—"

"Gracie." She puts up her hand, quieting me. "Just for tonight, let's not lie to each other. Okay?"

She lifts her eyebrows, and I nod in response.

"I know you have nothing. And it's because of me. I'm sorry for that."

I swallow hard. "I don't have nothing, Mom. I have you. I have an education. I'm strong, and I'm a survivor."

"Goodness knows that's true." She nods.

"And I have this beautiful dress." I shake the dress, laying it gently in my lap again. The plastic has grown moist from my sweaty palms.

"That's not all you have."

"No?"

She shakes her head, and the slightest twinkle returns to her eyes. "Go to the closet again. Look on the floor." She winks.

Standing, I lay the dress carefully across the back of

the couch and rush to the open closet door. I squat down and push aside material from coats and old bags until I spot a shoebox. "Shoes?" I pull the box out and turn toward the couch.

"Yes." She's not watching me now. It must be too difficult for her to turn my way.

Clutching the shoebox with as much care as if I were holding a sleeping puppy, I walk back to the couch. I sit next to her and place the box on my lap.

"Well, go on, open it."

I lift the top, and there, nestled with tissue paper, are two navy satin shoes with six rhinestones adorning the front of each shoe. I don't dare touch anything.

"Go ahead." She chuckles. "Try one on. I promise they won't break."

Kicking off my filthy sneakers and pulling off my short mismatched socks, I lift a high heel from the box and bend my knee, resting my bare foot on the couch. I hold my breath and slide my toes in, praying my foot will fit. With just a little force, my foot slips in, and I tuck the simple strap up over my heel, resting it on the back of my ankle. It's tight, but it fits. I curl my toes, standing on the heel. I'm wobbly, but after a breath, I catch my balance.

"Try the other one, too!" Mom is nearly giddy.

Holding the arm of the couch for support, I balance myself and slide on the other shoe. I feel tall—really tall—I must be six feet in these things and very upright. Do women really wear these things all day long? I glance down at my toes and the beautiful shine of the rhinestones. Wow, they're pretty. A little pain is worth it.

"Perfect!" Mom exclaims, clapping her hands

together. “You really are Cinderella!”

I chuckle, stepping away, and then I turn back and walk clumsily toward the couch.

Mom nods in appreciation. “You’ll get it. You just need to wear them around the house for a bit.”

Laughing, I walk back and forth from the couch to our tiny kitchen, stopping at the table. I use the old ladder-back chair for support. Pivoting, I turn and swing my hips from side to side as I walk an imaginary runway.

“The latest in Paris couture!” Mom says as she chortles and falls onto her good side.

Opening my plaid shirt, I slap my hands onto my hips and show off my ripped white tank top. “Nineties grunge is back, haven’t you heard?” I take another lap modeling.

Mom howls with laughter. Damn, it’s so good to hear her laugh.

“I love grunge! That was all I wore in college!”

“Ah!” I take another lap. “I see my excellent taste in clothing comes from you.”

She giggles as I stick out my hip, showing the butt of my jeans. I slap my own bony ass before catwalking back to the kitchen. Slipping, I roll my ankle but right myself quickly. I throw both arms into the air like a gymnast who’s just scored a perfect ten.

“Come sit before you hurt yourself, or I hurt myself from laughing,” Mom says as she pushes herself upright on the couch.

Smiling, I make my way to her and plop down next to her, kicking my feet out in front of me. I flex my feet, rolling them together and apart, mesmerized by the flash of the rhinestones. I don’t think I’ve ever before owned anything shiny.

“So, Cinderella. Going to the prom?”

“Mom.” I drop my head back against the lumpy couch and roll it toward her. “He hasn’t asked.”

“So ask him!” She’s chipper.

“It’s not that easy.”

“Of course it is.” She sits forward and takes my hand. “Gracie, what they say about life being short, it’s true. It’s so very true. Live, Gracie. Ask handsome Josh, who pretends to like seltzer water, to the prom. Do it tomorrow. Take control of your own destiny. Don’t put your life on hold any longer.”

I stare at her frail frame and the pain lines on her face. How much would she give to live even one extra day?

“Okay.”

“Okay?” She sits up, surprised.

“Well, now that you look so surprised…”

She leans forward and embraces me. She smells different now since her thin body is filled with chemicals and medicines, but her touch is the same. She is still Mom.

“Will you do it, Gracie?” she whispers in my ear. “Will you ask him?”

I nod, tightening my embrace around her. “Yes, Mom. I will.”

****

I stare at my locker, fiddling with my lock, reciting the same mental mantra I’ve been repeating all morning. *I will take control of my destiny. I will take control of my destiny. I will—*

“Hey.”

“Huh!” I jump, placing a hand to my racing heart, and completely abandon my mantra. It doesn’t matter, it was really just a pathetic attempt to get my nerve up.

Josh walks up beside me as I fumble with my lock. The damned lock is attached to the locker itself, so it's not like I can just get a set of wire cutters or something and cut it free. I do my locker combo again and nick the side of my finger, trying to lift the lock. I shimmy the lock once more, lifting it up and down, but it won't give.

"Can I?"

I nod and step back, too terrified to look at him. I promised Mom I'd ask him to the prom today, but I'm quickly losing my nerve. I glance up at his strong jaw and the slight scruff growing on his chin and sigh. Oh damn, I'm doomed.

He knocks the side of his fist against the door of the locker just above the lock and sure enough, it swings open. Obviously, he's working some kind of hot guy magic.

"You working at Shakes 'n' Slaw today?"

"Y—yes…" I nod toward the locker. "Oh, uh, thanks." My palms are so sweaty I wipe them on my ripped jeans before shuffling through the mess of books and papers on my locker shelf. I clear my throat. "Um, I work there every day."

He frowns. "Seven days a week?"

"No. I mean every day after school. Sometimes I do work seven. But usually six." Heat rises in my cheeks. Good grief, could I be any more of a mess? My grip tightens on the straps of my backpack. *Just do this. Just ask him.*

He steps behind me, and we both stare into my locker.

"What are you looking for?"

He reaches one strong arm over my head, and I catch

a whiff of him. He smells so good. I don't know what the heck to call his scent except…man. He smells like man.

"Bio?"

"Yeah, thanks."

He takes my bio book from the top shelf and hands it to me. Turning, I end up wedged against my open locker, looking up at him. I inhale deeply. How does he smell even better than yesterday? He's wearing a white T-shirt that pulls across his chest and hangs over a pair of faded jeans. The whiteness of the tee makes his skin even darker… The fingers of my free hand fiddle with the buttons of my lavender plaid shirt, the only thing I own that's even the tiniest bit feminine. Wait. No. I have my prom dress, too.

I exhale, trying to stay cool, and my breath comes out in little spurts like I'm a tiny, constipated, fire-breathing dragon. Sexy.

"Thanks for the drink last night."

"Yeah, sure. Thanks for following me home."

"How about I follow you home again tonight?"

An electrical jolt races straight up my spine. If I were a cartoon character, I'd suddenly morph into that carnival game where someone hits my feet with a huge mallet, and my head flies off and up to ring a bell. Well, dang, my bell's sure been rung.

"That'd be great." My words come out like rapid fire. "I'm done at eight. Want to meet me in the parking lot of the grocery store next door?" I raise my eyebrows. "The discount place?"

"Why not just meet you at Shakes 'n' Slaw?"

"I uh…" I chew the corner of my lip, and my words rush out. "I think Jerry might get upset if you're there again. He has a strict, no boyfriends—" *Crap.* "—Or uh,

I mean, friends around." I shake my head. "No friends. Boys or girls." I place my sweaty hand that's holding my bio book behind me and hunch my shoulders forward, hiking my backpack up higher. What an ass I am. "It's his policy, and I just can't."

"I get it. I'll meet you in the parking lot next door at eight."

"Okay." I smile. Despite the fact that I'm a nervous wreck about prom, just being around Josh relaxes me. "But uh, better make it eight fifteen, so I have a minute to change out of that stupid uniform."

"I don't mind the uniform." He lifts his chin, smirking. "I've always had a thing for milkmaids."

"Cute. I mind the uniform. Hate the stupid thing. And besides, Jerry doesn't like us to wear it home."

"No?" He furrows his brow.

"Uh-uh. I think he doesn't want to risk the wholesome Shakes 'n' Slaw milkmaid image—if we go out partying or drinking."

"Makes sense." He leans closer.

He reaches out with his free hand and takes mine. Quiet giddiness sits in my chest like a mint candy in a bottle of soda pop ready to explode. Currents of electricity rush through me, up my hand, across my chest, shooting up my neck and ricocheting into the back of my head. My head actually feels hot. This boy has made me a hothead. What the hell?

Ask him, Gracie... Ask him.

He smiles, and I smile back. It's now or never.

I stand straight, and he releases my hand that's now aching from zaps of electrical current. Is this what love is? Feeling like my extremities are tasered every time he touches me?

"Josh, I..."

He lifts his hand and brushes a stray piece of hair off my cheek, and I just about die inside.

"Yeah?"

The moment's ruined by first bell ringing way too soon and way too loud.

"Crap." I jump, placing a hand to my racing heart.

"You okay?"

I nod feverishly.

The hallway begins to fill, and it's a freaking eerie thing. Students look like apathetic zombies, all lined up at their lockers. Then, with the precision of synchronized swimmers, they move—locks turn right, left, right—grab a calc book, lit book, put away a lunch. After all these years, this will all be over in less than four weeks.

I take a deep breath. "Will you go to the prom with me?"

He takes a step back, and his face blanches like he's about to puke after a night of binging on cheap vodka. "What?" He leans down closer.

"Prom."

I bite my bottom lip. *Ow*. A slight jolt of pain will keep me strong. Kids fill in around us.

"It's next Saturday night. A week away. I know it's close, so if you already have something planned." I shrug.

"No." His eyes widen as he shakes his head.

"No?" Prickly heat washes from my brain to my toes. My cheeks burn.

"No, no." He inhales sharply. "I mean, no, I don't have anything planned."

"Oh." I exhale, and my entire body tenses to the point of contortion.

He just stares at me, not saying a word. I purse my lips together and close my eyes. *I did the right thing. I'm supposed to take charge of my life. Control my own destiny*. I open my eyes, and he's still staring at me.

"Well, uh, I can't be late for Gibbons." My jaw is so tight from stress and humiliation I sound like a robot. I hold up my book, willing my shoulders to unglue from my ears.

"Yeah." He steps aside so I can walk by.

My shoulders slump forward like a deflated balloon as I step past him. He reaches out and takes my elbow, stopping me. I glance up at him.

"I would love to go with you to prom."

My gaze drops to the floor as I swallow hard. "You don't have to."

"I want to."

I raise my head. "You don't owe me anything, Josh."

"Why would you say that?"

"It's just a stupid dance. You reacted like I gave you a death sentence or something."

He flinches.

"Like that." I point to his face. "Listen." Anger churns in my belly. "I told you before, I don't have time for games. If you're not into prom, or me, you're not. We'll both survive."

He places a finger under my chin and guides my gaze back to him. It's such the wrong moment for an intimate gesture, but yet it feels so right.

"Gracie? You just surprised me. Really. I would love to take you to the prom."

"You don't have to *take* me. I can afford to buy the tickets."

"Gracie. Please."

He traces my chin with his thumb, and I can't possibly think straight. He drops his hand, and I straighten up. The side of his mouth turns up into a grin.

"I was just surprised. I didn't know you wanted to go to prom, that's all."

"I didn't know either. But then I thought I should have some high school experience that happens in high school and not in a hospital."

He nods. "I'm glad you asked. Really." His brow furrows. "But did you think I wasn't going to ask you?"

I raise one shoulder to my ear and then let it fall. "I don't know. And it's just…it's stupid, but I've decided to take control of my life. To make my destiny instead of waiting for it to happen to me."

He flinches again, but this time just the slightest bit. "Taking charge of your destiny, huh?"

I shrug. "I'm trying. But who knows, maybe I'm too late. Maybe destiny already has a plan for me."

"Maybe."

His face contorts like he's in excruciating pain, and then he relaxes. It all happens so fast I'm not sure I actually saw it happen. But I did. What is his deal?

He steps back, lifting his arm and holding it wide from his body. Without thinking, I slip in next to him. I don't know what his deal is, but I don't think I care. We all have something. He wraps his arm around my shoulder, pulling me close. Together, we walk toward bio class just as second bell rings.

Chapter Seven

Josh

"I can't help it. I've got a weird feeling about that place." I speak quietly into my phone, shoving my free hand into my jeans as I stand like a conspirator in some covert plan that takes place at the Cheap Buys food store next door to Shakes 'n' Slaw.

"Her work? What kind of feeling?" I know I have Dad's full attention because there's no hammering or noise of sanding in the background.

"The 'something's not right' kind. Something about her boss."

"Coming on to her?"

"No…not exactly. It's not like it's about her…it's about me. But why?"

"You sure he's not being protective? Maybe he's a father figure."

"Maybe." I crane my neck to see into the side windows of Shakes 'n' Slaw. Nothing. I see nothing, and it bugs the crap out of me. I start pacing again, like some starving wolf stalking his prey. Maybe if I just risk a walk to the edge of the parking lot I'll see better?

"Josh? You there?"

"Yeah. Sorry, Dad." I decide against it, hurrying back toward my car.

"How long's she worked there?"

"A couple of years, at least."

"And she relies on that income?"

"Completely."

"Then don't mess with it. Her boss—"

"Jerry," I prompt.

"Jerry. He's had ample time to be an asshole. Don't come on too strong."

Don't come on too strong. He might as well tell a dog not to piss on the only tree in the yard.

"Joshua. You've got to back off a bit. She needs time to get to know you. She's not privy to your…plan." He nearly spits the word. "You've got time. Don't be in such a rush."

Don't be in such a rush. How often does he say that? Who the hell is in a rush? Why would I rush? I run a hand over my locs, frustrated. It's not rushing. It's fate. My fate.

And hers.

I use my fingertips to massage the shooting pain in my temple and close my eyes, breathing. Silently, I repeat the mantra that Hanh, my spiritual guide, taught me: *I only focus on things I can control.* It's true. I didn't choose to be who I am. I didn't choose any of this.

But neither did she.

I open my eyes and jam my thumb and middle finger into my temples, stretching my hand wide across my forehead. How the hell can I do this to her?

Dropping my hand, I turn toward the Shakes 'n' Slaw. I can't. I shouldn't. But…it's just I have this pull toward her, and I can't stay away.

"Dad. I'm not in a rush. I'm just doing what I need to do."

There's a long pause before he answers. "I know."

I glance at my watch—a lightweight titanium

number with a silver band and a thick face Dad gave me when I turned sixteen two years ago. It's ten after eight. "Hey, Dad, she'll be out in five. Sorry I bothered you."

"You didn't bother me, Josh. I want you to call me whenever you need to. That's our deal, right?"

"Yeah, Dad, that's our deal." Out of the corner of my eye, I see her leaving the building. She's wearing that same purple plaid shirt and ripped jeans from today. Her hair is pulled back in a soft ponytail that flows down her back. Damn, she's beautiful.

"Josh? Still there?"

"Yeah, sorry. She just came out. She'll be here in a couple of seconds."

"All right." Dad's voice softens. "Just take it slow, Josh. Please. For her sake as well as yours."

"Yeah. Thanks."

I barely hear his goodbye as I click off my phone and watch her. She slides in behind the wheel of her car and peeks into her rearview. She smooths some hair back from her face and then grabs something from the seat next to her. She sits tall, raising her chin as her head sways back and forth, her hand moving in front of her lips. She must be applying lip gloss or lipstick or something, although she sure as hell doesn't need it. She is beautiful. Just as she is.

She backs the car out of its spot and then eases forward toward the dark side road that connects to this parking lot. That connects her to me.

Watching her… It's like I've got something deep in my chest that's pulsating energy out to my extremities. My arms literally ache to hold her.

Pulling into our parking lot, she makes a wide turn to avoid a pothole and comes up perpendicular to my car.

I squint from the lights, so she cuts the engine. Bounding to her side, I grab her door and open it. Damn. Those long legs in those soft, ripped jeans… Damn.

"Thanks." She looks up at me and smiles. It's not one of those fake social media smiles, either. It's a real, warm, genuine smile like she's absolutely relaxed around me, and we've known each other forever.

She reaches down to unhook her seatbelt, and I grin. Who puts on their seatbelt to drive from one parking lot to another?

"What are you smiling about?" She talks while she struggles with the belt.

I shrug. "Just glad to see you."

"Good." She teases as she yanks on the latch. "Just give me a sec. This sticks sometimes."

"Gracie, that's not safe. What if you're in an accident and your car catches on fire or something?"

She shrugs. "I thought about it, but I figure it would be way worse if I got into an accident without wearing one."

"Yeah. You have to wear a seatbelt."

"It doesn't usually stick like this, though." She fights with the belt, and her ponytail bounces along with her.

"Let me see." I reach in with my left arm and extend it across her body. I keep it taut so it doesn't touch her lap and find the latch.

She breathes deeply. "It'll usually unlock if you shimmy it enough."

I wiggle the belt at the lock, but it doesn't want to give. Frankly, right now, I don't want it to. Taking a deep breath, I inhale her scent—a combo of fresh laundry, lemons, and *her… Damn. Damn. Damn.* It's all way more of an aphrodisiac than I need.

All right, Josh. My mind screams at me. *Concentrate on the damned seatbelt.* Yes. Seatbelt. I shimmy the latch, but it still won't give. I need more leverage, so, leaving my arm across her body, I squat down, one knee on the ground. Without meaning to, I allow my arm to go slack, and it rests on her lap.

"Sorry." I flex my arm, lifting it.

"No."

She takes her two soft hands and places them on my forearm, guiding my arm back to her lap.

"It's okay. It's not bothering me."

I look away for a moment, catching myself. I really don't know if I can be around her this close…in the dark…touching. Christ, with everything I spent last night fantasizing about…

I gotta move. Grasping the doorframe with my free hand, I hold myself away from her and give one more tug at the seatbelt. It pops loose.

She looks up at me with eyes half-closed.

Screw this.

Dropping to my knee again, I glide the seatbelt back beside her and then rest my hand on her leg, massaging her thigh. Sliding my other hand off the doorframe, I place it on the seat behind her and then onto her shoulder. She lowers her chin toward my hand, nuzzling against it as she closes her eyes.

I sigh, releasing a whole crapload of tension, but there's still a whole hell of a lot more. She opens her eyes—lazily—and a small moan escapes from her lips.

"Okay." Standing, I clear my throat and walk a couple of steps away from the car to compose myself. Casually, I come back to her. "Gracie, you shouldn't drive around like that. I'd like to fix your seatbelt. Any chance you can follow me home tonight? Shouldn't take more than a few minutes tops."

"I guess." She glances down at her phone. It's obvious she's torn. She's been at school and work all day and needs to get to her mom.

"If it's better, I can swing home and grab the stuff we need and then come by your place."

Shaking her head, she looks at her phone again. "No, no. Let me just…" She shoots a quick text and then steps out of the car, smiling. "It's really nice of you, I mean, I've been living with this stupid seatbelt for a long—"

Her phone chirps.

She glances at it and then immediately types something back. "All good." She waves the phone in her hand.

"That was fast."

"That's our deal." She leans back against her car, crossing her arms. "Wow, it's chilly…" She shivers.

"Oh, uh, here." Without thinking, I remove my leather jacket and slide it around her shoulders. Even though she's tall, the jacket hangs to her mid-thigh, practically swallowing her. I'm standing way too close.

"Josh. You'll freeze." She shakes her head but tightens the jacket around her.

"I think cold air would do me some good right now."

I wink, and she smirks and looks away.

"So, your deal?" I ask, hoping to prolong the moment as long as I can. "With your mom?"

"Yeah," she takes a deep breath and turns back to me. "My mom has to answer my text within five minutes, or I know something's wrong."

"What if she's napping?" We're standing so close

our conversation is a whisper.

"We have her phone set loud. She's not a heavy sleeper." She shrugs. "I know it's not a perfect system, but it's all I've got, you know? The best I could come up with. The five-minute rule."

"Sounds like a good plan to me."

"Yeah?" She raises her eyebrows, and her gaze catches mine.

"Yeah. Very smart."

"Thanks." She blushes the faintest pink, and she's even more beautiful. "So, uh, you sure you don't mind?" She points to the car. "Fixing my seatbelt. Should I follow you?"

"Yeah, uh, no, I don't mind." I take a step back. Dad's right. I'm moving way too fast. "Can you drive a stick?"

"Sure. Why?"

"You can?"

She nods. "Why'd you ask if you didn't think I could? You seem surprised."

"I…"

"My mom taught me when I got my permit. I might be rusty, but I can. Why?"

"I want you to drive my car. The seatbelt works."

Her brow furrows. "No, I'm used to the stuck seatbelt. Besides, what about you? What if you get in a terrible wreck?"

I chuckle. "Between here and my home? Nothing bad's going to happen to me tonight, Gracie. I can promise you that."

"You sound pretty sure of yourself."

"I am."

She looks at me quizzically, and my chest aches. It's

the weirdest feeling, like there's a giant hand squeezing my heart.

"So," I prod, wanting to lessen the crushing pain in my chest. "Switch cars?"

"I don't know…"

"Gracie, please." I step closer again, closing the gap between us. "Please."

"I…I guess." She's quiet. "But just this one time."

Her breathing quickens, and even in the darkness of the parking lot, I see her eyes flicker. Reaching up, I tuck a stray hair behind her ear and then stroke her cheek gently. She closes her eyes and opens them again, looking up at me through thick lashes.

She's so close. So…

No. I drop my hand, shaking my head. *Come on, Josh. Keep it under control.*

I fish the keys out of the front pocket of my jeans and then take her soft hand in mine. Turning it, I caress her palm with my thumb. She closes her eyes again and snuggles down into my jacket.

"Feels so good…" she mumbles.

I dare another step closer until our bodies are almost touching…

Crap.

"Um." I drop the keys into her open palm. "Just uh, follow me. I'll make sure you're behind me."

"Okay." Her voice is deep and earthy.

"Okay." Walking her to my car, I open the door for her and chuckle as she slides in.

"What?"

"You look good behind the wheel and in my jacket."

"Yeah?" She grips the steering wheel and then runs her hands across the leather seats.

"Oh hell, yeah."

She grins. "This car is amazing, Josh. I mean, I know nothing about cars, but wow. How long did it take you to restore it?"

"My dad and I just started when we moved here, but it came together way faster than either of us thought." I shrug. "It's not finished by any means, but it runs. My dad did most of the work. I helped out where I could."

"He sounds incredibly talented."

"He is," I agree. "Hopefully, he'll be home working in the workshop. I'd like you to meet him."

"I'd like that, too." She smiles again, and the world suddenly makes sense.

"Follow me, Gracie."

I close the door of the car, but she knocks on the window, and I open the door again.

"I'll avoid every pothole and bump in the road. I'll be super careful. Promise."

I force a smile, wishing I could promise her the same.

Chapter Eight

Gracie

"No, no, noooooo… Oh, crap." I mumble a string of obscenities as I pull up to his house, hitting every stinking tiny rock in the damned driveway. If the car's so valuable, why do they have a gravel driveway? "Please don't hurt the car, please don't hurt the car," I plead with the stones and pebbles as they bounce off the undercarriage.

Finally, we're there. "Whew." I throw the car into *park* and exhale.

As he walks to my door, the stones in the driveway crunch under his heavy boots. The same stones that could have popped a hole in the oil pan—or damaged any of the million other car parts I don't even know exist. He opens the door for me and gives me his hand. Climbing out, I release a pent-up chuckle.

"What?" He nods to me. Even in this dim light, I can see his face well, and his bruises and scratches are nearly gone.

"It's just, with all the door holding and standing up to those guys at school and waiting for me, and now the seatbelt…well, I think you've done more for me in the past two days than anyone has in my entire life."

"Gracie." He shakes his head. "I really, really hope that's not true."

"It kinda is. But it's okay, I mean. I'm not

complaining. My mom does her best, and when I was young, she would always cook dinner and have it waiting for me and stuff, but…uh, nothing like this." I risk a glance at him from beneath lowered lashes. "I think you're spoiling me."

He steps closer, places one strong finger beneath my chin, and then tilts my chin upward. When he touches me like this, it sets my insides on fire.

"Mmmm…" A moan escapes my lips.

His eyes have darkened, and he steps closer still.

"That noise, Gracie." He inhales deeply, exhaling audibly. Snaking his hand under my ponytail, he rests it on the back of my neck and then tightens his grip, pulling me toward him. I stumble and land flush against him. He intertwines our free hands, holding me tightly. "I don't think I can survive that noise."

My chest heaves as I look up into his eyes that, in the dark night, appear even darker. I shouldn't want this. I should know better, and yet… My eyes close as he holds me tighter. Zaps of electricity shoot through my body like I'm a downed power line flailing in a storm—and right now, I'm just as dangerous. Tentatively, I take my free hand and wrap it around his waist. My fingers collect the material of his shirt, fisting it.

"Gracie." He tightens his hold on me, and perspiration builds between our palms.

I yank on his shirt, pulling his body even closer to mine.

"Gracie."

He repeats my name over and over, and each time he does, my heart races a little faster, and my body aches a little more. This isn't anything like the last time I was with a boy. This is…warm and gentle and feels right. I lean closer, but he releases his grip, stepping back from me. I open my eyes, shuddering like I've just been dropped naked into the Arctic Tundra.

"What happened?" I search his eyes.

"I, uh, I'm moving way too fast. I'm sorry."

"I'm not."

My gaze falls to the driveway, and I kick a stone with my sneaker. I wait for the anxiety to wash over me, to flood me with the horrible memories of three years ago, but instead, I feel okay. No, I feel better than okay. Actually, for the first time ever, I feel safe.

Maybe I *can* learn to trust again.

I smile as he wraps his strong arm around me protectively, tucking it in at my waist, and turns me in the opposite direction. Finally, I see his house. It's a beautiful white cape with a large attached garage. A light is glowing near the front door, and there's a small porch but no rocking chairs or flowers like a house like this might have. It's definitely the house of two men. And to be fair, two men who've just moved in.

"This is amazing."

"Glad you like it." He pulls me tight to his side and kisses me on the top of my head. He walks me toward the garage. "Maybe my dad's working."

"Oh, uh," I stall. "I don't want to disturb him."

"No, it's okay. He'll want to meet you. I've told him a lot about you."

"You have?" I glance up at him. There's no way I'm being cool about this. I probably look like a kid on Christmas morning who finds a pony with a puppy riding on its back.

He smiles. "He wants to know what's going on in my life, so, of course I'm going to tell him about you."

I dig my heels in, and he waits patiently next to me.

"Gracie, I know it's moving fast. I'm moving fast. And I know I should slow down, but…"

"No." Reaching out, I take his hand that's grown chilly in the night air. "I don't want you to slow down, Josh. I like being with you." My sweaty palms and racing heart attest to that.

He nods, and in his eyes, I see a flicker of something I can't understand. Even with the darkness, I know it's there. Then, an eerie feeling stirs deep in my belly. I place a hand on my stomach and rub.

"Josh?"

"Yeah?" He gives me his full attention.

"I just had this weird feeling. Like a premonition. I feel like…like you're going to move away as soon as we get started."

He swallows hard, and I watch the outline of his Adam's apple bounce up and down.

"No, Gracie. Actually, I think I'm through moving. I think I found exactly what I was looking for right here."

He lifts our intertwined hands and kisses the back of mine. His lips linger, and then he drops my hand. "Come on, I want you to meet my dad."

I nod, feeling so full and complete every cell in my body is saturated. Glancing at the garage, I spy the silhouette of a man with short hair in the window. Who knows how long he's been there or what he's seen? Regardless, I smile at him, raising my free hand to wave, but as soon as I do, he disappears from sight.

Crap. That cannot be a good sign.

****

"You did it that fast?"

Josh smiles up at me. He's crouching near the

passenger seat of my car, reaching across to fix my stuck seatbelt. “Not quite.” He shakes his head. “The good news is that the handle on the door is tightened.” He chuckles. “But your seatbelt… Usually when the belts get stuck like this it means there’s something in the receptor. But yours is different.” He turns away, and his words trail off.

“Of course.” I throw up my hands in exasperation. Nothing is ever easy, except watching Josh. Standing here, bundled in his jacket, watching him work on my car, is very, very easy. With every turn of the screwdriver, I can see the muscles of his back flex. Good grief.

He pops his head out again and crouches on the gravel driveway with his forearm resting on his thigh. He wipes a drop of sweat from his temple with the back of his hand. “Usually, if there’s something stuck in the receptor, the male part won’t slide in. But here it does, no problem.”

I lean in to make sure I’ve heard correctly. “Excuse me? The male part?”

His smile starts at the corner of his mouth and spreads to a full-blown smirk as he stands. He’s holding a screwdriver in one hand, and his wrinkled T-shirt is tight against his bicep muscles. The veins in his arms are bulging. He looks like a model in a car ad. I turn away, but he walks right up to me and uses his free hand to guide me to face him. My cheeks burn, and I’m certain that even in this dim light he can see me blush.

“The receptor, or buckle, is female. It’s the part that takes the male component in. The male part is called the tongue, but I think male connector sounds better.”

“Uh, yes.” My throat is dry, and my entire body

tingles.

He doesn't move. He just stands there staring at me. I rock forward onto my toes, and he steps back and returns to the car. He nods to the car as he talks.

"I was able to remove the buckle and open the socket. There's nothing impeding it, and there's nothing stopping the movement. Honestly, I think it may just be age. And use. I noticed the dash on the way over, and you've got over a hundred thousand miles. What year is this thing?" He pats the roof over my door. "A ninety-eight, I'm guessing?"

"I think so. How'd you know?"

He shrugs. "I told you. Restoring cars is a hobby I do with my dad."

My nod is stilted. The same dad that left the garage when I approached.

He must notice that my mood has shifted because he walks closer to me again. "I'm sorry my dad wasn't around tonight. I would have loved for him to meet you."

I contemplate calling him on it, but really, what would we gain by that?

"It's okay. Another time." I look down at my ragged clothing and catch a whiff of the greasy ice cream topping smell on my clothes. While the rest of the world is getting healthier, we're adding more crap to our food—how ironic that Shakes 'n' Slaw barely has any dairy in their products. "It's probably better. I'm a mess." I hold my arms out to my sides.

He shakes his head and then takes a step closer to seal the gap between us. We're not quite touching, but I can feel his body anyway.

"Not a mess. You look beautiful."

Laughing nervously, I wrap my arms around my

body. “Thank you, but I’m a mess.”

“Beautiful.” He stands so still, just smiling. “I’ll order the replacement for your seatbelt,” he offers. “Should be here in just a few days. It’s best not to drive the car until then.”

I nod just to be agreeable. “Thanks, Josh, but there’s no way I can spare anything for a car repair. And certainly not for the luxury of a repair while the car’s still running. And besides that, I can’t go without a car for two days. I’ve got to work and shop and take care of my mom…” At that, I pull my phone from my back pocket and shoot her a quick text.

“Gracie, there’s no way I’d let you pay for it.”

I shake my head. “Josh, I can’t allow you to pay.”

“Think of it as a present. We’re going to prom together, right?”

I raise one shoulder and then drop it quickly. “Yeah?” I chew on the corner of my lip in time with the butterflies raging in my stomach.

“I’ll make you a deal. Instead of buying you flowers or a corsage, like most guys do for the girl they take to prom, I’ll give you a new seatbelt. It’ll cost me less than the flowers would. I promise.”

I stop gnawing on my lip to consider.

“You can even wear it if you’d like.” He taps himself just below the shoulder. “We can pin it to your dress.” He winks.

“Ha!” I laugh. “It’s an incredibly nice offer, Josh. Really. And as generous and kind as it is, there’s no way I can be without my car.”

“Of course not. You take my car.”

“What?” My head springs forward. “Your car? No. No way. But thank you.” I shudder at the thought of so much as dinging his prized possession.

"Why not?"

"Why not? Because I'm terrified to drive it and scratch it or something. No way. Out of the question. But thank you. Plus, I need to drive my mom sometimes, and she needs space, and I can't worry about dropping something in a car that's way more valuable than I understand. And with my sleep deprivation, I'm likely to drive it off the side of the road and into a ditch."

"All the more reason you should have a seatbelt." He winks at me.

I exhale loudly. "Josh, thank you, but no. This is just going to have to wait. I'll be fine."

He stuffs his hands deep into the front pockets of his jeans. "Gracie, I don't think there's a choice here. You're going to have to do what I say."

"I'm sorry, *what*?" A rumble of energy ricochets through my abdomen and settles in my lower back. "Do what you *say*?" I step away, at once befuddled by his audacity and appalled. But that's not all. *Damn it.* I'm flattered and disgusted and turned-off and turned-on simultaneously. "What?"

He nods, and it's freaking unnerving.

"Hold on a sec." I step back. "Maybe this whole thing *is* going too fast. I don't even know you. Where did you come from? And why are you always moving, anyway? What's your deal, huh?" What was I thinking to trust so much and so fast? How stupid can I be? My brain flashes a warning: *Think about what happened the last time you trusted someone. Screw this.* I slide out of his jacket and throw it at him.

"Gracie, please." He tosses the jacket onto the driveway. "Those are really good questions, and I'll answer them all, I promise. All I care about is that you're safe. Please. Maybe I worded that wrong."

"No, I think you worded it perfectly. You told me exactly what I needed to know. So if you'll excuse me." I storm past him and over to my car.

He follows. "Oh, Gracie, please don't leave like this. Please." His eyes are kind and soft and scared. Scared that I'm leaving.

My phone vibrates in my hand, and I glance at my text.

—All okay. Thanks. Mom—

With a smiley face. Whew.

"You have to understand I'm new at this, too," he tells me.

"At what?"

"At relationships."

I scoff, crossing my arms in front of my chest. "You can't tell me you've never had relationships before. Look at you. You're a gorgeous…*man*…for goodness sake."

"Yes, I've had relationships. But…" His face softens. "How do I explain this? I know. I know it's ridiculously fast, but this is the first time I'm with someone I really believe I should be with. I'm sorry about how I said it. But I'm not sorry about what I said. You can't drive your car."

I feel my eyebrows knit together, and a tiny, burning headache forms between my eyes. "You can't tell me what to do."

"When it comes to your safety, I think that I can." The eyebrow of his droopy eye raises in a dare.

"No, you certainly can*not*. I am a big girl. I have taken care of everything, *everything* in my crazy, f-ed up life better than most grown-ups who have half my problems. You have no idea what I've been through and what I do. Who the hell do you think you are, anyway?"

"Gracie, I'm just thinking about you."

"No, you're pulling some old-school male bullshit, and I don't have time for it. I don't have time for your jealousy and my giggling and…and"—my hands flail at my sides as my voice grows louder and my words come faster—"running home to bury myself in pints of rocky road ice cream when you decide to flirt with some other girl at school. I don't have the luxury of all that. I don't have the time to be young, and I certainly don't have the energy to be stupid."

Tears threaten my eyes, filling them until he becomes a tall, handsome blur standing before me. But I refuse to let them fall. Tears serve no purpose. I toss my head back, grinding my teeth together. I reach my hand out toward him, palm up. "I'd like my keys, please."

"Gracie."

"Now." I make my voice as threatening as I can.

He steps forward and places my keys in my hand. They're heavy and cold and so very definitive.

"Can I do one thing, please?"

I fold my arms across my chest again, squeezing the keys in my hand until they cut into my palm.

"Just wait here, just for a second, please." He steps past me and jogs to the garage. I turn my face to the sky, and the brisk night air feels good against my hot skin. He comes back out within seconds, carrying what looks like a short orange nightstick.

"What is that?" I nod to his hand.

"It's a seatbelt cutter and window breaker." He holds up the cutter, showing me first the end that looks like a very heavy razor and then the opposite side that looks like a strong piece of pyramid-shaped metal. "Just please. Please wear your seatbelt, and please, if you ever get stuck and it's an emergency, use this to cut your way out."

He holds the seatbelt cutter out to me, and I uncross my arms, taking it from him. My arms ache from holding their tense closed-off position for so long.

"Thank you." I swallow hard, unable to make eye contact.

"You're welcome."

He nods as I step toward my car.

"Gracie?"

I turn back to him.

"Can I ask you something?"

"Yeah?" Exhaustion and depression make it nearly impossible to speak.

"Just a few minutes ago, you were ready to be together. And now, because of one thing I said…"

I shake my head. "It wasn't one thing, Josh. I was wrong to think I'd have time for any of this. I'm sorry."

"But maybe if you just give me a chance."

"Trust me. It's better this way."

Swallowing a lump in my throat, I shift my weight from foot to foot. The gravel crunches under my feet, and the pointier stones stick through the thin soles of my sneakers, making this moment even more painful. I slide the key into the lock, and as I pull my door open, I glance at him. He looks…sad.

"Josh, um, thank you for fixing the door and for the seatbelt cutter." I hold it up, waving it. "That was very thoughtful."

Climbing in, I close the door quietly so I don't disturb his dad. I click my seatbelt closed and reach across to place my new possession in the glove box. Who knows? Maybe someday it really will help me, and I'll think of this moment and how Joshua Cadman saved my life.

Careful not to back into him, I put the car into *reverse*, easing a few feet before moving it into *drive* and rolling forward, away from Josh and back to my very real life. The only life I've ever known.

Guess what, Mom, you were wrong. Seems I'm not Cinderella, and Josh isn't my prince. Now, how do I let her know that without devastating her?

Chapter Nine

Josh

"Want to talk about it?" Dad's sitting at our rarely used kitchen table, the one that he made out of a single piece of red oak while we were living in Northern California. It's incredibly beautiful and the one thing I insist we bring with us whenever we move. He's nursing a beer.

"No, I don't want to talk about it." I let the door to the garage slam shut behind me as I storm to the fridge and grab a beer. I mentally count the number left: eleven. There were two six-packs, and now there are eleven beers. Damn, I can't even be mad about that. I twist off the bottle top even though it's a crown cap. It leaves little burning nicks in my fingers that match the ones on my brain.

Screw it. Storming to the garbage, I press the pedal to lift the lid on the silver can and toss in the cap. The lid closes with a dissatisfying hydraulic *click.* What happened to the days of big silver garbage cans? When you could crash the cover and create your own angry thunder? What happened to phones you could slam? To glass you could break? To knowing what the hell a girl wanted?

To having a relationship like a normal person?

I march to the table and pull out a chair, spinning it around so its back is to the table. I plop down into it, straddling the chair, resting my arms on the ladderback. Dad glances at me as he takes a long, slow draw of his beer. Then he grabs a random blue envelope from a stack of junk mail on the table and toys with the edge of it.

"Love isn't easy, Josh."

"I'm sure it's not. But I wouldn't know."

He looks directly at me. "I thought you were certain she was the one."

"Well, apparently, I was wrong, again. Maybe I should just list the house tomorrow."

"Does that mean…she's not marked, then?"

I see the relief and confusion in his eyes.

"She is." I place my beer on the table and let my head drop down, my hand running across my locs. "But I fucked it up."

"C'mon. It can't be that bad."

"Ha." Standing, I drain my bottle and then head to the fridge to retrieve two more beers.

He puts up his hand. "No thanks. One's my limit tonight."

I sneer. "They're both for me."

"Josh." He cocks his head. "Go easy."

"It's beer, Dad. Not heroin. Although, maybe heroin wouldn't be so bad. Hell, I deserve a little escape." I twist the top of another beer and take a long pull, half-emptying the bottle.

"I see."

He sits back, twirling his bottle on the table. Damn, this table's gorgeous. No matter what crap mood I'm in, I cannot let it be damaged. I jump up and get us each a paper towel from the rack by the sink and slide it under our beers. I can't stand the idea of allowing this table to be ruined.

"Thanks."

I nod.

"So, you need an escape, do you?"

I glare at him. "Why the hell not? Why don't I get to be young while I have the chance? Why don't I get to enjoy my life for whatever little time I have left?"

"Josh." He reprimands me with his voice. He's right. He doesn't want to talk about it, and I'm acting like a spoiled kid, not the man I'm supposed to be.

"Sorry." I mumble the word, staring at my beer, and then take another swallow. It tastes warm and stale even though I know it's neither of those things. I read the label. It's a mass brand, discount store buy. "You know, we should be drinking micro beers or something. Lager, I don't know. Something better. And stronger."

"I'll remember that next time I go shopping."

He nods coolly, and I just want to punch something. Standing, I walk to the sink and pour what's left of my beer down the drain, watching as the amber color bubbles up against the white farmhouse basin. I glance out the window above the sink—the one that's lined with two cherry-patterned curtains left by the last owner. Usually, we don't even bother removing things like curtains from the last owners because we're never anywhere long enough. But these curtains are so damned ugly with their what, "Life is a bowl of cherries" message?

A bowl of cherries? My ass. Life is a bowl of shit.

Leaving the bottle in the sink, I reach up and grab the curtains, tearing them off the window. Ducking, I shield myself with my hands as the rod comes flying at me and the curtains crumple and drop into the wet basin. Little bits of plaster fall, and a cloud of dust forms where

I tore the rod out of the wall.

Dad says nothing, and for whole minutes I stare into that sink, watching white plaster dust settle on amber bubbles like an extra helping of crystallized sugar on a burnt crème brûlée.

When the bubbles dissolve, I become more lucid. "I'm sorry." I place both hands on the edge of the sink, gripping as tightly as I would to a life raft in the middle of a storming ocean.

"Who left whom?"

"She left me." I stand tall now, staring out the window.

"Did she say why?"

"Her seatbelt gets stuck. I told her she needed to take my car, and I'd fix the seatbelt."

"And?"

I nod and turn to him. Leaning back against the sink, I cross my legs at the shins. "She didn't want to take my car. Worried about scratching it or damaging it in some way. But I said…"

He raises his eyebrows.

"I said she had to do as I say."

He looks away, drops his head to one side, and then rolls it back toward me. "Do as you *say*?" He chuckles. "What is this, nineteen fifty-seven?"

I glare at him.

"Josh." He stands and walks over to me, taking a spot right next to me at the sink, leaning back in a position almost identical to mine. He turns, and we're eye to eye. "You can't tell a woman to do as you *say*. Didn't I teach you better than that? Especially someone like Gracie. This young woman has been on her own for a long time. You've got to earn her respect, and then maybe she'll value your advice. As advice, not as law."

I nod, looking away and back again.

"That's not all, is it?" He doesn't have to ask. He knows. "What else is bothering you?"

"I like her. Like, really like her. She won't admit it, but her mom is dying, and she can't take anyone else she loves leaving."

He looks down at his feet.

"She's never had a life, Dad. How can I do this to her?" I swallow hard and take a breath. "What if…I mean, do you…do you think we can change our fate?"

He glances at me, and his eyes flicker with pain.

"Do you?" I repeat my question despite the agony this is causing him.

"Josh."

He shakes his head. "I don't want to answer that. I don't know how to answer that."

"Please." I soften my voice. "Tell me what you think. For the first time in my life, I'm confused. And scared."

His shoulders rise and fall with his breath. My hands hang limp at my sides.

"Dad?" My throat aches.

He looks at the floor and away from me before drawing his eyes to meet mine.

"I think you have always had the ability to change your destiny, Josh. Always. You just have to decide to do it."

He pushes away from the sink and, leaving his half-finished beer on the table, walks quickly from the room.

Chapter Ten

Gracie

"Gracie?" Mom looks at me sideways as I walk through the door.

Ugh. Not tonight, Mom. I really don't want to talk about it.

"Everything okay?" She cranes to see over the back of the couch.

I walk to the middle of the room so she's not struggling to see me and appraise the used tissues, empty ginger ale bottle, and unopened magazines. The television remote is perched on the coffee table. Narrowing my eyes, I try to remember…with the single exception of the ginger ale, everything is exactly as I left it. Exactly.

"Mom?" I sit on the edge of the couch, not wanting to rattle anything and risk her nausea. "Have you been on the couch all day?"

She shrugs. "You know. Sometimes it's more comfortable out here."

I nod. So that means she hasn't eaten and probably hasn't peed. "How about a trip to the bathroom?"

She smiles, and her eyes twinkle. "I suppose if you're heading that way, I could hitch a ride."

She tries to make a joke of it, but I hear the urgency in her voice. We have a doctor's appointment this Thursday, and she starts a new round of chemo on

Friday, the day before prom. Thursday, I'll ask her doctor if it's time to consider keeping a bedpan with her. I know she'll fight me on that. Who wants their daughter to clean their waste? But there's no option. I can't quit my job to be with her twenty-four-seven. There are only a couple of more weeks left of school, and despite my wishy-washy attitude on my extra-exhausted days, I really don't want to quit before I'm through. I'm so close I can almost taste my diploma.

"C'mon." Walking to her good side, I wrap my arm around her waist and lift her as carefully as I can. The blanket she was wrapped in falls from her lap, and I start, catching a whiff of pee. Without her noticing, I glance behind her and spy a wet spot on the sheet I've used to line the couch. Damn, that means it went through to the couch, and she's been sitting in urine for hours. Damn.

It's nearly impossible to move her forward, so I bear down and use all of my strength, dragging her legs.

"Just give me a second," she chirps. "I'm stiff from sitting. I got caught in that romantic movie about email that I love so much." She clears her throat, wheezing. Thankfully, there's no cough anymore, but now she seems to be struggling to take a breath. That doctor's appointment can't come soon enough.

I swallow the ache in my throat. Truth is, she hasn't been able to move on her own all day. We both know it, but neither of us will say anything. Well good. That means we're back to playing games, and whenever she plays games, it means she believes she has more time.

As I shuffle her forward, I make a mental plan to sit her on the toilet while I quickly strip the couch, spray it, and remake it with several hidden towels to help dry the spot. I'll run laundry as we prepare for bed, and then later, once she's asleep, I'll treat the spot, letting it dry overnight. Good, a plan.

I keep my arm tight around her waist. She feels thin, way, way too thin, and her light green old-lady-crocheted slippers make a scuffing sound as I half-drag her to the restroom. But her clothes…how will I get her to change? She takes showers only every other day because it's so much work for both of us, and she showered yesterday. If I offer her a change, she'll know that I know.

I sigh. All I really want to do is to climb into bed, bury myself under my mountain of blankets, and sleep, but that doesn't seem to be an option. At least not for the next few hours. As much as I don't want to, I try a different tactic.

"Mom?" I smile as we move, catching another whiff of stale urine. "It's chilly outside but beautiful. I think there's a storm coming in, but it's clear right now. What do you say we change into our warmest sweats and sit on the front steps for a bit?"

She looks at me sideways, and her cheeks begin to flush. She thinks I know. I'm sorry. Maybe I'm a horrible person, but this is more than I can take right now. I can't stand her embarrassment, and I really can't handle her vulnerability. I'm just not good with that.

I get her to the restroom, guide her to the toilet, and then step outside. Waiting by the door, I realize what I need to do. The only thing I can do. I speak through the closed door. "I, uh, I just had a fight with Josh. I was hoping maybe the fresh air would do me some good, and if you're feeling up to it, I could use your perspective."

There. It was the very last thing I wanted to do, but the only choice I had.

I hear a flush followed by her lilting voice. "I would

love to talk, Gracie, sweetheart. And yes, I think I could use something warmer to wear."

I nod. Whew. Crisis averted. "Good, Mom. Thanks. I'll grab us both some sweats, and we'll head out."

"Gracie?"

"Yeah?" I talk to the door.

"Do we still have some rocky road ice cream in the freezer? Why don't you grab that and two spoons? Nothing solves man problems like ice cream."

I nod, fighting back another bout of tears. "You got it, Mom. Thanks."

****

We sit, shoulder to shoulder on the front steps, a spoon in each of our hands, but neither of us has the strength to dig into the ice cream that waits on the step between us. A tiny puddle of melted rocky road floats on the top of the opened container.

"It's so beautiful tonight." She takes as deep of a breath as she can. Mom's always been a lover of the outdoors and of life in general, but lately, she's been extra appreciative.

"Mm," I mumble in agreement.

"So?"

She turns to look at me, resting the side of her head in her delicate hand as her fingers toy with the edge of her brightly colored turban. I bought her those turbans years ago when we first learned her diagnosis, thinking the bright reds and oranges would cheer her up. I still remember that day when I brought them home and held them out to her proudly. She stared up at me from her seat on the couch, tears filling her eyes while she forced a smile onto her ashen face. She insisted the turbans were beautiful, and she appreciated them very much, but as I spent the night watching her aimlessly touch her ringlets of strawberry-blonde hair, I wondered if I had moved too far, too fast. Just as Josh had wondered tonight.

I snap out of my daze. “So, what?”

“Let’s see.” She bends her knees up and wraps her arms around her legs, leaning forward, careful not to squash the area of her breasts. She rests her head on her knee. “You were really taken with Josh and were planning to go to prom with him. What was the fight about?”

Swallowing hard, I look down our short driveway and at my car. “He, uh, he told me I had to do as he *said*.”

She furrows her brow and rests her forearms on her knees where her head had been only moments before. “Excuse me? Do as he said, how?”

I debate how much I’ll tell her. I point to the car, and her gaze follows my finger before settling back on my face. She’s trying to read my expressions. “My seatbelt sometimes sticks. And he wants to fix it for me.”

“Okkkkaaaayyyy.” She tilts her head, fighting to understand. “I know I have chemo brain, but it’s been weeks since my last treatment. I think I’m fairly lucid. How is that a bad thing?”

“It’s not. But when I refused to take his car—”

“Wait.” She puts up her hand, and her eyes move wildly across mine as she processes the information. “He wanted you to take his car?”

“Yes. So I would be safe.” My voice is barely more than a whisper.

“Safe?” I can read the panic in her eyes. It’s more visible than any pain she may be feeling. No matter how much our roles may have flipped, and despite her own agony, she still worries about me.

"Mom." I do my best to placate her. "It's not a real safety issue, I promise. He just doesn't want me to be—" I struggle to find the right word. "—inconvenienced."

"I see." She nods.

"Wait. I'm just getting to the infuriating part. When I refused and said it was no big deal, he said there was no option. I had to do what he *said*."

"Oh. That was rather nineteen-fifties of him." She scratches an itch on her bony wrist. Even though the air is heavy with humidity, I know it's not a mosquito bite. No mosquito wants to be anywhere near her chemical-laden blood. She focuses on me. "And what did you say?"

I drop my head down, burying it in my hands. "Well, the gist of it is that I said I didn't have time for a juvenile relationship."

"And wanting you to be safe is juvenile?"

"No," I snap without meaning to. "Sorry. Acting all macho and commanding me to do something for my own good—is. Screw that."

Mom purses her lips together, fighting her smile. "Gracie. I love that you are so smart and strong, but you really know nothing about men."

That's the understatement of the century.

She lets her smile free. "It's not your fault. I gave you no advice on the opposite sex."

I shrug one shoulder.

"So let me start now. Gracie, honey, they're idiots."

Her words startle me, and I burst out laughing. My body shakes as I laugh, and she begins to chuckle, too. I cover my mouth with my hand, but my laughter dies off as hers turns into a cough. She puts up her hand to ask me to wait, and I do, studying her as she fights for another breath. Her eyes are still sparkling, though, so I know she's okay. Finally, she catches her breath.

"He sounds like he has the right instincts," her voice is raspy, and she speaks slowly. "He just said it in the wrong way. We all do that sometimes. All of us."

"But I don't have the time or the desire to get stuck with some Neanderthal."

"Of course not. But do you think this young man who drinks seltzer is really a Neanderthal?"

"I don't know."

She tilts her head, raising her eyebrows to question me.

"No." I slump down into myself, hunching my shoulders forward. "I just don't know him."

"That's true of everyone. You don't know anyone until you do. Sounds to me like what you and Josh need is a real date. A night out at a diner with cheeseburgers and milkshakes."

I roll my eyes at her. "Now it really sounds like we're back in the nineteen-fifties. Which, by the way, was way before your time as well."

"Well, so, go out and do whatever your generation does for fun."

I have no idea what that would be. I smile wistfully, trying not to show my melancholy.

She reaches out and rubs my shoulder. "Maybe it's high time you find out what that is."

I nod.

"Gracie. Don't throw away what could be a good thing on one fleeting misunderstanding. His heart was in the right place. He just said it wrong. He'll learn that to hang with a spitfire like you, he'll need to share the role of the Alpha. And honestly, would you be attracted to a man who was weak?"

"I guess not." I learned that the last time I thought I was attracted to someone.

"There's no guessing, I'm telling you. As your mother. The person who's lived with you for the last seventeen years." She reaches out and takes both of my hands in hers. "You are an amazing young woman. Smart, beautiful, brilliant, capable. Give him a chance to learn how to be with you."

I sigh, looking back at my car.

She pulls my hands toward her, and my gaze follows. "That's not everything, is it?"

I stare into her eyes. They're the only thing about her that hasn't changed. Over these past four years, her eyes have been the only constant—my anchor as I've been tossed all over this raging sea. Sure, her eyes look tired and sometimes cloudy or filled with pain, but they're still bright blue—where my color comes from—and smart.

How do I tell her I can't risk any more pain in my life? Any further abandonment? That I won't survive any more hurt? I can be sad about never knowing my father, but I will be devastated when I lose my mother.

It's just another thing that "they're" wrong about. It's not better to have loved and lost than never to have loved at all. I know this firsthand.

Frankly, it hurts like hell.

The headlights in the driveway keep me from needing to tell her anything. Shielding my eyes from the lights, I stab the softening ice cream with my spoon and then stand, dusting off my butt as the car cuts its engine. I know the purr of that engine.

Even in the dim light, I can still see him fairly well.

Reaching across to the passenger's side, he takes something from the seat and then opens his door, stepping out of the car. He's holding two bunches of roses, one red and one pink. He walks to me, but I don't move, forgetting even Mom for the moment.

"Gracie." He addresses me and turns to Mom. "Mrs. Jackson."

"Hello, Josh." Her voice is tender when she addresses him. "You can call me Nora. And it's a pleasure to finally meet you."

"You too, ma'am." He looks down at his feet, giving her a moment to process.

She turns to me and mouths the word *ma'am* and then fans herself like his presence is too much for her. I understand completely.

He lifts his head and smiles at her, and for the first time in years, Mom's coloring looks almost healthy. So, he made her blush. I'll be damned.

"Oh, uh, these are for you." He hands her the pink roses.

I tense as she takes them. She can't stomach the scent of flowers. I move to take them from her, but he speaks.

"I hope you like pink. And I also hope you don't think it too forward, but I brought silk roses that don't have a scent. Gracie explained your situation, and I remember when my father was undergoing chemo, he couldn't stand any smells in the house. I used to eat all of my meals out on the deck. Sometimes, that wasn't far away enough, so I pretty much gave up on regular food and began to live on cereal. It was the only thing I could think of that wouldn't smell like food."

"Wait, what?" I step closer to him, once again

ignoring Mom's presence. "Your father had cancer?"

"Yes, lung cancer. I was only seven. He's been clear now for a decade."

"Well, that's wonderful news." Mom smiles genuinely. "And that was incredibly thoughtful of you—to bring me silk flowers and to make sure they had no scent. Thank you, Josh." She glances at me.

"You're welcome, Mrs. Jackson, uh, Nora. And I'm sorry to just stop in like this. I said something stupid to Gracie, and I wanted to apologize."

I shake my head, still stuck on the idea that his father is a cancer survivor. "Why didn't you tell me about your father?"

"There are lots of things I want to tell you, and even more I want to learn about you."

"Well, that's my cue." Mom smiles and presses her hands against the concrete step but can't lift herself. I move to her, trying to be as inconspicuous as possible.

"Why don't I help you inside?" I take her elbow and guide her up easily.

She stands, but she's wobbly on her feet.

"Can I help?" Josh asks Mom and then looks at me in earnest.

I shake my head. "No, thanks. We're okay." I'm sure he understands that she's not ready to accept help from a relative stranger.

He nods and holds the door for us, still clutching the other bouquet of roses.

Mom makes it to the door and then turns back to face Josh. "Thank you again, Josh. Really. It was so incredibly thoughtful. And seeing as there's no school tomorrow, I hope you two will take some time to get to know each other."

He nods. "Thank you, Mrs. Jackson. I hope that, too."

I hold Mom tighter, taking the flowers from her as I guide her inside. As soon as we've crossed the threshold of her bedroom, she lets out an exhausted sigh, wheezing from the effort. I help her into bed, sitting next to her as I slide off her turban, exposing the surprise birthmark we both discovered when she first lost her hair. Tonight, small tufts of hair, like dutiful little soldiers, are rebelliously fighting their way back on the sides of her head, clueless that in just a matter of time, they'll be annihilated.

Like the rest of us.

My hand lingers, and I toy with the tiny, soft, red curls just behind her ear that are trying to make a comeback. I stare at her birthmark. It's much smaller than mine, but nearly identical. She moves my hand away.

"Gracie." She reaches out and strokes my hair, smoothing it.

No. No more reality tonight. I jump up with her flowers and grab the water pitcher we leave by her bed every night. "How about this for tonight, for a mock vase, and I'll bring you a glass of water?" I arrange the roses in the oversized plastic pitcher.

She smiles agreeably. "Gracie. The man is really, really trying. Hear him out. I beg you."

I beg you. Small shivers run up and down my spine as I worry she wants this for herself as much as she wants it for me. Can I take another layer of stress and guilt if it doesn't work out?

"I will, Mom." Suddenly, I remember the couch. It's going to have to wait. What happens if she accidentally pees in the bed tonight? I have covers on both of our beds to protect the mattresses, but it won't collect the wetness. The urine will run everywhere, and she'll be embarrassed and…"Hey, Mom, you want to take one last trip to the bathroom? Your bed's a mess, and I'd like to make it comfortable for you before you sleep."

She nods, beginning to sit up. "I suppose I could take one more trip."

I help her the rest of the way, and once she's safely in the bathroom, I layer towels under her sheets and quickly remake the bed. I make a mental note to buy towels soon because at this rate, we're running through them faster than I can wash them. Wiping my forehead with the back of my hand, I catch a whiff of myself. Crap. I've broken a sweat and now, I reek. The hell with it. I don't have time to worry. Retrieving her from the bathroom, I walk her to her bed and tuck her in.

Once she's settled, I rush through the living room toward the door, catching another whiff of myself. Okay, I don't exactly *reek*, but you can smell that I've been working and sweating. Oh well, some days just having the time to shower is a luxury I can't afford. I guess that's the next test for Josh. Does he run because I stink? If he does, good riddance.

As I walk through the door, I find him standing on the steps, still holding the flowers. He looks into my eyes.

"Gracie."

I step out onto the concrete step.

"Gracie, I'm sorry. Really. I really am new at this relationship thing, and I do understand that you're a smart, independent woman and—"

Letting my heart lead my mind for once, I step

forward and slide both hands inside his leather jacket and around his strong waist. I snuggle tight against his abdomen and turn my head, resting it on his chest.

"Gracie." He wraps his arms around me, pulling me even tighter to him. "I'm sorry. Really. It came out wrong." The flowers rest against my back.

Lifting my head, I look up into his gorgeous eyes. "Please don't. I'm sorry, too. Thank you for caring."

He leans down and kisses me on the top of my head.

****

"What time is it?"

He glances at the beautiful watch on his wrist. "Just after midnight. Should I run out and get some more?" He holds up the empty ice cream container and shakes it.

"No, thanks." Yawning, I stretch my arms overhead. "I need to get to bed soon."

We've been sitting here, talking and eating for over three hours, but it feels like minutes. Even though the air is heavy, I was wrong about the storm, so we've been dry the whole time. Behind us sit my beautiful silk roses propped up in a giant yellow plastic lemonade cup I got at a fair years ago. It was the only thing in the house large enough to hold an entire dozen roses.

"And by the way, you know you weren't supposed to get me flowers. Remember? That was our deal. You got me a seatbelt."

"These are 'I'm sorry' flowers. Different. Besides, they come from a gas station." He shrugs. "Only place open at this hour."

I smile. "I don't care where they come from. They're beautiful. Like that watch. I've never noticed it before."

"I don't wear it to school."

"I don't blame you."

"It was a gift from my dad on my sixteenth."

"Nice gift."

He nods.

"So." I clasp my hands together, fighting back another yawn. "You know everything from my favorite color—"

"Don't have one."

"To my favorite food."

"Vegetable pizza." He makes a screwy face.

I roll my eyes. "Don't knock it till you try it. And my favorite type of music."

"Yes, I have to admit reggae was a surprise."

I smile. "Your turn."

"I'm not so exciting." He waves me off with a lopsided grin.

Looking around at the blackness of the sky, I focus on the lighter gray clouds that are threatening above, and then my gaze finds its way back to him. "How did your dad kick lung cancer?"

He sits taller, and I can feel his energy change—like an imaginary brick wall has just gone up between us.

"Did they catch it early?"

"Yes. But I was a child then. I wasn't a part of all of this that you're going through with your mother."

"But you still knew it was happening. And with only you two…"

He nods.

I can tell he doesn't want to talk about it, but I press on. I need to understand. "Was it just chemo or radiation?" Maybe, buried in his memories lies the help that Mom needs.

Inhaling deeply, he leans forward, resting his arms on his knees. He looks back and forth at absolutely nothing, and he seems to be weighing some big decision. Maybe I should back off, but I'm too tired and too invested for tact.

Finally, he turns to me, and his eyes soften. He reaches out and brushes a stray piece of hair from my face, and then his hand runs down the length of my ponytail. I shiver.

"We did use chemo and targeted radiation. Since the cancer had not metastasized, it was easier for us, I think."

It's such a vague answer it's frustrating. I turn toward him, bending one knee so the entire front of my body is facing him.

"That's it? No additional meds?" I look away and back. "I guess if it was isolated to the lungs, there was no need for surgery, but did you try targeted therapies? How about immunotherapy? I've heard there have been good results with that. We tried one course here, but they didn't have all the resources she needed. I'm hoping that as soon as Mom is well enough to travel, we can get her to one of the big clinics in Texas. Try immunotherapy again. Try some other alternative approaches. If this round of chemo doesn't help."

He startles me by reaching out and stroking my cheek in a very definitive way. Instead of my heart racing like it usually does, this time I have to mentally remind it to beat. My whole body is limp and drained, and it takes real effort to look into his eyes.

"Gracie."

He takes both of my hands in his, holding and caressing them. It feels so good I pretend I didn't notice the concern in his voice. Then, out of the corner of my eye, I see something stir. He turns his head in the same direction; he must have spotted it, too.

"What was that?" I point just past the driveway and toward a sunken patch of lawn near our maple tree. The tree, along with a worn wooden fence, divides our property from our neighbor's. Behind the neighbor's house is a fairly thick acre of woods, so it's not uncommon to spot small animals roaming about—except at midnight.

"I don't know." He stands and walks toward the area.

"I hope it's not a lost cat." I follow closely behind him.

"No." He stops short and looks down into the shallow dip of our lawn. "Oh hey." He squats down, addressing something on the lawn.

I squat next to him and see that he's talking to a bunny. It's a tiny thing lying on its side, and its eyes are wide with fear.

"What do you think is wrong with him?" I notice three of his four legs are moving, but the top hind leg is immobile. "Do you think he broke a leg?"

Josh doesn't answer. Instead, he reaches down and scoops the bunny into his hands. He holds the bunny for a moment, stroking it, and the poor creature's eyes close. I draw a sharp breath as a wash of fear envelopes me.

"Are you going to kill it?" I whisper.

Josh turns to me, and the bunny's eyes open. It's such a surreal moment.

He smiles. "Of course not. I would never hurt an animal. I don't even eat meat."

"You don't?" I step back. How did I not know this?

He just shrugs.

I nod, caught in this mystifying moment of tranquility, fear, and peace. "What's wrong with it?" I point to the bunny.

"Nothing." He pets the bunny one more time, and it wiggles in his arms. Then he squats down and places the creature on the ground, facing it toward the woods behind my neighbor's house. The bunny hops away as Josh stands next to me, watching him go.

"But…how? What just happened?"

"I think he was stunned. Maybe bumped into the fence in the darkness and then fell into that dip in the lawn." He turns to me. "Does that bother you? That sunken area? I can fill it in if it trips you or if you're worried about your mom getting in and out of the passenger side."

I shake my head. "No thanks. We're okay. It's never been an issue. Except, I guess, for bunnies. Why was the bunny here? Isn't it late for rabbits?"

"Yes, actually, they're crepuscular creatures."

"I'm sorry, what?"

He smiles at me. "Crepuscular. No?"

I shake my head, mesmerized.

"It means they're animals that are active during twilight hours. Rabbits aren't diurnal like we are—active during the day…"

He explains in the most non-condescending way, and I'm grateful. I've never heard either of those terms before.

"…or nocturnal."

"That one I know," I exclaim, playfully triumphant.

He chuckles. "I figure you know a lot of stuff, Gracie."

"Apparently not as much as you. How do you know all this? Are you planning to be a vet?"

He stands very still in the darkness, looking out

toward the woods. He takes my hand and turns, pulling me back toward the house.

"Josh? Are you planning to be a vet? I don't even know your school plans for next year."

He nods, sitting us both on the top concrete step. "I'm planning to hang close. See how things work out."

"What things?" The energy coursing through my stomach tells me what I want him to say, but he can't be serious. We've only just met.

"Things."

He grins at me and nudges my shoulder with his. I grin back, but I'm not letting him distract me. Completely.

"School?"

He leans forward and rests his forearms on his knees. "I don't make plans for the future."

"Why not?" A shooting pain travels across my gut.

He shrugs dismissively. "I try to live in the moment, you know? Hey, as much as I don't want to say goodbye, aren't you working tomorrow?"

"Unfortunately."

"Let's get you to bed, then."

His words burn through me, and suddenly, I am feeling very, very awake. My eyes dash to his.

He stands and guides me upward. "I'll meet you tomorrow after work in our parking lot?" He forms it as a question, but there's no doubt in his voice.

With his arm still wrapped around me, we stall by my front door.

"Yeah. Thanks." It doesn't matter how good it all feels. I just can't let it go. "But you never answered my question. How did your dad get cured?"

The look in his eyes tells me I'm pressing him to

give more info than he wants to. But why? Shouldn't he want to help keep Mom alive, even if it means dredging up painful memories?

"A combination of Western medicine and alternative therapies."

"Immunotherapy?"

He shakes his head. "A healer on a reservation. We lived on the reservation for a year, and my dad was treated and fed herbs. When we left, he was given a clean bill of health."

"A healer?"

"Yes."

"You lived on a reservation, and your dad was treated by a healer?"

He nods.

"I… That's…amazing," I stutter, trying to make sense of the jumble in my brain. "Wait." I look at him through lowered lashes. "Do you think…can this healer help my mom?"

He stiffens. "I don't know."

"But is it something we can check into? Do you remember the place?"

"Of course. But you can't just walk onto a reservation and ask to be healed."

"Your father did."

"It's complicated."

"Explain." I plop both hands on my hips.

"My dad knew them, the people on the reservation. They believed they could heal him because he hadn't yet…finished his purpose in life." He's careful with these last few words.

"Which is?"

"I don't know. All I know is that the healers can read

auras, and my father's aura was unfinished. Because of that, they were able to cure him."

"So you're saying if someone hasn't yet fulfilled their what, destiny?"

I raise my eyebrows questioning, and he nods, staring intently at my face.

"Then there's the chance they'll be saved?"

"That's what these healers believe, yes."

"Well, my mother couldn't have fulfilled hers. I mean, she's done nothing with her life."

His head ricochets back like he's just been slapped. "Of course she has. She had you."

I smile as heat warms my cheeks. "I really hope, for her sake, there's something more."

"Why?" His brow knits together.

"Why?" I release a tiny, frustrated yelp. "Because who wants to think they've done nothing in their life?"

"She hasn't done nothing. She's done the most important thing in the world. She's given birth. To you."

I tilt my head. "But your dad is a parent, too. And there was more for him."

He nods, offering a small smile. "You're right. What do I know? I'm thinking about something from over ten years ago. Tell you what, tomorrow I'll ask my dad what he remembers, and we'll go from there. K?"

"K. Hey." The image of the bunny pops into my mind. "Maybe the healer wore off on you. Maybe that bunny was hurt, and you fixed it."

His face remains immobile. "The bunny was confused, Gracie. And I calmed it."

He seems to have lost his usual sense of humor and any trace of sarcasm. He's got to be as exhausted as I am. I step to him, slip my arms around his waist, and rest my cheek on his chest. He wraps his arms around me, holding me close, and I know exactly how that bunny felt…calm in his arms.

Still…

I can't help but think there's more—way more—he's not telling me.

Chapter Eleven

Josh

How the hell can I be this nervous? I mean, it's prom, for Christ's sake. I'm not performing open-heart surgery or anything. I check my reflection in the short mirror over my dresser one last time. Cuts and bruises—gone. Opened collar gray shirt looks good tucked under the sleek charcoal suit. No, I don't own a full-length mirror, but what man does? Most of the time, I just care enough that I'm not embarrassing myself in public—but tonight means more. Tonight is Gracie's prom, and I want it to be perfect for her. I lift one leg, trying to get it high enough to see it in the mirror to check if the fitted pants and pointed shoes look okay together. I catch a glimpse of shoe, and then drop my leg. Best I can tell, they're okay.

"Knock, knock." It's Dad at my open door.

As I walk toward the door, I pull my locs into a low ponytail. Dad's giving me that downturned smile he does when he's impressed but doesn't expect to be.

"Nice." He nods in appreciation.

I hold my arms out. "Yeah?"

"Oh, heck yeah. You look good. Should dress up more often instead of that leather jacket and ripped jeans all the time."

"Says the man who lives in flannel shirts."

"That's different, I'm a carpenter. A craftsman.

People expect artists to be 'cazh'…"

"Are you abbreviating 'casual' now?"

"Someone in town today thought I was a hipster. Just trying it out."

"A fifty-something-year-old hipster?" I walk past him, tapping him on the shoulder.

Chuckling, he follows me out of my bedroom. He definitely wants something. I glance at the time on my wrist.

"Dad." I stop short, and he nearly bumps into me. I reach out and take him by the shoulders. We're eye to eye as I move him back a step. "What's going on with you?"

"Nothing."

"Okayyyy…" I leave him standing there as I go to the kitchen and grab her corsage in its plastic container from the fridge.

"Pretty." He's too close again.

"Thanks." I shrug, appraising the flowers. "She told me she'll be in blue, so…"

"Wildflowers are a nice choice."

"Yeah?" There are tiny periwinkle blue flowers surrounded by some type of miniature white and yellow flowers. "I figure real flowers are okay as long as they don't go into her house. I dunno. I wanted something as unpredictable as she is."

"What's that flower called?" He points to the flower in the middle.

"Seriously?" I rush past him to grab my keys by the door. "I don't know. Some blue thing. Want to go make us a spot of tea, and we'll chit-chat some more?" I exhale and then turn to him. "Sorry. I'm nervous."

"Why? It's not your first prom."

"No, but it is my last."

He looks away.

"More importantly, it's Gracie's first prom. And I want it to be as great for her as possible." I adjust the sleeves of my jacket, stopping for a moment. "If you saw the amount of work that girl does in a day…"

"So, uh, as far as tonight being special." He faces me again. Good. He's finally—hopefully—getting to his point.

"Dad?" I'm hovering at the front door, fidgeting with the keys in my hand. "Dad. I don't want to be late, and I'm out of time. If you have something to say, please just spit it out."

"I just want to make sure you have everything you need."

"Sure, gas in the car. Flowers"—I hold them up—"tickets"—I pat my breast pocket—"plenty of money. Hoping to take her to a late-night dinner after since she didn't have time before."

He steps closer to me and runs a hand across his clean-shaven chin. "Josh, I mean, do you have protection?"

It takes me a moment until I realize…"A condom?"

"Or several." He stares at me, gauging my reaction.

"Dad, c'mon."

"Josh, I know you're a grown man, but—"

"Dad." I cut him off. "Nothing's gonna happen. It's too soon."

"Just be safe, Josh. Please. Things happen on prom night." His face scrunches into a scowl.

"Yes, Dad, I know." I just want this conversation to be over, but the look on his face is so worried I can't be mad.

"It's just if this girl is really the one…" His voice fades away.

I pat him on the shoulder. I don't want to dismiss him or his fears, but I don't want to think about that tonight. Any of it. Tonight, I just want to be young and go to prom with my girlfriend and have fun.

Shaking my head, I grab the door handle but stop myself. "Dad." I turn back to him and nod. "I'll be careful. I promise."

He nods back.

****

"Holy crap." I stare at her, transfixed. Her hair is wavy tonight, and it falls down around her shoulders. Some of her hair is pulled back off her face in a way that makes it look as if she should be wearing a crown. Her already giant eyes are even more so with a touch of something sparkly on her lids. Her pink cheeks glow, and her lips are stained a berry color, but it's the dress…

"I—I can't even." My gaze drops down the length of her—and then back up. The long gown is cinched tight at her waist, and two simple, thin straps hug her toned shoulders. And the rest of it…fuck! I didn't realize she was built like *that*.

*Look away, Josh…*I clear my throat as I reprimand myself. But Jesus, she looks like she should be walking the runway of some teenage All-American beauty pageant and not out with me. "I…"

"Does he like the dress?" Nora calls from inside.

Gracie stays at the door but turns her head to be heard by her mother. "We've gotten one 'holy crap' and a bunch of stammering."

She giggles as her mom chuckles behind her.

Shaking my head, I try to pull myself together. "I'm

sorry, I'm being rude."

"I rather like your reaction." She winks at me.

"I have flowers to give you. In my car." I point over my shoulder, finding it nearly impossible to formulate a thought. *Come on, Josh, pull it together.* "Uh, can I come in and say 'hi' to your mom?"

"I guess. Even though I was supposed to be wearing a seatbelt on my wrist and not flowers." She raises an eyebrow before stepping back to let me in. I walk through the doorway and into the tiny entryway of the house. I stall next to an empty old-fashioned wooden coat rack that must have been left here since the seventies.

"Well?" She moves around toward the front of the couch so her mom can be included in the conversation. "This is our place." She holds her hands out to her sides.

"I…" My gaze falls to the small kitchen off the main room, and I spot old damaged cabinets. My hands grow itchy, wanting to fix the damned things. The rest of the house matches—it's clean and picked up—but it's worn, and there's absolutely no sign of a male presence. This makes me happy and sad all at once. The baseboards are scuffed, and there's the slightest evidence of water damage on the far corner of the living room. I quell my impulse to ask how old the roof is. That's definitely not pre-prom conversation. Then I catch the sketch on the wall. A simple pencil sketch of a younger Gracie and her mom—obviously at a time before cancer struck.

I walk toward the sketch without meaning to, like I'm being pulled toward it.

"We had that done on a trip we made to the city once. A street artist drew it for us." She walks up next to me and tilts her head, looking at the picture. "I like it. Do you?"

"Yes, it's beautiful. You're beautiful."

"I told you." Her mother's voice is a lilting sing-song despite her pain.

"Nah." She waves me off.

I clear my throat. "I'm sorry. I'm being rude, but I just realized with all the time we've spent on the front steps, I've never been inside your house."

"Well, it's not much." Nora's voice is soft.

I step around to the front of the couch to stand next to Gracie so Nora can talk to us directly.

"No, no," I protest, smiling at Nora. "It's great. Really nice. You can tell two women live here. Not like my dad's house." I shake my head for emphasis. "All we have are car parts and microwave dinners."

Nora smiles, but I see pain in her eyes. I force myself not to turn away. If Gracie can deal with this day in and day out, then I can man up for the night.

"Well." Nora sits forward, holding her left arm toward her body like she's guarding. Her left shoulder is slumping lower than her right, but she fights to put on a brave face. I can only imagine the immense pain she must be in. "One day, you and your dad will have to come for dinner. Gracie tells me you're a vegetarian?"

"Yes, ma'am."

"I make a mean vegetable Pad Tai." Her eyes light up as she turns toward her daughter. "Right, Gracie?"

She nods. "Right, Mom. Best I've ever tasted."

"That would be lovely." Nora smiles again. "To have a group here, having a meal together, celebrating friendship and love."

She looks away wistfully, and I steal a glance at Gracie out of the corner of my eye. She's flushed. So, she's shy about the "L" word.

"Well, uh…" I stutter. I want to get Gracie away just for an evening, just to give her one night, but I don't want to force this or abandon her mother.

"You two need to get going," Nora chirps.

Gracie walks to an old reclining chair by the couch and retrieves a white shawl that was lying on the back. I step up to her and take the shawl, holding it open for her as she turns her back to me. She holds up her hair, exposing narrow, toned shoulders and small vertebrae that dot her neck. I wrap the shawl around her, hugging her gently as I do. Even though she may be the strongest person I've ever met, she looks fragile. My protective instinct is screaming to take care of her.

But the one I have to protect her from is me.

She lets her hair fall, and clutching the wrap with one hand, she turns her head and smiles at me.

"Have fun, you two." Nora nods encouragingly from the couch.

Gracie appraises her sternly. "Listen, Mom. If you need anything, anything at all, text me. Please."

"I—"

Gracie holds up her hand, taking control of the situation. She drapes another small throw blanket over her mother's legs, and I stand by as she moves about, putting the finishing touches on everything her mother may need.

"Mom. I won't have any fun unless you promise. I know you think you'll be ruining our night, but it would really be ruined if you didn't let me know if you needed something." As she speaks, she glides into the kitchen. She opens an upper cabinet beside the stove and balances on her tiptoes. She retrieves two cans of ginger ale.

"These are room temperature." She waltzes past me and places the cans on the tiny coffee table near the couch. "Listen."

She lowers herself carefully and sits on the couch with her mother. She reaches out to adjust her mother's head wrap just as her mother reaches for a tendril of Gracie's long blonde hair. They both smile.

"Mom. It's a new chemo. We don't know how it's going to react in you, and we know that the few days following your transfusions are always the worst. Please, call me if you need anything."

She takes her mother's hand, holding it gently. "Josh has been through this."

She turns her gorgeous eyes to me, raising her eyebrows expectantly, and it's like a crushing blow hits my chest, knocking the wind out of me.

"Right?"

She raises her eyebrows higher, and I snap to.

"Yes. Please, Mrs. Jackson. Uh, Nora. If you need anything, Gracie and I will be right back."

Her mother settles against the cushion. "That's what I'm afraid of."

Gracie stands, smoothing her beautiful dress. "This is no time for worrying about us." Her voice is strong and insistent, although the slightest tremor lies beneath. She's exhausted.

"That's right," I chime in, trying anything I can think of to help. "You save your strength now, and when you're better, you can make your famous Pad Thai, and my dad and I will be over for dinner."

Mrs. Jackson nods, forcing a tiny smile as her face blanches. *Crap.* It must have been my reference to food. I glimpse Gracie, who's scowling. No, I don't want to cancel tonight, but something is telling me we may have to.

"All right, Mom." Gracie adjusts her mother's old cell phone on the table, spinning it so the *home* button faces Nora. "You know the rule. Five minutes, or I'm sending the National Guard."

"Oh, Gracie." Nora sighs, but her breath is labored. She gazes up at her daughter with so much love in her eyes it's heartbreaking. "You look so gorgeous. I wish I could hold onto what you look like right now, forever."

"You can." I step forward, and both women turn to me. "Prom pictures, right? We'll snap some prom pictures. Everyone takes pictures before prom."

"I think that's a lovely idea." Nora sounds exhausted. Her words are slower, and sleep is overtaking her. "If you two stand by the TV, I'll take your picture. Can I have your phone?" She reaches out, but there's no way she can possibly hold the phone and snap our picture.

The panicked look in Gracie's eyes tells me she's thinking the exact same thing.

"Well—" I think fast. "—Would you mind if I took one of just Gracie?"

Gracie's chin springs up, and she stares at me.

"I'd love one, too," I babble. "And I'm not much of a 'being in the picture' kind of guy. But I'd love a picture of Gracie in that gown. Is that okay?"

Nora nods, smiling, and Gracie exhales audibly.

"Gracie? Want to stand there?"

I point to the spot her mother was planning to take our picture, and Gracie obliges without a word. As she walks, her dress sways gracefully around her feet, and for an instant, I'm caught in the image of Gracie as the wind softly blowing the curtains of an opened window. She looks up at me with a wild look in her eyes—exhaustion, fear, longing—but nowhere in those bright blue eyes do I see surrender.

Her mother coughs a chest-rattling bellow, and Gracie starts, her shoulders rising high, her entire body tense, ready to spring into action at the slightest need. The cough subsides, and Gracie's anxious expression relaxes. I pull my phone from my jacket pocket and hold it up—trying in vain to confine her beauty to a single frame.

"So can I take your picture?"

She shrugs. "I guess so. Go ahead." She raises her arms and drops them again, grimacing.

I look around the camera and directly at her. "Well, would you like to maybe, I don't know, smile?" I'm careful how I word this. I know women despise being told to smile, and who could blame them? It's condescending, chauvinistic, and just plain rude.

"Oh." She glances down at her feet and fidgets with her hands that are clasped before her.

"Gracie." I drop the phone to my side. She is so uncomfortable. It's evident this is foreign to her. "When was the last time you had your picture taken?"

She shrugs, glancing at her mom and back to me. "I don't know. Class photos in elementary school, I guess." She looks at me through lowered lashes. "Most of the time, I just blend in places. No one really notices me." She gives me an adorable straight-line smile, but this isn't the smile her mother needs. She needs to see Gracie happy.

I step a tiny bit closer, feeling that undeniable pull toward her. "You have to be kidding me. *Everyone* notices you. They just think you're unapproachable."

"Me?" Shock overtakes her face. "Why?"

I feign disbelief. "Really? Come on, Gracie."

Her forehead creases with her furrowed brow.

"Because you have what they all want."

She looks at me quizzically. "What's that?"

"You really don't know?"

Pink begins to brighten her cheeks.

"You have the key to Shakes 'n' Slaw for free milkshakes."

The look of shock and confusion on her face morphs into one of pure joy. I smile as she laughs, and Nora giggles from the couch. When Gracie turns back, her smile is radiant, and her cheeks are flushed, like she just sprinted around the football field at school. Reacting on impulse, I lift my phone and snap her picture. It's gorgeous, but still nowhere near as beautiful as she is in real life.

She furrows her brow. "Did you take that picture?"

I nod, suddenly without words.

She steps closer to me and points to the phone. "Can I see?"

I turn the phone to her. She studies the picture, and gently, with one finger, touches the screen. Shaking her head, she drops her hand and looks up at me.

"That's really me?"

I nod. Her proximity and fragility make my chest feel like it's caving in on itself. How can a woman who's so strong be so defenseless at the same time? Has she really never before seen what she looks like to the world? And that's just what she looks like physically. Her true beauty, as cliché as it sounds, is on the inside. Cripes, my thoughts have been reduced to sentiments in badly written Valentine's Day cards, and the worst part is, I don't care.

My arms ache as I hold them back. All I want is to pull her into my embrace and take care of her forever.

What the hell have I gotten us into?

"Can I?" She smirks her adorable half-grin and takes my phone from me. She crosses back to her mother. "Look." Triumphantly, she holds the phone out toward her mother.

"Gracie, you're stunning."

Gracie smiles and glances at her own picture again.

"Can I have a copy of that, Josh?" Thankfully, Nora's voice sounds a bit stronger. Now maybe Gracie can enjoy her evening.

"Of course." I stand where Nora can see me. "I'll send it to the store to print. It'll be ready on our way home tonight."

Nora nods. "Thank you."

Gracie smiles up at me again, but this time the smile is different. She is still stunning, still sweet, but this time, there's a different passion in her eyes—it's not about keeping her mother alive, or working seven days in a row, or fighting to graduate high school. This is passion for life—and for me.

Shit, I am going to need every ounce of self-control I have tonight.

I clear my throat. "Ready?"

She nods, handing me my cell and clutching hers tightly. "Oh." Her gaze darts around the room. She runs her hands up and down the bodice of her dress like she's feeling for something in her non-existent pockets.

"Did you forget something?" I walk closer. "Because everything looks pretty perfect to me."

She smirks. "My bag. I want to slip my phone into a bag. I think I left it in my room. If you'll excuse me for a minute."

Her room. As she walks away, I wonder what her room is like. Warm? Pink? A small bed? Posters? Is it as grown-up as mine, or is she still a kid?

"Josh?" Nora's faint voice wakes me from my daydream.

"Yes. Sorry." I step closer to hear her better. "Can I get you something? Ginger ale?"

She shakes her head, frowning as she uses her good hand to rub tiny circles on her abdomen. Damn, even the thought of a drink must be making her nauseated.

"Josh, I want to say thank you."

"For what?"

"For taking Gracie to prom."

"Nora." Now I'm feeling nauseated. She can't *thank* me. That's the last thing I deserve. "It's my pleasure. I'm…" What am I exactly? "I'm *honored* she's going with me." There it was. The word just slipped out, but it's the right one. I am honored to be with her.

And terrified all at the same time.

She smiles faintly. "You know, I'll never see her children. And I'll never see her wedding. I probably will never know what college she's going to, and I'm hoping—" Her words fall away, and then she turns back to face me."—That I make it until her eighteenth birthday, but that's five months away." She shakes her head. "But most of all, I'm praying I'll still be here the day she graduates high school."

"You will be."

Her eyes widen with surprise at my assurance.

"But Josh…" She holds out a hand toward me and,

kneeling down next to her, I take it. Her hand is soft but cold and spongy from dehydration. "Seeing her go to prom, looking like this, so happy with you…" She smiles as her eyes sparkle. "Thank you, Josh."

"What's going on?"

Letting go of Nora's hand, I turn to see Gracie standing in the entryway to the living area.

"Your mom and I were—"

"Oh, I know exactly what was going on here." She clamps both hands to her hips and tosses one foot out to the side. Then she storms into the living room and stands before her mother, crossing her arms in front of her chest. She's pissed.

"Gracie, I can't imagine what you're thinking." I stand, perspiration forming on my lower back.

"Oh, can't you?"

She glances up at me and winks, and all my tension falls away. I crack a smile that quickly widens into a grin.

"I see what's happening here." She chews the corner of her lip and nods to her mother. "You've got your fancy turban on for a reason. You're trying to get Josh to take you to prom, and you were going to make your escape while I was searching for my bag in my bedroom." She holds up a tiny blue bag, waving it. She beams at her mother.

Nora tilts her head, mocking a sigh. "He's just so handsome, Gracie."

"Oh, I know." Gracie flashes a radiant smile. "By the way, Josh, I meant to tell you, you look very handsome tonight."

"Thank you." So they use humor to survive this. The way Dad and I sometimes do. Of all the things they could be doing—the complaining, the misery they could be wallowing in—instead, they choose to enjoy their time together. Once again, I'm in awe of Gracie.

"Well…" Nora raises her good hand and drops it again. "Seems he didn't take the bait." She runs her hand up and down the blanket lying on her legs and points to the coffee table jammed with ginger ale cans. "For some reason, he chose you."

Gracie smiles at me. "Yeah, he did."

"Yeah." I step closer, raising a hand to her cheek, stroking it gently. "I did."

"All right, you two." Nora smiles at us. "Go be romantic at prom where it belongs."

Just like that, Gracie's expression changes again. "Mom." She shakes the tiny bag in her grasp. "Anything. If anything doesn't feel right…"

"I'll call, Gracie. I'll call."

"Here." She grabs her mom's phone and types something. "I just added Josh's number too." She glances up at me. "Is that okay?"

I nod as a cold sweat breaks out across my forehead. *Don't trust me, Gracie. That's the last thing you should ever do.*

"You can text or call him too, okay?" She speaks to her mother.

"Yes. Gracie, I'm fine. Please. Go."

Gracie nods as she walks to me and slips her hand in mine. It feels so natural and so right, I smile.

"What are you smiling about?"

I raise our intertwined hands. "I've got a lot to be happy about."

She gives me her closed-lip smirk and leads me out the door, locking it behind us.

Chapter Twelve

Gracie

"It's beautiful." I turn in a full circle as I look around our high school gym. This usually hot, smelly, oversized room has been morphed into Paris, or, at least, a really pretty make-believe version of Paris, which is fine by me…I could use a little make-believe in my life.

Holding me by the hand, Josh walks us along the side of the gym and down a long plastic runner with a cobblestone print that serves as a street. The "street" is lined with five-bulb streetlamps borrowed from the retro diner in downtown. Across the gym is a cardboard silhouette of the Eiffel Tower.

"I had no idea we had a prom committee that could do this," I whisper as he walks us toward an empty white cloth-covered table with a small silver l'Arc de Triomphe centerpiece. Without a word, he helps me out of my shawl and leads me onto the dance floor.

He pulls me toward him and holds me so close our intertwined hands are tight between our chests. His free hand wraps around my waist, and I lift my arm, resting my bag behind his neck. My eyes close as he begins to move our bodies so…so…slowly…

****

Kiss me. Kiss me. Kiss me.

We've been together on the dance floor for *hours*. Through fast song and slow, I've been nestled in the strong arms of Josh Cadman, and I don't ever want it to stop. Ever. But I do want him to kiss me. Desperately.

Kiss me.

The heels I slipped off an hour ago dangle behind his head with my clutch, and our bodies are melded together. What I never expected, what I thought would never happen…has.

I'm ready to be with a boy again. Maybe I'm not ready to go as far as I did that summer before my sophomore year… That was…

I shiver, and he tightens his arms around me.

But it won't be like that summer. Everything with Josh is different. Josh is different. Special. That's why I'm ready to take a step.

More than anything, I'm now sure that I'm ready to trust again.

I open my eyes and glance up at him as he looks down into my eyes. His eyes are so dark. So soulful and so smart.

Kiss me.

Maybe I can will it to happen before I have to break away and call Mom.

Snuggling even tighter against him, I lift my chin, trying anything I can to signal him. Since the moment he took that beating for me, I've imagined what his lips would feel like on mine. Would he be forceful? Gentle? Would he know, despite everything I've done, that it's my first real kiss? Would it matter?

The song draws to a close, and I stiffen. As much as I don't want to, I have to check on Mom. It's been a couple of hours.

He pulls back and gazes down at me. "You have to check with your mom?"

"I'm that predictable?"

He shakes his head, smiling. "No. I felt your body tighten. As much as I don't want to let you go, we should check on her."

We should check on her. It feels so good to have someone to share the responsibility with, even for one night.

"Thanks." I drop my arm from around his shoulder and still holding my hand, he leads me to our empty table at the edge of the gym floor. He hurries to remove a couple of used plastic cups, tossing them into a nearby trash, before pulling out my chair for me. I plop down kind of ungracefully, but oh well, and take my cell from my bag. While I pull up Mom's contact, he toys with the tiny table centerpiece.

"*L'Arc de Triomphe*," he mumbles.

I glance up from my phone.

"What?" He narrows his eyes.

"Your pronunciation. *Arc de Triomphe*." I do my best to copy his accent. "Do you take French?"

He nods. "Did."

"How well do you speak it? Are you fluent?"

"Fluent?" He chuckles. "Because I can pronounce one thing?" He glances at my phone. "How's your mom?"

He slides his chair next to mine.

It's unnerving, but I stay focused. "I haven't checked yet—but—you are fluent, aren't you?"

He stiffens. "What if I am?"

I search his eyes, but they're unreadable. "Did you live in France or something?"

"Or something."

"I thought we weren't playing games."

He nods. “You’re right. I did live in France, for six months my sophomore year.”

“Were you an exchange student?”

He shakes his head. “My dad and I went. A sort of vacation, I guess.”

“What a vacation.” My words fall away as I consider the very real possibility that Mom and I will never take a vacation like that together. I clear my throat and collect myself. “What was that like?”

He smiles at me in a way that makes my insides melt.

“Josh? What was that like? Living in France?”

He reaches out and strokes my cheek. “Not nearly as rewarding as being here.” His voice is a whisper.

Warmth radiates through me. We’re so close. I’m sure he can hear my heart racing and see the perspiration forming on my top lip.

“Well…” Still holding my tiny clutch, I plop my hands on my hips and shake my head. “You’d better spend some time speaking to me in French, mister. Honestly, if I’d known you were fluent, I would have asked you to the prom a heck of a lot sooner.”

I wink, and he grins at me.

“Are you fluent in any other languages?” I lean closer as I speak.

“Nah.” He bounces his head back and forth. “Well, English, I guess.” He leans over and whispers in my ear. “Except when you’re wearing that dress.”

Heat rises in my cheeks, but the moment’s dashed when he points to my phone.

“Come on, we need to check on your mom.”

“Yeah, right.” It’s too easy to be sidetracked when I’m this close to him.

He stares at the statue in his hands while I shoot a quick text:

—Been three hours. All good?—

Then I sit back, watching him. He doesn't make eye contact.

"You okay?"

He looks up, and his brow is furrowed. "Of course." He places the statue back on the table and looks down again.

"Uh-uh."

I lean forward to reach for him but get caught up in my dress. Good grief, I am so not used to moving in anything like this. Leaning back, I shimmy myself up, loosening the dress and freeing the bodice from its taut position. Finally, I reach out and take his hand, and he turns mine over in his, gently rubbing my thumb.

"What's going on?" I ask. "You definitely disappeared."

"No." He shakes his head. "Sorry. I'm right here with you."

Before I can protest, I catch a glimpse of the school assholes making their way into prom.

Oh, no. No. I close my eyes and wish them away, but when I open them, Black and his group have just crossed through the double doors of the gym. They're holding their hands out to their sides, ripping down crepe paper banners like they were charging onto a football field, slapping hands with fans in the stands. When the last of the little gang makes it into the gym, they swagger onto the middle of the dance floor, howling and laughing. Black's wearing a white tux and a stupid grin, and his four assistants, Brown, Red, Green, and Yellow, who's now become Green-Two, are dressed in light blue tuxes. No doubt they think they're being ironic. Like any of them actually knows what that means. They're all wearing unbuttoned dress shirts and no ties.

"Let's get this party started!" Black pumps his fist into the air as he howls like a wolf.

"*Aww-woooo*!" the other four respond.

Kids rush off, creating a blur of pulsating taffeta that settles on the edges of the dance floor. We're frozen in a circle of fear.

Prom halts as everyone collectively holds their breath. Jeannie, a girl who transferred to our school last year, grasps the sides of her dress in her fists and sways back and forth. She's clearly terrified, and she's not the only one. A few of the boys stand in front of their dates, but no one dares to talk to Black and his band of assholes. Even the one male chaperone in the gym—Mr. Soltz, who teaches ELA—has disappeared. The assholes walk the perimeter of the dance like they're stalking their prey. I sink back into my chair, trying to disappear, praying they won't remember me or Josh.

"Boo!" Black startles a girl in a peach-colored dress. He laughs as she bursts into tears, covers her face, and runs from the gym. Once she's gone, he continues on his path of terror.

"Josh." I whisper his name. The last thing I want is to call attention to us. My shoulder muscles are so tense they're glued to my ears. "We should just go."

I sit forward, trying to take his hand so we can slide out the side exit unnoticed, but instead, Josh stands and steps out into the middle of the gym. Black glares at him.

"Josh." I whisper his name. "Josh, please."

Black stops before Josh and turns his head comically, like a bad actor in a zombie movie. He raises an orange-colored eyebrow. “Josh, is it?” He nods. “Well, nice to make your acquaintance.” He offers his hand.

Don’t do it, Josh. Don’t take his hand. It’s a trick.

Josh places his hand in Black’s, and they shake. My heart races in anticipation. It’s like I’m watching a scary movie, and the killer clown is just about to attack.

“We’ve met before.” Josh drops Black’s hand and stands tall. “Under similar circumstances.”

“Oh, I remember. One sucker punch, and you went down like an f-ing pussy.”

Black turns to his gang, and they all laugh.

“Interesting choice you’ve made to come to prom without dates.” Even though I see only his profile, I can tell Josh smiles and then makes steady eye contact with each boy in Black’s group. They mumble and shuffle their feet.

“You looking for another beating, dumb ass?” Black opens his arms wide and steps into Josh’s space, swaying his head like a hungry hyena.

“I think you should leave.” Josh speaks matter-of-factly.

Black has to crane his neck to look Josh in the eye. “And what if I don’t?”

Come on, Josh. Just back away. Let them be. I stare in disbelief.

“You should go,” Josh repeats.

Black mumbles to his gang.

What’s happening here? Why aren’t they fighting? Are they just waiting for us to get to the parking lot to attack? Oh crap. That’s exactly what they’re doing. They’re waiting to attack us, to hold Josh while they do whatever the hell they want to me. I place a hand on my stomach, fighting a cramp of nausea. I can't afford this. Not ever, but especially not now. I have to be okay to go home to Mom to take care of her. Oh crap! I use a shaking hand to pull out my cell and look for her text. Nothing. But then, it's only been four minutes. I turn my attention back to Josh, who's as still as a boulder.

Black breaks eye contact first, looking down at his feet, and then he glances tentatively at Josh.

"You need to leave," Josh commands as he steps closer.

The other four boys in the gang walk up behind Black, tensing and snarling like rabid dogs.

"Now," Josh adds.

"Yeah? And why would that be?" Black tries to stand toe to toe with Josh, but his tone has lost some of its cockiness.

"Because there's nothing for you here. You're nearly a grown man, Noah."

Noah? His name is Noah? How does Josh know?

"Be better than this," Josh tells Black.

"What the fuck? Be better than what? Huh, *bitch*?"

Before Black can react, Josh reaches out and places a hand on his shoulder.

"What's going on in here?" Mr. Gibbons interrupts the moment as he comes in waving his aluminum bat.

I never thought I'd be so happy to see him.

Josh removes his hand from Black's shoulder, and Black drops his head, shuffling his feet. One foot gets caught on a filthy, untied shoelace. He rights himself and then lifts his head and nods to his group.

"There's nothing here. This guy's a pussy. He won't fight us. Come on." Black waves to his posse, and three of them follow him toward the door. All move with eyes down and sloped shoulders, like their cocky football team just lost the state championships.

Mr. Gibbons stands by, resting the bat in his hands.

Only Green-Two hangs back. He walks to a girl who's waiting on the edge of the dance floor. He reaches out and toys with a tendril of her dark curly hair that's hanging loosely from her fancy updo. She pulls away, and he laughs. Black glares at him.

"Jim. Don't be an asshole, man."

"James McDonald," Gibbons yells, "kindly remove yourself from the premises before I call the cops."

Jim? Noah? This is the first time I've ever heard any of them called by an actual name. Green-Two bows his head and walks toward the door of the gym, following Black like a dog with his tail between his legs. Gibbons escorts them out.

I turn to Josh. "What the hell just happened?"

He lifts his chin. "Did your mom respond?"

Mom. Crap. I shake my head as I process my feelings of relief, fear, awe, and anger. Despite the occasional inquiring glance thrown our way, prom pretty much returns to normal all around us. Although I'm annoyed as heck that he's not answering my question and explaining what the hell just happened, he's right. Mom is more important. I look at my phone.

I exhale when I see the text from her.

—Sl gid—

"Everything okay?" He nods toward the phone as he speaks.

I furrow my brow, trying to understand. "I'm not sure."

"What does it say?"

I hold out the phone to him.

"What does *Sl gid* mean?"

"I think she meant to text *All good.*" I shrug, swallowing hard. An ache forms in the pit of my stomach.

"People mistype all the time." He smiles, but the smile doesn't reach his eyes.

"You don't believe that, do you?" I whisper, suddenly filled with fear. My hands tremble as I hold the phone and reread the text.

"I think you should text her again." Concern fills his eyes.

I nod, fighting to steady my thumbs so I can text faster.

—Really okay?—

I send the text and look up at Josh. Despite everything and the weirdness that just went down, I'm so grateful I'm not alone right now.

"Let's give her a couple." His voice is deep and reassuring.

He moves around the table and comes up next to me. He pulls up a white folding chair and sits, draping his arm around the back of my chair. Despite it all, I feel safe and protected. He's here. With me. For whatever happens. He brings his hand to my shoulder and rubs gently.

I glance at my phone. Two minutes. I look over at Josh, but he smiles reassuringly. Two minutes is nothing. We have a five-minute rule for a reason. What if she's in the bathroom? Except… She really can't get to the bathroom on her own right now. She's there. On the couch. She's just not answering my text.

His hand drops to my lower back, and he rubs in small circles that work like magic. My too-tight muscles melt with his touch. All I can think is how good this would feel the next time I have those horrifically painful cramps—the ones that make me pop four painkillers at a time so I can be on my feet for my shift at Shakes 'n' Slaw. I lean toward the table, and he increases his pressure as he rubs away any last bits of tension. My eyes close as he places his hands on my waist and uses his thumbs to knead at the knots in my lower back. It hurts all the way around to my abdomen but feels so good at the same time.

"Mmm…" I moan, releasing pounds of pressure.

"Feel good?"

"Good grief, yes." I don't think I've ever had anyone touch me like this…ever.

He works his way around my lower back, and my body gives over to him. But still, no matter how good this feels and how magical it feels to be connected to Josh, I need to know if she's okay. I steal a peek at my phone. Nothing. Damn it.

"How long's it been?" He removes his hands from my back.

Shivering, I face him. "Six—almost seven—minutes."

"Text her again." His voice is authoritative, and his face is filled with concern.

As fast as I can, I text: *—Mom? Are you okay?—* and send.

We sit in silence for another whole minute. "Josh, I—"

The phone vibrates, and I glance at the text.

—te—

He nods toward the phone, and I hold it out.

He scowls as he reads it. "*Te*? Do you think that was

supposed to be—"

"*Yes*? Yes, I do. T is next to Y on the keyboard." I place the phone on the table. "She meant to text 'yes.'"

Without a word, he stands and grabs my phone, which I just put down. He fishes in his pocket for his car keys. "Where's your wrap?"

I point across the room, but before I can tell him to leave it, he sprints across the gym, grabs my wrap from a chair, and sprints back. "Come on." He takes me by the hand and pulls me out the gym door.

****

Running red lights and passing slow cars on back country roads, Josh gets me home in record time. We race through the front door, and the smell hits me immediately. Fresh vomit. I cover my mouth and nose with my hand and turn to Josh. I pull my wrap off and hold it out to him. "Here."

He takes the wrap but shakes his head, not understanding.

"Cover your nose and mouth."

"No, Gracie. Who cares about the smell? Go. Find her."

I rush forward. "Mom?" I look around frantically, but she's not on the couch. Damn it, damn it, damn it. Did she try to make it to the bathroom on her own? I hurry past the couch and down the short hallway, barging through the bathroom door. Nothing. "Mom?" I'm frantic as I hurry to her bedroom.

"Gracie!" It's Josh.

I rush back to the living room, and he's squatting on the floor by Mom, his arms wrapped around her. He lifts her from a puddle of her own vomit. She somehow ended up out of sight, hidden by the chair. She glances at me, and her eyes are filled with despair.

"Mom." I run to them and take her bad side, and together, we lift her carefully and sit her on the couch. She wheezes and coughs and her body contorts with abrupt, jagged movements as she fights for breath.

"Is she having a seizure?" He holds her shoulders as he speaks.

"I don't know. It's a new chemo."

Taking the shawl he's somehow still carrying, he wraps it around her shoulders and holds her tight. She settles some as he does.

"Gracie, call 911."

"No!" Mom winces as she yelps her protest.

"I can't afford 911 unless it's an absolute emergency, Josh," I explain.

"This is an emergency," he snaps.

Mom clutches her stomach as she shakes her head. "Nooo."

"Fine." His shoulders race up and down with his breath. "Go get her a bucket or a bowl or something."

I nod and obey, rushing to the kitchen in search of the old purple bowl we once used to hold Halloween candy for trick-or-treaters but has since become the designated vomit bowl. It's the right size and easy to disinfect. I dig through a high cabinet, pushing aside refillable water bottles and sippy cups from when I was a baby. "Come on, come on…" Taking a deep breath, I spy a silhouette of a witch against something purple. The bowl. I yank on it, and it falls onto the counter, along with bunches of plastic cups and plates that land on the floor. I leave them and dash back to the living room. "Here." I hold it in front of Mom, placing it on her lap carefully.

She shakes her head, still shaking and wheezing. She looks up at Josh, and I know she's embarrassed.

"Mom, it's okay. He's my friend. Please. He doesn't mind." Selfishly, I can't stand the thought of him leaving me all alone with this tonight. Not now. Not now that I've known what support can be.

"I promise, Nora. I've been around this many, many times." He holds her as she allows her body to give over to Josh.

"Oh, I'm—" She tries to stand, but of course she can't. He leans her forward and rubs her back as she vomits up the little ginger ale and bile she has in her stomach. She sits back, and her head drops to the side like a broken baby bird. "Josh. Should…n't see." She pats his hand. "Or Gracie."

"The only thing that bothers me is that you're not feeling well," he reassures her.

"And it doesn't bother me, Mom."

"Bathroom," she ekes out.

"Mom. Just use the bowl."

Her head rolls from one side to the other. "Bathroom."

"Gracie, I think she wants…"

"Oh, yeah." I jump to her good side and scoop her up, dragging her to her feet. She's so thin, but it's still so much for me.

"Bath!" Her voice is filled with urgency.

"Gracie, let me—"

Josh moves me out of the way and scoops Mom into his arms, cradling her, and then rushes her to the bathroom. Placing her down on her feet, he leans her against the wall, and I bolt past him to get to her. He closes the door behind himself, and I drag her to the toilet, helping her with her sweats. Thankfully, she made it in time. She leans her head against the bathroom wall.

"Mom?" I kneel down next to her.

She bats her eyes in response.

"Mom. I need to call 911 and get you to the hospital."

"Noooo." She rolls her head back again.

"Mom, I'm not equipped for this. Josh is right. We can afford it. I promise. You're having a bad reaction to the chemo. You need a doctor."

She closes her eyes and steadies her breath. "No."

"Mom!" I shriek but then calm my voice. "Please. Let's consider it."

She shakes her head, and frustration rushes through me like a raging fire.

"Ugh!" I stand back and run my hands through my hair, flummoxed. "Why not?"

"No am—ambulance." She waves her hands to cue me to help lift her. I do as she yanks at her sweats, but I'm still fuming.

"Please, Mom."

She doesn't respond, so I help her to the bathroom door and pull it open. Josh is standing there, waiting. His brow is furrowed.

"Nora, what if I drive you? Rather than an ambulance?"

He's heard everything.

"Don't nee—"

Suddenly, she drops her entire weight into my arms.

"Mom?"

I struggle to hold her upright, but Josh jumps in again and slides his arm around her.

"Nora? Mrs. Jackson?" He turns her head to look

into her eyes, but they're closed. He pulls out his cell.

"Can you drive us, Josh?" My words are a fast whisper.

He shakes his head as he presses the emergency button on his phone. "The ambulance is better. They have equipment she'll need."

I nod and hold Mom's hand as he gives our address to the 911 operator. As we wait, she drifts in and out of consciousness, but thank God her heart never stops, and she's able to breathe.

"What do we do?" I'm shaking from head to foot, but I stay strong for her—and for him.

He moves her to the couch, and we lay her down. Yanking my gown over my knees, I squat by her and smooth tiny tufts of hair back from her face, tucking them into her turban. "Did they say how long?" I turn to Josh, who's perched by the window, waiting to flag down the ambulance.

"Just a few minutes. They're not far."

"Okay."

Mom moans in pain as her beautiful face hardens and her body contorts. I hold her as best I can, but I'm terrified, and my own limbs are shaking uncontrollably.

"It's okay, Mom. It's okay." All I want is to fix this for her—to make her feel safe and protected as she used to do for me.

She moans again in response.

"Josh?"

He comes to my side and reaches out to smooth a piece of hair back from my face, just as I had done for Mom.

"I'm here."

I nod as a rush of emotions overtakes me. I want to

ask if this is the end. I want to know if it's finally done. If the monster wins. I want to know if it's horrible that I feel…relief. Instead, I turn to him and look directly into his gorgeous eyes.

"Please don't leave me."

His eyes flicker with surprise as the flashing lights of the ambulance flood the living room.

Chapter Thirteen

Josh

Please don't leave me. Christ. What have I done?

We stand outside Nora's critical care room, waiting for information. Waiting for anything. I fidget in my suit, pulling my cuffs down over my hands and then pushing them back up to expose my forearms.

I hate hospitals. No, it's more than hate. I loathe them. I loathe the steady sounds of machines that suddenly *ding* or *beep*, announcing some fucked-up situation has just gotten worse. I despise the sights—the bedpans and walkers, the white sheets on adjustable beds, but most of all, I abhor the smell. It's not even the smell of hospital-grade antiseptic that turns my stomach. It's what's underneath that smell—the smell of death lurking under hope.

If smells could have a size and shape, a hospital's would be a lightning bolt with jagged edges that scrape and cut as it fills each nostril and every bit of lung.

I inhale as shallowly as I can, feeling my face scrunch into a scowl. Christ, there it is. Sour milk. That's the smell. It's a thick, lumpy, foul, sour milk smell that clings to whatever victim it's chosen. And once that smell is on you, it never leaves.

And once you're gone, the ones left behind can never forget it.

"Here." Dad walks over to Gracie and me and hands

us each a coffee. "It's loaded with cream and sugar. Had to do something to make it tolerable."

The coffee's lukewarm and stale, but my nose is grateful for the reprieve and so am I. I nod my thanks to Dad.

Gracie takes her cup and lifts it to him like she's toasting him. "Thank you, Mr. Cadman." Her voice is weak and tired. She's exhausted.

Dad stares at the ground as he answers her. "Call me Ben. Please."

She smiles sweetly at him, but he just nods and steps away. He stands on the opposite side of the narrow, sterile hallway as we wait outside Nora's room. His gaze is downward as he drinks his coffee.

"Gracie." I put a fist to my mouth, clearing my throat. "Are you able to get some rest? There are couches down the hall in the waiting area. I'll wait here. I promise I'll get you as soon as I hear anything."

She shakes her head. "No, Josh, thank you, though." Her voice is so frail she sounds like a young child. She glances at Dad and back to me. "But you two shouldn't wait. It could be all night."

"I'm not going anywhere," I assure her.

My dad looks up at us but doesn't move from his position with his back against the wall.

"Thank you." She smiles.

A sharp pain shoots across my head, stretching from temple to temple, but then it leaves as fast as it comes. I was taught that pain is the manifestation of sorrow, so if you don't deal with your sorrows, you're doomed to a life of pain.

Shit. That's what I've done to Gracie. I have doomed her to a life of pain when all I wanted—all I *want*—was and is to be able to protect her from all the pain and sorrow coming her way.

Instead, I'll be the cause of most of it.

Dad pushes himself off the wall and crumples his empty coffee cup. "I'm going to go get some folding chairs." He walks down the long antiseptic hallway and turns the corner.

Gracie gives me a half-smirk. "He doesn't like me much."

I shake my head. "That's not true. Really. He just has a hard time with me growing up."

She nods. "I guess that would be tough on a parent." She gazes at the door to her mother's room.

Crap. What an asshole I am. Like Gracie would have any idea what that feels like.

She yawns, covering her mouth with her hand.

"Why don't you go get some rest?" I repeat my earlier question, hoping she'll take me up on it. "I promise I'll get you if I hear anything."

"What time is it?" She grabs my forearm with my watch, and I like that she feels close enough to me to do that.

"Three ten."

She nods, glancing at the door and back again. "I guess if you don't mind taking a shift, maybe I will try to sleep for a few minutes."

"Yeah. Sure. That's great." I slip my arm around her and begin walking her down the hallway before she can change her mind. She falls heavily against me.

"I have to open tomorrow, so I'm going to have to leave by seven so I can clean up the house and grab a shower before work."

"Wait." I shake my head. "You're working

tomorrow? It's Sunday. Day after prom."

She shrugs. "There's a little league game in town. Jerry said he needs me to open."

"Why can't he do it?"

"Some obligation."

An obligation. For the man with no wife and no kids. He couldn't let her have off the day after prom?

"I can't say no, Josh. Not now, for sure."

"I know. It's just you're going to sleep for what…a couple of hours? And then clean and work a full shift?" We turn into the empty waiting room, and I guide her toward the couch against the far wall.

"It's not that big of a deal. You do what you have to do, right?" She sits as she speaks and covers her mouth again as she yawns.

"Yes." *You do what you have to do.*

"I'm just going to…" Her eyes grow heavy as she turns onto her side. She's out before she makes it to a parallel position.

"Wait a sec." I yank off my jacket, ball it up, and then slip it under her head.

She rouses enough to smile, and she adjusts her makeshift pillow. "Smells so good," she murmurs, and she's out.

I stand there for a moment, taking in her beauty. Her long blonde hair falls over her shoulder and across the top of her gown. Her face is relaxed and peaceful, and her chest rises and falls with her breath. Underneath the fluff of her gown, I see her foot twitch as her body lets go. She is perfect.

"She asleep?"

"Jesus, Dad." I turn to him, startled. "How'd you know we were here?"

"I went back with the chairs and guessed. It's good she's sleeping."

"Yes."

"You okay?" He keeps looking forward, cracking the knuckles of one hand by fisting it in the other.

"What does this have to do with me?"

"Josh." He mutters my name as his gaze drops to the ground. He lifts his head again and resumes staring at Gracie. "I mean, the whole hospital scene. Haven't been to one in what, three years now?"

I shrug. "You do what you have to do."

He nods.

We stand there for a minute in silence. Finally, I can't take it any longer.

"Dad, I know why I'm staring at her; why the hell are you?"

He releases one short chuckle. "You wouldn't believe how much she looks like Celia."

"Mom?" I turn to him.

He nods. "Yeah. It's startling. I saw it that first night you brought her by. I saw her get out of your car, and for a moment I…I just forgot where I was and what was real."

I tilt my head, taking in Gracie. "I've seen the pictures of Celia, but I never put it together."

"Why would you? The nose is different. Celia's was pointier. And Celia's eyes were a brighter blue." He glances at me before turning back to stare at Gracie. "But the rest." He shakes his head. "The hair color and length, the heart-shaped face, the strong forehead, pointy chin, her height, and even body type." He sighs. "She could be Celia's daughter." He makes eye contact. "And from what I'm seeing of her, she's incredibly strong. A spitfire, like your mom."

I nod. "Is that why you've been avoiding her?"

"I haven't been." He looks back at Gracie sleeping on the couch and drops his head. "Maybe that's part of it, anyway. I don't know." He raises his chin and looks down the hall toward Nora's room. "I wonder if she'll pull through this."

"She will. But I don't think she has very long."

Suddenly, he reaches out and grabs my forearm, turning me toward him sharply. His eyes plead with me. "Josh. This girl—her whole life has been taking care of her sick mother. Are you really going to do this to her?"

He points to Gracie sleeping on the couch, and finally, I understand. He loves me, but he *blames* me.

Because to him, once again, I stand in his way of saving Celia.

****

"Josh?" Gracie glances around her living room, which has been cleaned and sanitized. "What happened here?" She gazes up at me with exhausted eyes.

"Please don't be mad."

She shakes her head. "Mad? I…" She turns to me. "When and how did you get this done?"

"As soon as you agreed to get some rest, I called a service we sometimes use when we're renovating a house. I got your key from your bag, and my dad drove over to let them in on his way home."

"Wait, your dad?"

"Yeah, why?"

"It's just…" She furrows her brow, thinking. "Nothing. That was really nice of him. I'm sorry if I put him out." She looks away. "Huh."

"What?"

"No, nothing."

"He likes you, Gracie."

She tilts her head.

"It's just—you remind him of someone. I think it's painful for him."

She nods. "I'm sorry if he's in pain, but I hope that's what it is." She moves around toward the front of the couch, where the rug has been removed and the floor sanitized. "You have connections that will come clean in the middle of the night? You've only lived here for a couple of months."

"It's because of our business. We make connections quickly. And the guy who runs this business used to live on the West Coast near us. We worked with him. I called in a favor."

"To clean *my* house at four a.m.? That's some favor. Josh, I can't let you do this."

"It's done."

She bites the corner of her lip. She doesn't look happy.

"Gracie. Please. We had a tough night."

"But this is…" She turns in a full circle. "Josh, they cleaned the kitchen." She marches to the bathroom. "And thc bathroom." She throws her hands up and then lets them fall. "It's too much."

"I just wanted to help."

"But why?" Her eyes search mine. "Why are you so nice to me?"

"Gracie." I shake my head. "Please don't say that. I'm not all that ni—"

Before I can finish my word, she walks up to me, lifts her chin, and balances on her tiptoes. She kisses me softly on the lips.

Pulling back, she smiles. "Sorry. I've been waiting for you to do that all night, and it just got the best of me."

I freeze. Looking down into her gorgeous blue eyes, my tight abdominal muscles unclench.

Sliding my arms around her, I pull her closer. "I wanted to kiss you. I *really* wanted to. I just didn't know if you were ready."

She's tight against my body, and her chest heaves as she speaks. "I guess I need to work on my signals then."

"Oh, I think you've gotten pretty clear." I lean down and kiss her on her soft lips, over and over.

She presses her body even tighter to mine and snakes her arms around my shoulders. Her lips mash hard against mine as she kisses me more passionately. There's no room between our bodies, so I shift back, giving myself some sort of fighting chance. She opens her mouth and without thinking, I press our bodies tight together again, and my tongue finds its way in. She moans in response.

"Gracie." I pull back, holding her at arm's length.

She blinks her eyes lazily at me. Her hair is tousled, and the soft skin around her mouth is red from kissing. She's gorgeous.

"We have to stop." I take a deep breath, releasing it through parted lips.

"You don't have to stop for me, Josh." Her chest rises and falls as she speaks. "I thought maybe I wouldn't be ready. But…"

"But?"

"But I think I am." She smiles. "It's the strangest thing, but it's like I have this pull toward you. Like I'm a ball rolling around one of those old pinball games, and no matter where I'm shot off to, I can't help but roll back to you. That's where I want to be anyway—around you. When I'm with you, maybe for the first time in my life, I feel peace." She looks up into my eyes. "Is that crazy?"

"Maybe. But it's the same for me."

She reaches out and takes my hands in hers. "Will you stay? With me, tonight? Or, I guess, more accurately, will you stay for whatever we have left of this morning?"

An icy chill washes over me. "Gracie…I…I can't."

"Why not?" Her eyes flash with hurt.

"It's your mom's house."

"I wish that were true," she answers sadly. "Please, Josh. I don't want to be alone."

She looks away for a moment, and when she turns back, her eyes are full of sorrow. I can't say no.

"I'll stay as long as it's on the couch."

She tucks a hair behind her ear. "The couch. It's, um, kind of my mom's sick bed. I don't want you stuck on that."

I exhale. "Well then, I'll stay on the chair." I point to the old wingback.

"You're sleeping on a chair?"

"Yes."

"Okayyyyyy. Well, I'll grab a quick shower and then get you some sheets and a pillow for the *chair*." She shakes her head and walks off smiling. Suddenly, she stops and turns back. "Josh? I'm glad you're staying."

"Yeah. Me too."

She smiles again, and then she's gone.

****

Who the hell invented the wingback chair? I turn to my side, trying my millionth position of the night—or morning—but the chair is the most freaking uncomfortable thing I've ever attempted to sleep on. That's saying a lot considering some of the places I've slept, like those two months in Tibet when I slept in a meditation box—nightly. I turn to the other side. Maybe the guy who invented this thing wasn't as tall as me. Maybe it was okay for him, but my head hits the very top of the chair, forcing my back into some crazy, unnatural shape. Damn. Even the greatest yogis I've known wouldn't be able to contort into this shape. And the seat—Jesus. It's like sitting on lumpy concrete. The floor has to be better than this.

I grab my pillow and sheet and begin to lower myself to the floor.

"Hey." Her voice is soft.

I stare dumbly as she walks into the living room and squats down next to me on the hardwood floor. She's wearing faded plaid pajama bottoms and a see-through white tank top. I take a deep breath as she takes my sheet from me and reaches around to get the blanket from the chair. Without a word, she lays the sheet down and then places the blanket on top of it. She smooths it out as if we were about to have a picnic and then sits, balancing her elbow on her bent knee.

"I figured you weren't sleeping either."

I shake my head and hold my half-squatting position against the chair. She pats the blanket and smiles.

"You can sit with me."

Easing myself the rest of the way onto the floor, I raise one knee and lean back against the chair. I try to maintain some distance.

She adjusts so she's sitting cross-legged. Her long hair falls around her shoulders, and she busies herself, picking at the pills on the blanket. Then she looks up at me through thick lashes and places a warm hand on my knee.

I feel like I've been tossed into a bipolar ocean—pinpricks of energy sting me, and then waves of calm wash over me.

Reaching out, she takes my hand in hers and turns it, palm upward. She caresses the calluses on my skin as I close my eyes.

There's a gentle tug on my arm as she tries to pull me closer, so I open my eyes and let my body move toward her. She places two warm hands on my chest and gently eases me to the floor. She slides in next to me and nestles in the crook of my arm. This isn't the first time I've held her tight to me like this—but it is the first time we're doing it lying side by side. In an empty house.

She drapes one arm across my chest and one leg up over me, dropping it into the hollow between my thighs.

It all feels way too good.

She lays a hand on my chest and traces tiny circles. "Josh?"

"Yes?" Her touch is like magic.

"I love you."

"I—" Her words are so unexpected I stutter.

She pulls herself up and balances on her forearm but leaves her other hand on my chest. "It's okay. You don't have to say it back. I can see it in everything you do for me." She pulls her hand away and motions to her cleaned house like she's an old-fashioned game show hostess showing the daily prize.

My chest is cold without her.

Leaning down, she kisses me, and then she sits up abruptly. The way she's posed, with a long, straight spine, she looks like she's getting ready to answer her side of an argument in debate club.

"I was with a boy only once before," she tells me. "Two years ago, when I was fifteen. Mom's cancer was accelerating, and I was so…lost…" She looks off. "There was a boy who lived next door then. A year older than me. I was lonely. I thought it would help."

"Did it?" I sit up next to her.

"Of course not. It made me feel even worse. Especially when it was over, and he pretended it never happened."

"I'm sorry that happened to you."

"That isn't all of it." She takes a deep breath. "It was only one time, but it was enough." Her hands shake as she tells the story. "I never told my mom. We had too much to worry about without having to plan for a baby. But I was…surprisingly okay about all of it. Yes, I was terrified, but I was also strangely happy. I was grateful that I wouldn't be alone anymore. I was grateful that I wouldn't have to be shuffled to some foster home all by myself. I knew that with the baby, I would always have someone." She stares into my eyes. "Is that horrible?"

"No," I assure her. "No, it's not. What happened?"

"I was almost five months and barely showing. Mom didn't notice because we were dealing with her new diagnosis, and I just wore loose shirts over yoga pants every day. One night, I woke up with cramps. I still remember the time: three-o-seven. I had this little battery-operated clock, the kind that folds up because it's made to travel, and it sat on my nightstand. It was three-o-seven when I sat up in a cold puddle. There was blood everywhere. I wrapped a towel around my waist, snuck out of the house, and drove to the hospital. When I got there, the baby was no longer alive." She sighs. "They induced using a drug that I had a serious reaction to. It was awful." She closes her eyes and shakes her head. "I was hospitalized for days. I lied to Mom, told her it was my appendix, and the lie worked because she couldn't drive to come see me. She was weak from her chemo. I was all alone except for Jerry. When the hospital demanded a parent or guardian, I lied again and said he was my father. He signed paperwork for me, but all in all, it still cost me a fortune. I lost a lot of time at work, but Jerry stepped up again. Gave me a bonus to help me out with bills and such."

I swallow my aversion to Jerry and hold her hand tightly. "I am so sorry you went through that."

"I'm still going through it," she whispers. "Always will be."

"What do you mean?"

"The pregnancy, the operation… The scar tissue was so extreme, I'll never be able to have a child."

"What?" I sit back, distancing myself from her, trying to process this. "Wait. You—you can't get pregnant?" There's no way. No way I could be wrong about her. "You're sure?"

She nods. "Not that it matters. Not now, anyway."

"Yes, it matters." My words are a whisper.

"Josh?" She tilts her head. "You seem, uh, really affected by this. You okay?"

"Yeah, um, yes." I take a deep breath, trying to pull myself together. This isn't possible. I know she's the one. She's *marked,* for Christ's sake. "I'm just so sorry that happened to you."

"Thank you." She leans toward me like she's letting me in on an even bigger secret. "Want to know the weirdest part?"

Trying to slow my breathing, I nod.

"The weirdest part is, when I got home after they released me, I plopped down on my bed and looked at my clock, and it said three-o-seven. The exact time it was when I left. It's like time had frozen." She looks away. "I guess it did."

Three-o-seven. Three-seven. March seventh. My birthdate.

This is just too coincidental.

"So?" She looks down at the ground and then back up to me. "Now what?"

Cripes—what *do* I do now? I was so sure, *so sure*. How could I have been wrong about this? She's marked. Time stopped on my birthdate. The whole drive from North Carolina here, I could feel her presence. She even looks like my mother. I know she's the one. But she can't be. What the hell do I do now?

I'm desperate for an answer, but tonight, there's no sign, no signals, no premonition. There's only us. So there's only one thing I can do. I stare into her smart eyes and tell her the truth.

"Gracie, I have no idea what we do next."

She smiles and nuzzles against me, pushing me back down onto the floor.

"I do," she whispers.

She lays her body on mine and covers my mouth with hers.

Chapter Fourteen

Josh

"Josh, hi." Her eyes light up when I approach her window at Shakes 'n' Slaw. She grins and winks at me. Her gaze drops to my T-shirt just for a second, and then her eyes meet mine. It only came up in passing this morning, but I'll bet anything she's thinking about the birthmark on my chest that's the exact complement to hers.

"Hey." I grin back. I glance past her, but it doesn't appear anyone else is working. "You alone?"

She nods. "Just to close."

I shake off a shiver that starts deep in my spine and shoots up my back. I hate that she's working today. I hate that she works so hard. I hate that she's alone, but I hate it even more when she's alone with Jerry.

More than anything, I hate that I was wrong about her.

Except…except now, at least she'll be safe.

It dawns on me. "Wait." I place my hands on the cold steel window counter. The sleeves of my zip-front sweatshirt are pushed up to my elbows, and I catch her eyeing my forearms. "You're opening and closing today?"

"Uh, yeah. Jerry needed the help."

"Wait, so that means he's in back?"

"Nope. Haven't seen him all day."

It's like ten pounds of stress falls off my shoulders. What is it about Super Nice Guy Jerry that rubs me the wrong way? "It was a lot for him to ask you to open and close."

She shrugs. "It's just the two of us as managers." She holds up an oversized rag stained with chocolate ice cream and points behind her with her thumb. "I still need to wipe down the machines and then mop the floor. Will you wait for me?"

"How about I help you?" I lean forward on the tiny window counter.

Her face scrunches. "I'd love it, and thank you. But Jerry would be pissed."

"But you just said he's not here."

She points overhead and then toward the front of the building and the back. "He's not. But he can still see if he wants to. Cameras everywhere."

Cameras everywhere. My body stiffens, and I stand straight. That hollowness in my belly suddenly turns to lead. This is what I've been sensing, not as some psychic premonition or some crap like that, but as a boyfriend.

Where the fuck does he hide the cameras?

"Gracie." I keep my voice as cool as possible. "How many people work for Jerry?"

She furrows her brow as she wipes down a vat larger than she is. She looks off and back again. "I dunno. Um…" She stills her rag while she mentally counts. "Counting all the part-timers, a dozen." She goes back to wiping.

"And how many men work for him?"

She shakes her head. "All women. Jerry said he wishes he had girls."

"Oh, I'll bet."

"What was that?" She tilts her head, and her expression clouds over. I have to be careful here.

"I like girls more than boys, too." I swallow my anger until I'm certain. If this asshole is watching these women…

"Mmm…" She reaches up with her forearm, wipes away a few hairs that are sticking to her sweaty brow, and then goes back to her frenetic scrubbing. She turns her back and starts wiping down the bottom levers of the machines. "Luckily, I did all the inner parts earlier. We were slow once the little league teams left. All I have to do is finish this."

She pops back up to eye level. "Done." She holds a mop in her hand. "Let me just get the floor. I start up here."

I glance up at the cameras. Okay. One problem at a time. First, get her away from the cameras and her scumbag asshole boss. What can I do to get her to agree to leave without changing? *Think, Josh, think.*

"So, uh, the part for your seatbelt came in yesterday. What do you say you finish up as quickly as you can, we visit your mom, and then we go fix your car?"

"Really?"

"Yeah, really."

"Aren't you exhausted?" She balances her forearm on the tip of the mop handle like someone who's handled a mop a million times before.

"No more than you." My adrenaline has me on fire right now.

She smiles. "Okay. Thanks." She spins the mop around and works feverishly.

I hate that I can't help.

She pauses at the entryway to the backroom. "I just

need to rinse out the bucket and change. Give me ten and meet me in the parking lot? We can meet here tonight." She points overhead to a random camera. "He'll be glad I'm not walking out to the parking lot alone. He's a really nice guy." She spins the mop into the far corners past the windows.

Really nice guy. Shit. Let's see how nice of a guy he really is. "Why don't you just throw a jacket on over your uniform and change once you get home?"

She turns back to me and furrows her brow. "Well, we're going to the hospital first, and besides, you know Jerry gets angry when we wear our uniforms in public."

"It'll be covered."

She chuckles. "I appreciate it, but I need to change here."

"Nah. Change at home, later."

She stops and smirks at me. "The milkmaid outfit is that much of a turn-on?"

"On you?" I grin back. "Hell, yeah. Didn't I tell you I had a thing for Heidi when I was growing up?"

"The model?"

"No. The Swiss girl with the braids and the yodeling and such. Drank gallons of hot cocoa—even in the dead heat of summer—just to stare at her on the box."

She giggles. "I don't think that was Heidi on the box, and this isn't a Swiss girl costume, but I guess if it means that much to you, Jerry will understand I have to run to get to the hospital ASAP."

"Great." I nod, and at least a few of the knotted muscles release in my gut. "I'll stay here while you stash the mop and grab your jacket and clothes." I point toward the backroom. "Then I'll walk around the building and meet you in back in five."

"Okay." She smiles. "In five."

I hold up my hand, and as soon as she disappears into the back, I start plotting how I can bust in and check for cameras that Super Nice Jerry has hung in the breakroom to watch the girls change.

****

"Hey." She smiles as she climbs into the passenger seat of my car.

She's stunning, and probably exhausted, but I attack with my usual tact. "Gracie, we need to talk."

She tilts her head. "What's wrong?"

Her face scrunches into a scowl. I turn and look out the front window, laying my wrist on the steering wheel, dangling my hand.

She leans forward and places a warm hand on my forearm. "You're worrying me, Josh."

"Are you working tomorrow?"

"Of course. Pretty much every day. I'm going to try to get off by seven so I can see Mom. C'mon. What's going on? You're all closed off and serious." She sits back. "Are you…sorry about last night?"

"What?" I turn to her. "No, no. Of course not." I reach out and stroke her cheek and then tuck a stray piece of hair behind her ear. "Never. Last night was…the best night of my life. The part when we were alone, I mean."

She beams at me.

"I'm sorry if I made you think that." I turn to face her, resting my arm on the back of my seat. There's so much energy between us the engine might spontaneously ignite. "It's just, do you ever get *feelings* about things? Like gut feelings that something's not right?"

"Sure. Everyone does."

I nod, sitting up taller. "I've had a bad feeling

lately."

Her face blanches. "Is it Mom? She's not going to pull through?" Her voice wavers. The tremors of hurt and uncertainty in her voice radiate through me.

"It's not that." I take her hand. "I'm talking about Jerry."

Her eyes widen. "He has been acting strange lately. Oh no. Do you think he's sick, too?" She slips from my grasp and covers her face with both of her hands. Then she drags her fingertips across her forehead to her temples and rubs. "I know I sound selfish, but I can't take any more illnesses or the thought of anyone else leaving me. I…I know it's not about me, but I don't think I can survive another reason to grieve." She rests her hands in her lap.

Another reason to grieve. Fuck.

I inhale deeply. "He's not sick, Gracie. And the last thing you are is selfish. I've had a bad feeling about him since the day I met him, and well, I've been putting things together, and today it finally hit me."

"What?"

"I think the reason he wants you all to change in and out of your uniforms at work is because he's watching. He's filming you while you do."

Her jaw drops, and then she blurts the tiniest giggle that works its way into a full-blown laugh. "Josh. You scared me. When you were talking about having a *feeling*, I thought you were serious." She slaps me on the chest playfully.

"I am serious."

Her face whitens, and then she shakes her head. "What? Why would you say that? What makes you think that?"

"It's just a hunch. But it all makes sense."

"I…" Her words fall away, and she turns sharply, staring out the front window. Her arms wrap around her waist. "Why would you say something like that? You know Jerry has been like a father to me." Her tone is hurt and inquisitive, not angry like I'd expect it to be.

"Yes. That's why I would never say anything if I didn't really, really think it was possible."

"You *think* it's *possible*? What are you basing this on? One glance at him and a casual reference I made to cameras in the building?" Her face blanches again as she considers the possibility. She shakes her head. "No. No, you're wrong."

"I don't think I am."

"You don't *think* you are. That doesn't mean you know for sure."

"Then do me a favor. Close the breakroom now. Immediately. My dad has this equipment that can sense if there are cameras in a room. I'll teach you how to use it and then please take it in with you as soon as possible. If I'm right, the sensor will alert you to the camera in the—" I stall, swallowing hard. "—Women's changing area, and then you get the hell out of there, and we call the cops."

"Call the cops?" She looks at me like I've lost my mind. "I can't call the cops on Jerry. It'll close the business. Do you know what I make there? And I have health insurance. I couldn't possibly make that anywhere else, and I'd never get health coverage for both my mom and me. And then what do I do? How do my mother and I survive?"

"But if he's filming you, he deserves to be in jail."

She shakes her head again. "It's all so black and

white for you, isn't it? I thought you were someone who understood life for what it really is—it's not some fantasy they tell us about in movies. I…I thought you understood. I can't afford to be a kid. I can't have a jealous boyfriend swoop in and take away the only thing keeping my *mother alive* just in the name of chivalry. Unless Jerry physically hurts me, I can't afford to leave. And frankly, I wish you'd never told me your…your *hunch*." She sighs so heavily her shoulders rise up and down with her breath. "If you want to protect someone's honor, then go find someone who can afford to be saved." She shakes her head and places her hand on the door handle.

"No, Gracie. Please don't go."

Ignoring me, she gets out of the car and holds the door open. She leans down to speak to me. "Thank you again for helping me out these past few weeks. It's been really"—she bites the corner of her lip—"great. Really." She shrugs and walks off.

I don't even dare breathe as she gets into her car and turns the key.

When her engine revs, I know I've lost her.

I turn my engine too, and then suddenly, red brake lights shine through my window and her engine cuts. She climbs out of the driver's seat, walks up to me, and stands by my door. I unroll my window. She rubs her hands up and down her arms, fighting off the cold, and looks me dead in the eyes. "You really think he's filming us?"

"Yes."

She nods. "Well then, as a manager, I have to do something. I can't allow those other women who work for him to be victimized."

"I can help you."

"No." She runs her hands across her face, rubbing her eyes. "Thank you, though. I'll…I'll come up with a bogus reason to close the breakroom immediately and tell all the women to change at home. I'll keep it up for as long as I can, and hopefully, in that time, in between school and my mom, I can find a job." Her voice trails off. "Even if I have to leave school. I'll get my GED eventually."

It dawns on me. Holy crap. I've never seen this girl cry.

"Do you ever cry?"

"What?"

"Sorry. Stupid question. But do you? Cry?"

She raises one shoulder and then lets it drop. "I don't see the point in it. Tears can't drown cancer. Or find me a new job. Or help me graduate school. Or get me health insurance. Or keep my perverted boss from posting half-naked images of me online." She shivers. "If that's what he's doing."

"Maybe not." My throat aches from choking back emotions. "Maybe tears can't help, but I can. At least with some of it."

Her face scrunches into a scowl as her eyes search mine. "How can you help?" Her voice is a whisper.

I nod, staring at her, this girl I barely know, yet in every way, I have known all my life. What I'm about to do…it will seal my fate.

Staring into her smart blue eyes filled with hope, I wonder, for the first time ever, if maybe I don't care about fate or my destiny.

"Marry me." The words fall out before I can think. Before I can stop them. Before I can warn her. But the thing is, they feel right.

"Excuse me?" She steps back from my car, distancing herself as any normal person would.

I get out of the car and stand next to her. "Marry me." I repeat my request.

"*What?*" She tilts her head, trying to understand.

I move closer, eliminating the gap between us. "Marry me."

"But…" Her words fall away as she looks off at nothing in particular.

"But what?"

She turns back. Her face is stamped with all the words she's unable to speak.

I take her hand and place it on my chest, covering my birthmark that matches hers.

"Marry me. Marry me and leave the damned Shakes 'n' Slaw, and we'll make it a safe place for the other women to work. I make enough money to cover our expenses, and you'll be on my health care. We'll set it up to make sure your mom is covered, too. We'll move into your house so you can take care of your mom when she gets home and still go to school. We can graduate, and then we'll figure out what to do from there."

I leave out the part about our very limited future.

"I…I need to work."

"You can work with my dad and me. We could use the extra hands."

"I'm sure he'd love that."

"He will. Give him some time to get to know you."

"But you can't leave him."

I take a deep breath. "I'll have to eventually." No one knows that better than him.

Shifting myself even closer, I reach out with my

hand, running it down her beautiful cheek. Her eyes close. When she opens them again, we're staring at each other.

Is this what love is? Being willing to sacrifice the rest of the world to keep her safe?

"When would we even…?" Her eyes search mine again, looking for the catch. But the catch, how could I even begin to explain that?

"Now. Tomorrow. As soon as possible."

"It would be nice for my mom to see my wedding." She's contemplating this, but then her face hardens again. "This is ridiculous, Josh. You can't marry me just to help me out." She crosses her arms. "You deserve so much better than marrying some girl in high school you kind of know just because you're a nice guy."

"Don't say that." I shake my head. "I'm not a nice guy, and I'm marrying you because I love you."

Her arms fall limp to her sides, and she turns away. "But, Josh."

"Marry me, Gracie."

I reach out and take her by the bicep, spinning her toward me. Her head seems too heavy to hold anymore, and she lets it slump from one side to the other.

"Gracie. Marry me."

She looks up at me, and her eyes dance back and forth across mine. "Don't say it if you don't mean it."

I take a deep breath. She's giving me an excuse. She's giving me the opportunity to change my fate.

But I may just do that all on my own.

"Marry me."

"Okay."

"Yeah?"

"Yeah."

She smiles, and I pull her tight to my chest. All I want is to take care of her forever.

And now all I have to do is to explain.

To everyone.

****

I cross the threshold into Dad's kitchen, and he's staring out the small window over the sink. He's holding a glass of orange juice and takes a long drink as I make my way into the room.

He doesn't turn to me. Instead, he lifts his wrist in an exaggerated move to check his watch. Classy, Dad.

Okay, I'll talk first. "Morning." I'm not going to deny it's morning. Why would I? I'm a grown man. And I'm not being rude. I texted him last night to tell him I was staying at Gracie's. Again.

"Morning." He keeps staring out the window. "Orange juice?" He lifts his glass. "Fresh squeezed. There's more in the fridge."

"Thanks." I cross to the cabinet and take down a glass, which is really a Mason jar, but who cares? These are better for the environment, and we don't need fancy drinkware. We're two men living alone. But not for much longer. I take a deep breath as I open the stainless fridge and grab the container of OJ.

I pour the juice and drink it down fast. It burns my empty stomach, so I rub at it with the side of my fist. Dad still hasn't turned around, so I go to the table, pull out a chair, and plop down.

"Don't you have class?"

"Not until third period. I'm gonna grab a quick shower and head over."

"Good." He nods.

"Dad."

He doesn't move.

"Dad?" I raise my voice, but he still holds his position. "Jesus, are we really gonna be girls about this?"

"That's probably offensive in about a hundred different ways. Your mother would have—"

"Dad. Please. Cut the crap."

"I don't know what crap you're talking about."

"No? How 'bout the near silent treatment you're giving me?" I spin the empty glass on one of the coasters I've been keeping on the table. "It's been ongoing since prom."

"The last time you were out all night?"

I raise my eyebrows.

"I'm not giving you the silent treatment. We're talking."

"You're not looking at me."

"Fine." He puts his glass into the sink and turns, leaning back against the counter. He crosses his strong, dark arms in front of his chest. "I'm looking at you."

He's so hostile all I want is to shout, "Fuck this," and storm off in some childish rage, but I can't. I'm not a child anymore. I'm going to be a husband, and it isn't going to be easy on him.

I think of how to do it—the bandage way, I suppose. Quickly.

"Dad. I'm going to marry Gracie."

He nods. "I suppose if you discover she's the one, then in time…"

"There is no more time."

He glares at me.

"I'm marrying her. Now."

His forehead creases as he squints to understand. "What?"

"You heard me."

"But why?" He walks toward me and pulls out a chair. He spins the chair and sits straddle style. If he was wearing a baseball hat, he'd probably turn it toward the back. Is this the beginning of some midlife crisis? "Why would you…" He takes a deep breath and measures his words. Dad has always measured his words around me. "Why would you rush this any more than you have to?" He sits up and then leans forward again, uncharacteristically fidgety. "You have time."

"Not much."

"Enough."

"Her mother doesn't. We're getting married as soon as she's released from the hospital. They think she'll be out in a week or so."

He exhales a deep breath. He must like that justification. "I understand you want her mother to be at her wedding, but does Gracie…*know*? Any of it?"

"Not yet."

"When are you planning to tell her?" He scrubs his face. "*What* are you planning to tell her?"

"You know what I have to tell her."

He nods solemnly. "Yes, I do."

"But it doesn't matter. I'm marrying her. I love her, and she loves me. The rest…doesn't matter."

"It matters."

Sitting forward, I tip my juice glass in one direction and then the other. I drop the tone of my voice. "I'm tired, Dad. I've lived with this for the past eighteen years."

"Who hasn't?" His eyes level on mine.

I still my glass and change my tactic. "I have a reason to marry her now." Again, I omit the part that she can't have children. I'm just not ready to share this yet. "I think her asshole boss is filming the girls when they change in and out of their uniforms."

"He's doing what?" He rests his arms on the back of the chair and leans forward.

"I don't know for sure, but I want to send her to work tomorrow with your camera detector if that's okay."

"Of course."

"Thank you."

"But Josh, we can help them in other ways. Pay for their health insurance. Take over the mortgage. I can pick up extra work. Whatever it takes. Please, Josh. A bad job isn't a reason to get married."

"It's not the reason." I raise my eyes to his. "I love her."

He stands so abruptly it startles me. He flips the chair back in the correct direction and shoves it tight to the table.

"Fine." He looks off, and his chest heaves with his breath. "You're a grown man. Do what you want." He grabs his keys from the side table and marches out the door to the garage, letting the kitchen door slam behind him.

Chapter Fifteen

Gracie

"Are you pregnant?" Mom whispers her question so the nurse who's changing her IV can't hear.

My cheeks heat. I look around the chemo room, making sure no one but the one nurse is within earshot, and I whisper back. "Pregnancy is not the only reason young people get married." I stare at her. She's rocked me for a moment. She has no idea how difficult this question is for me. How much I've wanted to tell her. How much I want to tell her. Would the thought of a grandchild make her happy? I take a deep breath and push away my emotions, focusing. "He wants to help me work less. I'll get even better insurance working for Mr. Cadman, uh, Ben, and won't have to work six days to make my income."

"But Gracie, *marriage*."

"Yes." I nod.

She doesn't burden me with all the useless things a normal mother would say to her normal teenage daughter who's just announced she's getting married. She doesn't guilt me with "Find yourself first" stories or "Go to college and then if you still want to" speeches. Both of us know how precious life is, and both of us know it could end in an instant. Both of us have learned to seize the day.

"It's just, I can't help but feel your life is on fast

forward. And I'm afraid it's because of me. Aren't there other experiences you should have before getting married? You're just so young."

"Mom." I have to be extra careful. After a week in the hospital, she's just been released, and they're hitting her with chemo again. The last thing I want is to exhaust her and for her to worry about this. "Even if you were completely healthy, could you ever imagine me getting drunk at a graduation party or joining a sorority in college?"

She chuckles. "I suppose not."

"And you like Josh, right?"

She nods. "Very much." She closes her eyes, and her face contorts. "Ohhh…" Her moan is barely audible.

"Mom?" I shoot a look to the nurse, who steps back from the IV and stoops down to speak to Mom.

"Nora? Are you in pain?"

"No, no." Mom pats the nurse's hand. "I'm just reacting to my teenage daughter."

The young nurse smiles. "I used to make my mother crazy, too, sometimes. But seems to me Gracie's pretty cool. Right?"

She flashes a pearly white smile, and I smile back, glancing at her freshly washed hair pulled back in a perfect Dutch braid. I've never been able to braid, and despite the fact that we're both blondes, I'll never look like her—bright and sunny—with expertly drawn plum eyeliner and pink cheeks. Nah, sitting here in oversized sweats, my look is a perfected "rumpled mess."

"She is that." Mom pats my hand lovingly.

I move her empty wheelchair out of the way and scoot my chair closer to hers.

The nurse finishes with the IV tower. "All right,

Nora, this is your flush. The chemo will start as soon as these two bags are complete." She turns to me. "Gracie, if you or your mom need anything, just—"

"Buzz you. I know."

She tilts her head. "Yes, I guess you do know. You also know where snacks and magazines are if you want anything."

She winks and then scampers off to tend to the next patient.

"Mom? Want anything? Soda?" Why they stock the chemo fridge with diet soda, I'll never know. Seems to me you're just adding chemicals to chemicals, but maybe that's the point. "Sparkling water?"

"No, thanks."

We're separated from the other patients by long curtains, and Mom and I are in our own little cubby, tucked into a subtly colored corner. There's a private TV and stacks of blankets. We've been in this chemo room so many times it's like a second home, yet I'm kind of shocked we're back again. It seems too soon to start all of this again.

A shudder runs through me at the same time Mom shivers. Opening a soft white blanket, I lay it across her lap, gazing longingly at it. What I'd really like is to wrap that blanket around my shoulders and climb onto her lap, having her sing to me about the ant who had "high hopes." Just like she'd do when I was little and scared. Every time she'd get to the chorus of, "*He'd have hi-i-gh hopes*," she'd open her knees wide and let me "drop" an inch or two before catching me in her graceful arms. We'd laugh and laugh until whatever was worrying me was long forgotten. What I wouldn't give to have high hopes today.

But today, it's all so painful I turn away. Thankfully, we have a window location, so I pull up the shade to let in some sun.

"Too bright?"

She shakes her head and fidgets with her PICC line.

"Mom. You've got to leave it alone. You know that."

"It's just itchy." She scratches at the bruised area of her inner elbow.

I take her hand and guide it away. "How about a magazine? I saw a stack of new—"

I'm interrupted by the sound of a loud bell. "*DING! DING!*"

We turn toward the far side of the chemo ward where a bald man, maybe thirty years old, dressed in running pants and a zip-front sweatshirt, is balanced on crutches. He's standing near the chemo bell, which is placed prominently at the entrance to the ward. He's grinning, and he damn well should be. That bell means he's kicked cancer's ass. The ward erupts in applause.

"Ring it again!" someone shouts.

"*DING! DING! DING!*" The man rings the bell again and then raises a crutch into the air, waving it triumphantly.

"Congratulations!" People all over the room embrace one another and shout their best wishes to him. A woman about his age falls against his chest, hugging him. The nurses applaud and holler.

Mom claps along and then raises her free arm into the air and pumps her fist. "Go him!" she squeals.

It's a good day.

I glance at Mom, who's gone right back to her enthusiastic clapping. From her first treatment, all she ever talked about was ringing that damned bell. No matter what chemo she was on, she never doubted it would be the next one that worked. From the Red Devil that first took all of her hair to the immunotherapy they tried when all else seemed to fail. Through it all, she was always optimistic.

Until she wasn't.

Neither of us has mentioned that bell in a very long time.

She turns away from the man and, still clapping, looks directly at me. "Gracie." She nods to my hands, raising her eyebrows.

I snap out of my daze and clap along. She's right. I should be happy for him, and besides, it's not just this guy who's won. It's all of us.

She leans toward me. "Gracie," she whispers. "This is no longer about me. It's so much bigger than that. It is 'Us versus Them.' But the 'Us' is mankind, and the 'Them' is disease. I wish everyone understood that. Even if only one of us survives, like that handsome young man over there, then we all do. I have to believe that. I have to believe we're fighting for all of us. For our…collective spirit. I'm never going to ring that bell, Gracie. But at least someone has."

My throat aches, and we stare at each other for a very long time.

Finally, she speaks. "Do you love him?"

"Yes. Very much."

She nods and rests her head against the highbacked cushioned chair. She continues to stare at me. Her lips purse, and then she offers a tiny smile.

"Why don't you go take a look at the new magazines that came in. Maybe there's a bride's magazine." She blinks slowly, no doubt pushing away a wave of pain. “Maybe we can get some ideas to knock off.”

I nod, swallowing the lump in my throat. “Sure, Mom. That’d be great.”

She smiles again, and I walk away.

Chapter Sixteen

Josh

Gracie sits at my dining room table, staring at the portable Radio Frequency detector, or RF detector, we're borrowing from Dad. It's on the table before her. "Sorry for the crash course." I nod to the machine.

"No, it's good. I needed to learn."

She insisted we wait for this until her mom was released. It bugged the crap out of me, but I get it. I can't expect her to handle all of it at once. At least she closed the breakroom at Shakes 'n' Slaw right away.

I jump up from the kitchen table and grab her a bottle of her favorite orange battery acid from the fridge.

"Thanks." She takes the bottle from me, leans forward in her chair, and drinks. Then she places the drink on a coaster and traces little hearts in the condensation on the side of the bottle. "And thanks for helping me get Mom home from chemo." Her voice is soft. "This time, it's—" She looks away and then back again. "—Different."

Slumping forward on the table, she stretches her arm long and rests her head against it. "Mom's so beat," she continues. "The side effects usually don't hit until the next day or the day after that…" She traces over the hearts she's drawn on the side of the bottle. "I can't imagine why they went with another course of chemo so soon. We know there's fluid in her lungs, and she was just hospitalized for a bad reaction to a different chemo…but I'm not a doctor." She drags herself up to a seated position and wipes her hands on her jeans. "I just wish she could have rung that damned chemo bell just once."

"Chemo bell?"

She nods. "It hangs in the chemo ward. Once you're done with your treatment and you've kicked cancer, you get to ring it."

"That's awesome."

"Yeah. Anyway, the side effects from the chemo will make this weekend a bitch, and unfortunately, I'm scheduled to work all day both days."

"Work?"

"Well, assuming the only thing our little covert operation exposes is my boyfriend's paranoia."

"Try fiancé." It's now or never. I reach into the front pocket of my jeans and pull out a small diamond ring. There's no velvet ring box, and for a moment, I consider dropping to one knee, but that all feels so cheesy and contrived. Instead, I hold it out to her. "It was my mother's." I clear my throat.

"Josh, I…" Her eyes widen as she stares at the ring I'm holding. "It's…it's beautiful. All those little diamonds around the center one. I've never seen anything sparkle like that. Is it silver?"

"Platinum."

I turn it upward, and the facets catch the rays coming through the kitchen window.

"It's like wearing the sun on your hand," she mumbles. "That must be nice on your dark days. To have the sun with you." She glances at me and blushes. "Sorry. That was stupid."

"Not stupid. True." I take her hand and slide the ring onto her finger. It's a perfect fit. "Like it was made for you."

"Josh, I…I can't." She shakes her head. "It was your mom's. Your dad will be devastated."

"It was meant for you. Trust me."

"It's gorgeous, but I couldn't."

"Please. I want you to have it. You could use a little sun in your life." My voice is a whisper.

Her gaze dashes to mine. "What's wrong?"

"When they released Nora, you heard what that doctor told us, right? You know it's not just fluid in her lungs. You know the cancer's spread to the lungs, and it's in the lymph nodes."

"She's fought worse."

"Gracie."

She reaches out for the RF detector and slides it toward her. "Do you think other people do this the day before their weddings?" She toys with the button on the side of the detector.

I smile at her. "You understand how to use it?"

She looks over the device once more and then picks it up and holds it in her hands. "I think so. I feel like a secret agent. Or one of those detectives on TV or something."

"Just remember to go slowly and be thorough. Tiny cameras can be hidden anywhere." It's killing me that I can't do this for her.

She nods, placing the small black device onto the table. Running her hand over the varnished tree rings on the table, she murmurs, "So beautiful." Then she gives her attention back to me. "Why does your dad have this, anyway?" She nods to the detector.

I chuckle. "Once, years ago, my dad thought he was alone in a house. This big, beautiful place out in the Hamptons."

"Long Island?"

"Yeah."

She nods. "Must be so beautiful there. I'd love to see the beach one day."

"You've never been?" It dawns on me that this girl has maybe never left this tiny landlocked town.

She shakes her head. "Nope. I would love to, though. One day. That's my dream."

"We'll make sure of it."

She looks up with expectant eyes. "Really?"

"Really." I force a smile as I lie through my teeth.

"So?" She holds the device toward me as she speaks. "Your dad? Why does he use the detector?"

"He was installing this custom high-end cabinetry, all pecan wood, dovetailed, really beautiful. The woman was away from the house for the summer, and the air conditioning wasn't set very cold."

"That's surprising." She takes another sip of her drink and then places it carefully onto the very center of the coaster.

"Just wait." I grin. "He got hot and took off his shirt."

"Thank goodness that's all he took off." She giggles.

"It wasn't."

"No!" She grasps the bottle, and her knuckles whiten. Her eyes are giant. "He didn't?" She asks in a deep, gravelly voice that sidetracks me for a moment.

"And you can guess the rest. Apparently, the woman was watching live feed from her brownstone in Manhattan, and she"—I laugh as Gracie giggles—"saw him and just about flew out to the house. She must have been traveling ninety miles an hour the entire way. She bursts in, and there was Ben, working away in nothing but his black boxer briefs."

She clamps a hand to her mouth. "Oh no."

"Oh yes. The woman thought she would meet him in the kitchen and also strip to her bra and underwear…"

Gracie laughs.

"She was certain they would make a perfect couple—my dad, on the other hand, wasn't convinced."

Gracie's jaw is open. "What did he do?"

"He says he went right on working and finished the install."

"What did the woman do?"

"Got out her juicer to make him a fruit juice." I raise my eyebrows, chuckling. "And removed her bra to ask him if he'd like melons in his!"

She laughs so hard she bangs her hand on the table.

"It was a fruit smoothie." Dad walks in, chuckling. "If you're going to steal my story, Josh, the least you can do is tell it correctly."

"Did you drink it?" Gracie's beaming at him as she asks.

He smiles back, and it warms my core.

"Hell, yeah. It was hot in there."

"I'll bet." She laughs again.

"Nah, not like that." He shakes his head, grabbing a chair and turning it so he can sit in it backward again. Apparently, this is the new thing we're doing. "Only ever been one woman for me."

She nods and smiles sweetly at Ben. "I understand. So—" She bites the corner of her lip. "—Didn't stay for appetizers?"

He mock-shudders. "Lord, no. Could you imagine? Skeeves me out just thinking about it." He peeks at Gracie out of the corner of his eye and then glances down at the table. Progress. At least they're sitting in the same place, and he's acting civilly toward her.

"So, you kids hungry?" In a grand, sweeping, peacock-ish move, he gets up, spins the chair to its correct position, and makes his way to the fridge. He pulls it open and stands there, staring into it. "I've got some of my amazing, homemade, perfectly spiced guac, or equally awesome leftover mushroom pizza?" He turns, lifting his eyebrows.

He's trying, and I smile at him in appreciation. He nods.

She smiles back. "No, thank you, Mr. Cadman, uh, sorry, Ben." She holds up her bottle. "Josh just gave me my favorite selt—"

Suddenly—everyone freezes, and it's like time stands still.

I look from Gracie, who's stopped mid-sentence, to him. His face is blanched, and he's immobilized at the refrigerator with the door open. She's frozen, with her drink still raised in the air.

"Dad?" It's like we're in a movie where some mad scientist casts a spell on everyone, and I'm the only one who escapes. Wouldn't that figure.

"Is that…" He steps forward, allowing the door to close behind him. "Celia's ring?"

I stand, heading him off. "Yes, it is."

My gaze travels to Gracie, who's lowered her drink to the coaster. She rests her hands in her lap, and her chest is heaving in time with her hurried breath. She looks from my dad to me and then down at the table.

"I…I told him it may not be a good idea." She raises her eyes. "I'm sorry, Mr. Cadman."

"You have nothing to be sorry about," I tell her, and then I speak directly to him. "Dad. You know we're engaged. The wedding is tomorrow."

He starts. "*Tomorrow?*" His word is thunderous.

"We can't wait. We want Nora to be there and feeling as well as she can. And you knew Gracie was going to wear my ring."

"But that ring, Josh?"

He shakes his head, and I move closer, wedging myself between the two of them. I'm standing so close to him that for the first time in my life, I wonder if this conversation is going to come to blows.

"Yes, because it was Celia's ring."

"Oh, I know exactly what that ring is and who it belongs to."

"Belonged."

"*Belongs* to, because I bought it." He raises his voice, and behind me, I can feel her cower.

"Dad, you're acting like a bully. Stop it. You know that ring was meant for the woman I marry."

"Christ, Josh."

He steps away and then turns to me sharply. He storms up to me until we stand toe to toe. His shoulders are wider than mine, and his body is stronger. But I'm faster. For the first time ever, I see genuine fury in his eyes. Not the pain or sadness I usually see. Today, this is ire.

But there's no freaking way I'll back down.

His breath races, and his eyes narrow. He's a lone wolf snared in a trap, desperate for any way out. There's no way he's in his right mind. Right now, he'd chew off his own damned leg if it meant escape.

With his eyes still locked on mine, he shakes his head and steps back.

"Christ," he mutters under his breath. "This is…"

"What, Dad? Huh?" I push. "Crazy? Is that what you want to say? This is all just *crazy*?"

"I never said that," he mutters under his breath as he grabs the keys for Ol' Sally. He stalls for a moment and makes eye contact with me. "I would never say that." Then he storms out the garage door.

"It's tomorrow, Dad," I call after him. "We're getting married at Gracie's house. Six o'clock!"

The door slams, and he's gone.

I turn back. She's standing next to the table, her brow furrowed and her eyes filled with sadness.

"I'm sorry, Josh."

"What?"

I walk to her and stroke her biceps. Her eyes close for a moment, and then she opens them again. They're clearer now, and she gives a small smile.

"Why would you be sorry?"

"For putting you in this position." She breaks away from my hold. "For being the reason you and your dad are fighting."

"It's not you, Gracie."

"Of course it is."

"It would be any girl I was serious about."

"Any girl that reminded him of your mother."

"You guessed that?"

"Josh." She sticks out her hip and plops her weight to one side. "It wasn't difficult to figure out." She shakes her head. "The way he looks at me. It's rather sad, really."

I nod.

She drops her head and begins to slip the ring from her finger.

"No, don't do that." I place my hands on hers, stopping her midway. She glances up at me.

"I can't keep it, Josh. I don't need a ring. I'll marry you tomorrow with a twist-tie wrapped around my finger. It doesn't matter to me. But…"

"But what?"

"But while we're talking, what happens if I go to work and find nothing?"

"No cameras?"

She nods. "What if there's no reason for me to quit?" She stands strong and keeps her eyes on mine, but I can see the question. And it lands straight in my gut.

"Are you asking me if we'd still get married?"

"Yes."

"Gracie." I step to her and wrap my arms around her. "You leaving that job has nothing to do with me wanting to marry you." I inhale deeply.

"Maybe. But chances are we wouldn't be getting married while we're both still in high school."

I grip her arms and stoop down to look into her eyes. "Are you having second thoughts?"

She laughs, smiling. "I haven't had time for first thoughts." She reaches out and places a warm hand on my cheek.

I close my eyes and breathe her in.

"Yes, I want to marry you, Josh."

I open my eyes, and she removes her hand, pulls off the ring, and hands it to me.

"But I can't do it wearing your mother's ring."

"It's meant for you. My mother would have wanted

it that way."

"Maybe so. And I'm sorry, but your mother isn't here. Your dad is. And I refuse to be the reason for someone else's suffering." Her eyes brighten as she looks deeply into mine. "Why would we hurt him if we have the option not to?"

Christ, she has no idea how poignant those words are. How many people am I hurting by marrying her? And what happens—to everything and *everyone*—when I can't fulfill my destiny?

But then…looking at her smiling at me, I don't actually care.

Some freaking savior I am.

"What if you're supposed to wear that?" I ask her.

She pulls back and tilts her head. "Here's the thing about 'supposed to,' Josh. It runs on a totally different track than 'what actually happens.'"

She folds my hand around the ring and stretches up onto her toes. She kisses me quickly on the lips and then turns and grabs the detector. She waves it in the air.

"I've got to go. My shift starts in a couple. Thanks for this. I'll text you if it doesn't work or something."

I nod as she scoots out the door, leaving me completely alone. *WTF?* The two people I love most in the world have both left and gone totally off-script.

How the hell can I help the world when I can barely help myself?

What the hell is happening here?

Chapter Seventeen

Gracie

My keys are shaking in my hands as I let myself in the backdoor of the Shakes 'n' Slaw. I'm as sure as I can be that Jerry's not here; it's his weekend to go fishing with a group of his guy friends. His weekend away could not come at a better time—it's the perfect reason for not inviting him to the wedding.

Although, until recently, I'd always thought Jerry would be the one to walk me down the aisle.

Shrug it off, Gracie. Taking a deep breath, I let it go. So what? So what if I have no one to walk me down the aisle? That's something else I'll do on my own. Won't be the first time I do the job of two people. I can handle it. And when I make it down that aisle, Josh will be waiting for me. And from that moment on, I'll have someone to share the burden of life with.

Huh. Maybe I shouldn't write my own vows. *To love, honor, and cherish* sounds a hell of a lot sweeter.

My arms feel dead, like I'm carrying Mom to the bathroom, but I force myself to focus. I have trouble just turning the key in the lock, but I really, really need to get it together. I'm Manager on Duty today. Thankfully, we're not anticipating a big crowd.

Moving inside, I'm hit with the scent of old grease and charred hotdogs. Must have been a Mommy 'n' Me play group come through on their way home for naps.

That's usually who comes during lunchtimes as we near summer. Well, mommies and old people. I'm always strangely wistful when I give an exasperated mommy of a four-year-old a cut-up hotdog and then hand a vanilla milkshake to an elderly man. It's like all of life shows up at my window at one moment. It's not because of new life versus old or anything as poignant as that—it's more that I'm amazed at how we're never happy. How the mommy can't wait for this day to end, and the elderly man prays for just one more.

I shake off my weird melancholy and tighten my grasp on the bag where I've got the RF detector safely stowed. I've got a job to do. People are counting on—

What the heck, Gracie? Who do you think you are? And just like that, my mind starts tormenting me.

No. I take a deep breath, trying to drown my negative self-talk while I quell the panic rising in me. This panic, it's a slow-moving but all-encompassing feeling—a tsunami of fear. I felt something like it once before when I trimmed my own hair in the bathroom mirror and accidentally cut off seven inches instead of two. But that was just hair, and for me, anyway, it grows back. What happens if I have to leave this job? How can I work for Mr. Cadman, a man who hates me and thinks I'm stealing the love-of-his-life-dead-wife's ring?

No way. I can't do it. I tighten my grasp more and pull the bag to the front of me, cradling it. Sorry, Josh. I just can't risk knowing.

Heading toward the breakroom where we change, I stop at the door and pull down the bogus, handwritten *Do Not Enter* sign. When I posted it, I told everyone it was because I had seen a very large mouse. I exaggerated the word so they'd think it was a rat, and I just didn't want to alarm them. I even shoved insulation strips beneath the door to seal the mouse in. I instructed all employees to change in and out of their uniforms at home while we waited for the exterminator. Thankfully, this time of year, exterminators are incredibly busy. That bought me some time. Even Jerry believed the lie. Frankly, he seemed a bit queasy about the whole thing.

As I stare at the door, disappointment washes over me. What's wrong with me? Why can't I do this? Why can't I—

The door to the breakroom opens, and I just about jump out of my skin.

"Gracie, baby?" It's Louise, a thirty-five-year-old with three young kids and no husband. She adjusts her uniform as she exits the breakroom. "Gracie!" She throws her arms open wide and then embraces me, hugging me hard. The sign crumples between us, and her homemade wooden earrings bang against my cheek.

"Gracie Girl! I haven't seen you in weeks. We've been on different schedules."

She steps back from me, and for the first time ever, I really *see* Louise. With her flowing blonde hair and heavy eye makeup, she looks like an old-fashioned country singer. My gaze drops downward, and—Holy crap. I never realized she was…built. She's beautiful, and with the size of her top and the length of her legs, the stupid uniform is even skimpier on her.

"Were you…in the breakroom?" I point to the room as I ask.

"Hope you don't mind. A little mouse or two won't scare me. But I was super careful to keep the door plugged up even while I was inside. I promise." She mimes an *x* over her heart. "There's no way he's getting away, the little bastard. No way! My Gracie Girl won't let 'em!" She leans forward like she's sharing a secret. "Gracie, baby, truth is, I've been changing here all week. You know I hate to drop off the boys when I'm in my uniform. The way them other mothers look at me…" She shakes her head. "Well, screw 'em." She smiles radiantly. "They'll all want to be my friend once my jewelry business takes off. Hell, they'll probably start dressing like this"—she holds out the sides of her uniform—"just to be like me!" Laughing, she moves her head from side to side, showing me her earrings. "By the way, whatdaya think of these?"

They look like feathers with delicate laser etching. "They're beautiful, Louise. You are really, really talented."

"Sheesh, Gracie Girl! You are going to make me blush. You know, making my jewelry is my passion. I do it when-ev-er I have a sec. Which isn't often!" She laughs. "Oh! And get this! There's a little festival outside of Columbus that said I could have a booth. Could you imagine? I'm making some wood cuff bangles now to bring with me. Wanna have a whole lot of stock. This is it, Gracie. My break. Imagine *me* selling *my* jewelry to people *at a festival!* Well, damn. Next stop for Louise Miller, *TV*!" She throws her arms in the air. "Anyway"—she nods to the sign in my hand—"does that mean we've caught the bastard?" She smiles and flashes cigarette-stained teeth.

"Um…" *Caught the bastard.* I look into Louise's bright blue eyes as she waits for my answer. What a party Jerry must have watching her. I shudder.

"Baby, you cold?" To Louise, I'm either "Gracie Girl" or "Baby." She mothers me the way she mothers her own three children: ferociously.

"I'm okay." I shake my head. "Thanks." I look at her again and give a half smile. Maybe I'm okay. Maybe we all are. Maybe I need to do this. Maybe.

"Louise, could you do me a favor?"

"Anything for my Gracie Girl, you know that."

She hoists herself onto the stainless counter near the freezer. I don't have the energy or desire to tell her it's not sanitary to sit where we prep food or to ask her to get down. Why would I bother? This may be her last day on the job. All of our last days. I glance at her. Can I risk her job? She needs it…unless Ben would be willing to bankroll the entire staff of Shakes 'n' Slaw. I roll my eyes without meaning to, and she leans forward, studying me.

"What was the eye roll about?"

"Nothing."

"You sure you're not keeping secrets from me? 'Cause you and me, Gracie Girl, we've always been like plastic wrap."

She means transparent, and she's right. Which makes me wrong. There's no maybe about it. She does need to know if Jerry's filming her. She needs to have the option. We all do.

"Louise, could you cover a few more minutes? I need to scour the room. Look for any telltale signs."

"Absolutely."

She slides off the counter and plops down onto her old tennis shoes with a thud and a bounce. I look away.

"Be careful, baby, but go see if you can track that slimy lil' bastard."

Taking a deep breath, I enter the breakroom and shut the door tight behind me. Reaching into my bag, I pull out the RF detector and turn it on. When Josh was teaching me how to use this, I'd argued with him.

"What if Jerry sees me and figures out what I'm doing?"

He looked at me like I had three heads. "How would Jerry know what you're doing unless he was spying on you?"

Good point.

Thankfully, the detector's not all that large, and it's fairly easy to handle. It fits in one hand, so I begin as Josh instructed, with the largest, most obvious places first. I hold the detector out and run it along the edges of the two framed posters—the only artwork in this place. One is a motivational poster I hung. It has a rainbow and a slogan about giving your best effort. The other, a poster Jerry hung, ironically explains our rights as employees. Then I do a sweep of the three standing lamps and the couch. Nothing. Not a beep or a blink. I exhale. Good. Maybe Josh is just being paranoid. I check the floorboards, the rug, and get out the ladder we store in the tiny closet, and sweep the top window ledge. Nothing. Whew.

My shoulders release from my ears. Maybe I won't havc to rely on someone else's health insurance or work for a man who despises me, after all. Maybc I can stay right here, working a job I know as we nurse Mom back to hea—

I stop myself mid-thought. There's no nursing her back to health. And the sooner I face it, the better. I force myself to push back the tears that have been stopped so many times, I'm certain they'll eventually leak out my ears.

Feeling way more confident, I wave the detector

past the small desk we use to store our bags and move to the opposite side of the room to check the few lockers and freestanding full-length mirrors. At least I don't have to worry about the mirrors. That would be way too tacky. There's no way Jerry would put cameras in the—

The sound is low as I wave the detector past the mirror, but it's a definite *beep.*

My breath hitches and catches in my throat as I pass the detector back over the top of the mirror. Nothing. Thank God. It must have been a fluke—a false positive. Still, just to be thorough so we can all sleep better tonight, I scoot the detector down the ornate scrollwork on the sides of the mirror.

The sound intensifies, and this time, there's no denying it. The RF detector is picking up cameras around the mirrors.

Shit. My stomach drops so far and so fast, I'm worried I might step on it. Dammit. I'm lightheaded and woozy, but I push myself to keep going and move the detector down the opposite side of the mirror.

There it is.

The loud beep that signifies the end of my health insurance and Christmas bonus.

Sweat drips down my lower back, and my hands flail as I try to shake off the feeling of a thousand bugs crawling all over me. Closing my eyes, I imagine Jerry at home, pants unbuckled, fly undone, eating pints of chocolate ice cream—ice cream that *I* packed for him—while he watches us strip to our underwear and change into our uniforms. I draw in a deep breath as I imagine him tossing his spoon and empty pint so he can have his hands free to…

Shit. Shit. Shit.

I place a cool palm to my head. How many times have I done a bra change here? Or an underwear change? How many times have we helped each other in and out of these stupid uniforms, unaware that while we did, Jerry was getting a little girl-on-girl action? I drop my hand to my stomach, trying to steady it, but it aches and flips, and I think I might puke all over the floor.

But I won't. There's no way I'll give Jerry the satisfaction.

Think, think, think. I have to move fast.

I swallow my nausea as I imagine Jerry, and all his fishing buddies, huddled around his phone as they watched Louise change this morning.

Then, I smile as I imagine the panicked feeling in Jerry's stomach right now as he realizes he's been caught.

"You'd better be panicked," I hiss at the mirror.

Okay, move. There's no time. Who knows where he is and how quickly he can disable the feed? As fast as I can, I race to the lockers and open door after door.

The beeps are loud and clear. Locker after locker. Shit. Louise was right. That slimy lil' bastard.

With a shaking hand, I fish my phone from my bag and text Josh.

—You were right.—

My throat aches, and my head's heavy.

He texts back immediately.

—I'm outside. Let me in.—

I rush from the breakroom to the backdoor and fling it open. Josh is standing there. His eyes look wild as his shoulders move up and down with his racing breath.

"Let me have the detector."

Stepping back, I press myself against the wall to try

to keep from falling over. I hand him the detector and don't even care that he's double-checking my work. I'm just grateful I'm not alone.

With the detector held out before him, he rushes past me and into the hallway. "Where?"

I point in the direction of the breakroom, and he charges in. I follow after him.

"Here?"

I motion to the lockers and mirror.

He rushes to them and runs the detector up and down the sides of the mirror and over the lockers. *Beep! Beep! Beep!* Each beep sounds louder than the last.

"Son of a bitch," he mutters under his breath.

He picks up his phone and presses a button.

"Who are you calling?"

"The police. They need to get here before that asshole has a chance to get away." He turns his attention to the phone. "Yes, hello. We've just discovered hidden cameras in the women's changing room at the Shakes 'n' Slaw on old 101." He pauses. "Yes, that's right, Jerry's place. We used an RF detector and it lit up like a Christmas tree by the mirror and the lockers." He nods. "Thank you."

"They'll be out in a minute. We have to hang tight." He looks at his phone again and types something.

"Who are you texting?"

"Ben."

"My mother can never know."

"I know." He looks at me. "Now we just have to hope Jerry doesn't have any good friends on the force."

I shake my head. "I don't think so. The guys who patrol the area aren't all that friendly with him. They stop in at least once a week to check on us."

"Too bad they didn't think to sweep the room."

"Josh." I tilt my head. "How could they possibly know?" I pause for a moment to think. "How did you?"

"I told you I had a feeling."

"Gracie Girl?" Louise peeks into the changing room and spies Josh. "Well, hello. You're Gracie's boyfriend, right?" She steps into the room, appraising him from the corner of her eye.

"Yes." He steps forward and shakes her hand. "Fiancé, actually."

"What?" She claps her hands together and breaks into a beatific smile. "Oh, baby."

She grabs me by the shoulders and pulls me tight to her breast, the way Mom used to. It—Louise's embrace, the cameras, Josh and the engagement, the guilt of not inviting her—it's all too much, and I start hyperventilating. I wanted to invite her to the wedding, but it's all happening so fast… No. That's a lie. I don't know what's happening with our wedding, and I just can't imagine adding wedding guests to our already frantic lives.

Louise pulls back and holds me at arm's length. "You okay?"

I force myself to slow my breathing, but I can't manage to utter a word.

"Aw." She strokes the side of my head lovingly. "Don't you be nervous. I was just about your age for my first marriage."

She nods encouragingly as a wash of fear rushes through me.

"So." She plops her hands on her hips and turns to Josh. "Tell me, handsome, did you catch the slimy bastard?"

"Excuse me?" Josh steps forward.

"The rat?" She turns from Josh to me and back again. "Aren't you here to help Gracie with the rat?"

"You knew?"

"She hung a sign. And I know our Gracie Girl. I knew she'd catch the bastard."

"Gracie?" Josh looks at me for clarification.

"Guys." I put up my hands and step forward. "You're talking about two different things." I turn to Louise. "I need to talk to you, Louise. Let's step out of this room."

Louise's brow furrows. "You're scaring me, Gracie, baby. You're not firing me, are you?"

I shake my head. "No. Of course not."

"Good, because I don't know where I could go to get this rate or these hours. Be home for dinners and weekends. You've always taken care of me. Fought Jerry to get me the time off with the boys when I needed it. Have I ever thanked you for that?"

"Yes." My voice is quiet.

"Did I tell you Bo needs glasses now?"

I shake my head.

"And that with the price of the injection for Dillon's peanut allergy…" Her words trail off.

Sighing, I think I understand what Mom feels like when her lungs are filled with fluid—like I'm drowning in air. This is so much worse than being swallowed by the sea. At least water has the decency to offer the chance to sink or swim.

Right now, I'd happily settle for the illusion that I could swim.

Louise scratches an itch on her arm, and her eyes shift from me to the door of the breakroom and back again. What's going to happen to her? Maybe…I don't?

No. It's too late now, and she deserves to know.

"Louise, we have reason to believe Jerry has been filming us."

She straightens up and adjusts the V-neck of her uniform top. "Filming us? While we work?" She shrugs. "He's always told us about the cameras around the building."

"In the changing area. That's the reason he insists we change here."

"What?" Her normally tanned skin whitens.

"We've called the police." Josh walks out of the breakroom and over to us. "They're on their way. They'll do a sweep for us when they arrive."

"Gracie? You called the police?" Her tone is incredulous.

"I had to, Louise."

I try to take her hand, but she shoos me away.

"I have to protect you and all the other women working here."

"Protect me?" She turns to me and narrows her eyes. "And who is going to protect my boys when they're getting picked on for not having clothes that fit? Or when they have nothing to eat for dinner because I can't make a living?" She steps so close I can smell her spearmint gum. "And who's going to protect Dillon if some kid decides to eat a peanut on the bus ride home from school, and I can't afford his injectable? Huh? You?" She turns to Josh. "You?"

I lift my chin. "He's not involved in this."

"The hell he's not." She carves the air with her hand like she's swinging a tennis racket. She's exasperated. "He's the reason you can afford to do this." Her hand floats to her side. “You tell me honestly, Gracie, if Josh hadn’t swooped into your life with promises of marriage, could you have afforded to be so indignant about the whole thing?”

“I—” She’s right. “Louise, I had to do it. I had to stop Jerry.”

“Why?” Her eyes search mine. “So what if he’s getting off to us at home? He never touches us. He pays well. He’s always respectful to our faces.”

“You don’t mean that.”

“The hell I don’t!” Her face contorts, and then her expression changes from anger to sadness. “I have always, always respected you, Gracie. I always thought, ‘Christ. She’s just a kid who’s got a whole load of shit dumped on her, but she handles it. Day after day. Never a tear. Never a complaint.’ Didn’t matter how young you were.” She looks deep into my eyes. “I thought you *got* us—all of us women working for you—because you were one of us. But the first chance you get to get out, you’re gone, without even a thought about the rest of us.”

I shake my head. “That’s not true, Louise. Of course I thought of you. That’s the reason I did this.”

“No.” She shakes her head. “No. The reason you did this was because you’re selfish. You can afford to be offended. I can’t.”

She heads toward the changing room, and I follow her in. She grabs her small brown pleather bag stored on the desk and tosses the straps over her shoulder.

“Louise, please, I’m really sorry. What can I do to help?”

“Oh, you’ve done plenty.” Shaking her head, she fidgets with the fringe hanging from the strap of her handbag. Then she takes a deep breath and lets it go with a huff. "After all this time, Gracie, I would appreciate a solid recommendation if"—her voice cracks—"if I can find anyone willing to hire me."

"Louise." My feet are immobile, so I turn my head over my shoulder as I watch her slink out of the room.

She stalls in the hallway, tilts her head up like she's contemplating something, and then looks directly at me. "If Dillon dies because I can't afford his injectable, it's on you, Gracie."

Then she turns and storms out the backdoor of Shakes 'n' Slaw.

Red lights strobe through the windows.

"Gracie?"

Josh steps toward me, but I drop my head, cradling it in both hands.

"Gracie." He repeats my name as he walks to me and pulls me toward his chest.

"No." I push him away. I'm not sure I can stand on my own, but I am certain I don't want or deserve consoling. I stumble to a corner of the room and squat down, fisting my hair. All I want is to throw up and scream and cry, but I'm unable to do any of it. Instead, I just rock myself, allowing my body to take control of my decisions.

Maybe it'll do a better job than my brain did.

"Hello?" A voice comes from the backdoor.

"In here," Josh answers.

Peeking through my hair, I see two policemen enter the room. Thank goodness I don't know either of them. That's the only thing keeping me going right now. I cling to my anonymity like a starving, injured lioness protecting her kill.

If I had to face people I know… I don't think I could

handle it. They would forever look at me differently. Once I was Gracie, the seventeen-year-old manager who worked to keep her mother alive. Now, I'll be Gracie, the girl who was filmed naked.

My cheeks are flaming hot, and I raise a trembling hand to cool them.

Josh shakes hands with each officer. Their voices are only a drone to me, but I think he's giving our cell numbers and explaining the situation. He points toward the mirror and lockers. The second officer steps forward with a device similar to mine but larger. He sweeps the room and nods affirmingly. Crap. I was hoping I was wrong.

I want to yell at them to stop. To demand a do-over. One where I inform the women at Shakes 'n' Slaw of what's happening but don't call the police. One where I'm smart enough to let the women make their own decisions.

Nice job, Gracie, I chide myself. *You have single-handedly set women's lib back decades.* Who am I to take away their right to choose?

The officer with the detector pulls out a phone and presses a bunch of buttons.

The first officer, the older one, nods toward me. "She okay?"

"I'm not sure." Josh runs a hand down his locs. "It's a major blow."

"I'll say." The cop nods in agreement. "We're having the signal traced now. We'll be able to tell you where it's going. Best case scenario, it's for private viewing only. Worst case…" He shakes his head. "Worst case, it's being broadcast live on the internet. But either way, we'll pick up Jerry." The officer turns to me. "We'll get him, miss."

Obviously, he's talking to me, so I raise my head, nodding my thanks. He narrows his eyes, inspecting me like he's reading an expiration date on a carton of eggs.

"She's just a kid." He speaks to no one in particular as he steps closer to me. "You eighteen?"

I freeze, not sure of what to do. If I tell the truth, then Jerry will go away for sure, and that's the end of Shakes 'n' Slaw and any chance of Louise keeping her job. But I have no interest in lying to the police. Or anyone. Ever.

"Hey." He squats down to be at eye level with me but maintains a comfortable distance. "You okay?"

I make eye contact, and for a moment, I'm comforted by the officer's kind eyes. They're deep brown and soft. Not at all what I'd expect for someone who spends his days corralling drunks and responding to domestic violence calls. I glance at the officer's graying hair. He must be around Mom's age. The age my father would have been. Closing my eyes, I breathe in the moment. I'll bet my father had kind eyes, too.

And, I'll bet if my father were here, none of this would have happened. I wouldn't be working fifty hours a week at the Shakes 'n' Slaw, caring for Mom alone, and sentencing Louise to a life of what? Prostitution? And her son to his death.

But my father's not here. And it did happen. All of it. And I'm the reason.

"Kid." The officer nods to me. "You eighteen?"

I snap to and shake my head. He'll find out one way or another.

The officer scrubs his face with his hand. "Well, that's a whole other boat. Jerry will be going away for a long time. A long time. That's child pornography."

I sigh.

"Look." The officer stands and turns to Josh. "Why don't you take her home? We'll let you know if we need anything."

Josh nods. Without a word, he walks to me and slips his arm around my waist, and I allow myself to be half-carried out of the Shakes 'n' Slaw and slid into the passenger seat of his car.

"We'll get your car tomorrow," he tells me.

I'm barely able to nod a response. I glance at the back window of Shakes 'n' Slaw as Josh starts the car. I came to this place as a young girl with plans to work hard and save my mother's life.

I'm leaving as an almost adult who's ruined someone else's.

Chapter Eighteen

Ben

The screen door rattles as I rap on it. "Nora?" Cripes. No doubt she's sleeping. I remember sleeping a whole hell of a lot when I fought off my cancer.

I drag my hand down my chin and bang on the door of Gracie's house a bit louder. "Mrs. Jackson?" What the hell am I doing? Nora probably can't move from couch to door. Why would I bother her? What's wrong with me?

What isn't? Here I am, fifty-three years old, and I holed up in a cheap hotel on the outskirts of town for the past few hours because I just had to get out of the house, and then once I did, I just couldn't go back home. I couldn't face what I've been preparing for, for the past eighteen years.

And all of this is over, what exactly? A dead woman's ring? Shame washes over me like a sudden summer rainstorm.

Truthfully, it's not about the ring. I'm here bothering Nora because I'm angry. I'm angry that I've taken care of him for eighteen years and now…I'm just supposed to let go and leave it to the hands of fate.

But I can't do that.

Hearing some muffled sounds from inside, I know I can't do this either.

Shaking my head, I turn and hustle down the front

steps. I make it as far as the hood of Ol' Sally before Nora's at the door.

"Ben?" Her voice is a whisper, and she coughs deeply.

Asshole, asshole, *asshole*.

I drop my chin and nod. There's nothing I can do now, so I turn and sprint back up the steps. "Hi, Nora."

"It's nice to see you."

"You as well." I smile. "Truly."

She nods in understanding. "Come on in." She pushes the door open. It must take every ounce of her strength.

I grab it quickly and step inside. My text chirps, but I keep my cell in my pocket, pressing the volume down. I can handle work later. Glancing about as discreetly as possible, I look over their home. It's what I expected it to be: old and worn but clean and organized. That's all Gracie. She is an amazing kid, and I'm certain I would really like her if it wasn't for what she represents. I shudder.

"Ben? You cold?"

She furrows brows that catch me by surprise. When I saw her in the hospital, it never dawned on me that she still had eyebrows.

"No, no." I force my shoulders to drop. "Nora, I'm sorry to barge in on you."

She makes her way to the couch, and I offer her my arm. She accepts gracefully, and I help ease her down until she's seated.

Even though she looks like she's in immense pain, she smiles, and her eyes twinkle. "I'm surprised it took you this long."

"Sorry?"

"Oh please, Ben. We're both grown-ups. Have been for a long time. We both know you're here because you want to stop the marriage, and I'm guessing that you've struck out with Josh and you're hoping I can talk some sense into Gracie."

I nod, and suddenly, my body feels like it weighs a million pounds.

"You look tired." She points to a wingback chair near the couch. "Sit before you pass out."

I plop down gratefully. "It's not that I don't think Gracie is a great girl."

She tilts her head and adjusts her turban. "Gracie is a great girl. Amazing. I can't imagine any other child doing what she's done for me. But I understand she'll still be a great girl even years from now. And you don't want them rushing in."

"Yes." That's a plausible enough reason, so I go with it.

"I understand. I really do."

I nod, barely able to look this woman in the eyes.

"I'll do what I can," she assures me.

"About what? Mom?"

I spring to my feet, and there is Gracie in her uniform, with Josh protectively at her side. I didn't notice them slip into the house while Nora and I were talking. She moves to her mother's side and squats on the floor before the couch.

"Mom? See what you can do about what?"

Josh glares at me with narrowed eyes. "Dad." He shakes his head, and his voice is a low growl.

"Mom?" Gracie looks from her mother to me. "Oh." She stands, turning toward me. "I understand." She swallows hard. "You're here to ask my mother to stop the marriage. She's the only one who can do it, because Josh is eighteen, but I won't be for a few more months."

"Yes." What can I say except the truth?

She nods, and leaving her mother's side, she walks closer to me. There's no intimidation in this kid, no fear. "Well, here's the thing, Mr. Cadman."

I motion to tell her to call me Ben, but she puts her hand up, stopping me.

"Mr. Cadman, I know you don't like me. And I know at least part of the reason why. But all you've done here today is to make an even bigger mess of everything. Everything." She steps closer, and her eyes are full of fire. "Let's say your plan worked. Let's say my mother agrees and keeps me from marrying Josh right now. All you've bought is a few months. Because as soon as I'm eighteen, we'll get married." Her eyes are filled with sadness now. "And what if my mother doesn't make it until I turn eighteen? Then what? Then all you've succeeded in doing is keeping my mother from my wedding. Is that something you want to live with for the rest of your life?"

"No." I choke on my word.

"Did you read your text?" Josh steps to her side and links his hand in hers. She glances up at him and smiles in the same way Celia used to smile at me.

I pull out my phone and scroll through.

—Found cameras. Closing down Shakes 'n' Slaw. Nora CAN'T know.—

They're both so damned pragmatic for such young kids. But still… "There are ways to get her on our insurance as an employee…"

"Employee?" His voice is filled with disgust. He steps to me, standing toe to toe. Man to man. "The least you can do is have a little respect for the woman. I love her."

I look deeply into my son's eyes, and I know this is my time to stop being so damned selfish.

But I can't.

I turn to Nora. "I'm sorry, Nora. I'm sorry I bothered you. That was wrong of me. But I cannot and will not condone this wedding. And if I could explain, and if the tables were turned, I guarantee you'd do the same. Thank you for your time."

I hurry to the door, and Gracie follows after me. We stop on the front step.

"Gracie, I—"

"Goodbye, Mr. Cadman. I'm sorry for what you're going through, but I have to ask that you please leave and never come back here again. My mother can't take this kind of stress."

"I…yes." I'm a fifty-three-year-old man, and this girl puts me to shame. Turning, I scamper down the front steps and hurry to Ol' Sally like a dog with his tail between his legs.

Chapter Nineteen

Josh

"Asshole." I storm into Dad's kitchen. He's sitting at the table with three empty bottles before him. "So, what? You gonna self-destruct now?"

"Of course not. Have you told her yet?" He lifts the bottle to his lips and takes a long pull.

Anger rages through me, and I can't take it anymore. I storm to him, reach over, and knock the bottle from his hand. It ricochets off his tooth and splatters as it flies, landing with an unsatisfying *clink.*

He stands, as pissed as I am. His dark eyes are wild, but I don't care. I reach out and push his shoulder just enough to knock him off balance. He catches himself and stands upright. I push him harder this time, and he stands straight again. He's like the inflatable punching clown I had as a kid—I'd punch that clown as hard as I could, and it would just bounce back, time after time. It was the ultimate lesson in defeat.

"Josh." He drops his chin like a virile animal. "Stop it."

I step even closer. "Stop what? Huh?"

This time, when I push him again, he reaches out, grabs my hand, and twists it up behind me in a move I've seen cops do on TV. Fuck it hurts, but I won't give him the satisfaction.

"Is this what you want?" he growls into my ear.

"You want to feel pain? You want to know you're alive? That you deserve to be alive?" He lifts my arm higher, and the ache radiates down the entire side of my body. "Well, you're never going to feel pain the way I do, and Gracie will. Never. You're the lucky one."

"Lucky?" An adrenaline boost breaks me free of my father's hold. I spin around to face him. "How dare you."

I push him back again, and this time he stumbles. Quickly, he collects himself and comes at me. My hand balls into a fist, and before I can think, I clock him on the jaw, landing a right hook. He doubles over, holds his chin, and glares at me.

"Dad."

Charging at me, he takes me down by the torso. We're on the damned kitchen floor, and I'm trapped beneath him. I struggle against his weight, but he's too heavy. He's got me pinned beneath him. He presses all his weight against my wrists and hands, and I'm immobile.

"What the hell are you doing, Josh?"

"I'm marrying her. I love her. She needs my help."

"Then help her some other way." He pushes against me and rolls off. He drags himself a few feet and then leans himself up against a cabinet, bending one leg. He rubs his chin.

"I—I'm sorry." I nod to his chin as I push myself up and lean against a cabinet opposite him.

He looks at me like I've lost my mind. "I don't want your apology."

"What do you want?"

"You. I want you alive."

"We don't have that option." I slam my hand against the floor.

"Yes, we do." He sounds exhausted. "We have a choice. *You* have a choice."

"You're just pissed, because I'm not following my fate."

"What are you talking about? According to you, you're following your fate exactly."

"No. You're wrong." I turn my head to look at him. "She can't have children."

"What?"

"She was pregnant once. Had a bad loss. She can't get pregnant again."

"Does that mean…" he's choosing his words carefully, "you're walking away from all this?" He lifts a hand and makes a big, sweeping gesture.

"It means I'm risking everything, and everyone, for her."

"Josh, I…"

A small smile turns up the corner of Dad's mouth. That tells me everything I need to know. He doubts me. Although he's never said it, he's always doubted me.

"I guess love has the power to change our fate," he offers.

"No," I snap. "This doesn't change my fate."

"It could. Maybe you go to college together and—"

"No." I stand abruptly. "Nothing has changed. Can't you understand that?"

"Josh." He looks up at me. "You've lived almost all of your eighteen years looking for your mate—someone who's marked like you. Now you found her, and she can't fulfill your"—he struggles with the word—"prophecy. What do you think that means? What the hell do you think fate *is*?"

"What are you saying?"

"I'm saying maybe *this* is your fate. To find Gracie and then have a normal life with her."

"A normal life? You think I can lead a normal life?"

"I think you can if you'd like to. Son…"

He reaches his hand out to me, but I knock it away and leave him sitting there. All of this time. I should have known.

"You don't believe in me," I mumble more to myself than to him.

His eyes plead with me as he scrambles to his feet. "That's not true, Josh. I've been here all along. I know who you are. I know how great you are. And I know you can do great things for the world living a regular, normal life. Like your mother did."

"It always comes back to her, doesn't it? Well, Ben, she didn't lead such a normal life did she? She was chosen. She had me—a son who is marked."

"I gave you that birthmark. Not her."

"But you're here, and she's not. She was the one chosen to lead a special life. She was the one who died young."

"Yes." His face contorts with pain. "And I live with that. Every. Single. Day. You can't do that to Gracie, Josh. Do you understand how…how suffocating it is to lose your life partner? How you reach out in the middle of the night for her hand, and all you find is emptiness…? An emptiness that fills you with a hatred for everything."

"You're being dramatic."

"You know the worst part? It's not the empty bed. The worst part is the forgetting. Forgetting she's gone forever. Thinking she's out with a friend or at a yoga class and she'll be home later tonight. But then you remember, and the devastation washes over you again, each time more powerful than the last. Because you will never again hold that hand that was your only reason for living."

I stare at him.

"Josh. Everyone in Gracie's life that she's trusted and loved is gone—or will be soon. Think of her. It's time she knew who you are and what you're planning."

Without another word, I turn around and take off, leaving Dad standing in the middle of the kitchen floor.

****

Think of her. All I ever do is think of Gracie.

I grip my steering wheel until my knuckles whiten. There was no late-night traffic, so it only took me twenty minutes to the highway and eight hours to the Midtown Tunnel. But now I'm sitting in morning rush hour traffic in Jersey, holding my breath like an overinflated balloon float, praying someone'll come along and pop me with a giant pin. A normal life. Does he really believe I can live a normal life with Gracie? And what is fucking normal, anyway? *Normal*. It might as well be Greek the damned expression's so foreign to me.

"Hey!" Some beaten-up number with a loud engine and two-toned doors that make it look more like a spotted heifer than a car cuts me off. I draw in a deep gulp of air and then let it go, forcing myself to calm down by meditating on the one red brake light on the spotted heifer.

Normal. I'm pretty freaking sure this isn't what a normal guy does for his bachelor party.

I'm also sure that a normal guy doesn't ghost his fiancée on their wedding day. Even if it is for her own good.

Christ, Gracie.

*Vroom, vroom…*The spotted heifer revs its engine and weaves back and forth, confined to its lane. That's exactly how I feel. Confined to my fate.

Sitting up in my seat, I yank at the collar of my shirt and try to breathe.

What the hell am I doing? Why am I running? After all this time?

A sharp pain throbs behind my eyes. Hell, yeah. Why not? This would be such the perfect moment to get a damned headache—the kind that makes me totally immobile and helpless. Breathing deeply, I wait for the telltale blur of my eyesight and for the ground to feel like it's shaking beneath me. Like I'm trapped in an earthquake of my own mind.

In the meantime, I'm suffocating in here. Why the hell did I buy such a small car? Why can't this damned traffic move?

I lay on my horn, and the guy driving the spotted heifer glares at me in his rearview and stops the car.

I do it again, and this time, the heifer's door opens. A short, wide man wearing a dark blue jacket steps out of the car and ambles toward my ride. My heart races, and I grip the wheel tighter.

For some reason, I beep at him again. And again. Shaking his head, he pulls up his sleeves, exposing thick forearms. Good. Maybe he'll come beat the shit out of me so I won't have to think anymore.

He looks through my window and knocks on the glass. I ease the window down.

"You got a problem?" he asks.

"Yes."

"With me?" He leans over my window, stretching his arms on my door and widening his stance.

I turn to him, but my vision is still clear. If the headache was coming, it would have happened by now. Which means… I've only had one headache since we moved here, and never while I was with Gracie. How is that possible?

"Hey, asshole"—the spotted heifer guy slams his hand against my roof—"you got a problem with me?"

I know leaving Gracie is protecting her, but every cell in my body is screaming to be with her. A wish flashes before me of all the places I want to share with her: the bakery in the West Village with croissants better than France; the hidden bookshop that reeks of mothballs but has first-edition Hemingways; the galleries and museums. And that's just here. What I want is to explore the entire world with her, running far and fast, stopping only to hold her as we watch the sun rise over the ocean.

We'd be so happy even fate couldn't catch us.

"Hey, asshole!" The spotted heifer guy slams his hand on my roof.

Behind me, a car beeps. "Move it, jerkoff!" the driver yells out the window of his black SUV.

Spotted heifer guy nods to the man and then flips me off before heading back to his car. Traffic inches forward.

The black SUV finds a break in the traffic and pulls around me. "Hey, cumwad!" he yells out the passenger window. "Go back to fucking Ohio!"

Sometimes, the signs are so cryptic I almost miss them.

Sometimes, they come in the form of an asshole who reads my license plate.

Go back to Ohio.

Go back to Gracie.

Devastate her completely.

Either way, we lose, and she hurts.

Suddenly, I understand what Dad was saying. Fate isn't some externally drawn blueprint of life that's randomly assigned to us and that we're forced to follow.

Fate is our reason for being.

And my reason for being is her.

I need to tell her. I need to explain everything. I have to make it back in time. That means… I glance at my watch. Eight twelve. I have nine hours to get through this tunnel, turn around, go through it again, and make the eleven-hour trip back. And it all starts in Manhattan at rush hour.

Come on, fate. If ever I've needed you, it's now.

Chapter Twenty

Gracie

Glancing past the cardboard cutout of the two wedding bells I hung this morning, I look out the front door window. Still only my car. I know Josh is not supposed to see me before the wedding, but how far is he pushing this exactly? I haven't seen him or heard from him all day. In fact, we've had no contact since he took off after his dad last night. Isn't he cutting this a bit close? I pace back to the kitchen and glance at the clock on the wall. Five forty-eight. Just about ten minutes of six, and there's no Josh. Thankfully, there's no Ben, either. Good. That means I must have been clear last night. He needs to stay away because Mom does not need any more stress.

I peer into the living room that's decorated with a few white strands of crepe paper hanging from the doorways. My elaborate plan was to walk from the kitchen into the living room, where I would hand my plastic flower bouquet—the one Josh had given me—to Mom. After, we'd all celebrate with heart-shaped cucumber and cream cheese sandwiches, and to toast, I picked up extra seltzer—the orange flavor Josh likes.

I cleaned all morning and tried for a theme of light and airy, but I think I made the room darker and even more depressing. I have a knack for that. Along with a knack for thinking things are going to turn out one way right before they turn in an unexpected direction.

Sighing, I glance at Mom. She's propped up on the couch, wearing a floral kimono robe and her best turban. I can tell she's doing her best to don a happy expression while she fights back her pain. The turban is hanging lower on one side than the other, so I kneel before her and adjust it. Instinctually, she reaches out and strokes my hair in response.

She smiles through a grimace. Damn, I don't know why they did this last round of chemo, it just seems to have made everything worse. Now she's sick from the chemo, and her pain's intensified. One of the fingers of her good hand starts tapping—it's a way she self-regulates pain. She obviously needs this to be over. I glance at the time again: five fifty-five. They say you can make a wish when the clock has a triple number, so I do. I close my eyes and wish for pain to lessen.

Everyone's pain, everywhere.

The Justice of the Peace sits quietly on the wingback chair, palms in her lap, not looking at us. I imagine she's thinking I'm a jilted, pregnant teenage bride. And it seems she's right. Only, I can't imagine how it's possible.

An off feeling develops deep in my belly, radiating pain through my fingers and toes. Why would Josh no-show? Why would he have taken me this far just to devastate me? Why would Josh and Ben leave Mom and me with no insurance and no form of income? I place a shaking hand on my belly and grab a kitchen chair, easing myself into it. I'm careful not to wrinkle the white dress I bought just for today—a knee-length fitted satin dress with cap sleeves, a tight torso, and flowing bottom. I got it for fifteen bucks on the clearance rack at the secondhand store in town I like to call the vintage store. Makes me feel like I'm choosing to shop there.

Closing my eyes, I slip my feet out of my prom high heels and flatten them on the floor. The cool of the linoleum feels good against the balls of my feet. I lift my toes and then spread them wide and place them down gingerly. Maybe Ben is holding Josh hostage? Nah. Neither Josh nor his dad would leave us stuck without so much as a note explaining. No matter how much Ben dislikes me.

But…my eyes fly open. What if Josh was in an accident on his way here? I stand, pacing the kitchen. No, that can't happen. Not to him and not to Mom.

What have I done?

I hear a *clink* and *pop* coming from the driveway. A car. Whipping my head toward the front door, I rush to it. Feeling about a hundred pounds lighter, I yank open the door and float down the steps. I don't care that I'm barefoot. I just want to get to Josh. It *has* to be him, and no silly superstition is keeping me from him now.

Only… I stop dead in my tracks. It's not Josh's car, it's Ol' Sally, Ben's truck. My cheeks heat, but I stand perfectly still. There is no way I'm going to let him mess this up for us or for Mom. This is my wedding day, and I deserve one day without drama. The driver's door opens, and Ben jumps down wearing navy dress slacks, a white button-front shirt opened at the collar, and a dark blue sports jacket with dark brown dress shoes.

"Gracie." He nods to me. "You look beautiful."

"Thank you. You look very handsome yourself."

He smiles.

"Is he in there?" I nod to the truck.

Ben's brow furrows. He turns back to look at the

truck and then faces me. “Josh?”

I nod.

“No. I thought he was already here.”

“Not yet.” I take a deep breath. “He’ll be here any second, I’m sure. But listen, Mr. Cadman, what I said yesterday was true. You can’t be here if you’re going to cause drama. If you’ve come to try to stop the wedding—”

He puts his hand up. “No, no. Not at all. Gracie, I’m here to apologize for yesterday. It doesn’t excuse my actions, but there’s a lot you don’t know yet about my relationship with Josh. A lot you should know. My—” He takes a pause and steps forward, scrubbing his face with his hand. “—Reluctance for you two to get married never had anything to do with you. I hope you believe me. I think Josh is incredibly lucky to be with you.”

I cock my head. “Why the sudden change of heart?”

“It’s not. I realized I wanted to stop the wedding so I wouldn’t lose my son, and by trying to stop it, that’s exactly what happened.”

I give him a small smile. “Funny how life’s like that, isn’t it? It seems the harder we hold on, the farther away we get from whatever it is we wanted.”

“Yes.”

“You’re welcome to wait inside with my mom and the Justice of the Peace.”

“I thought I’d wait with you, if that’s okay.” He steps closer. “I was thinking maybe we could make an entrance together. Maybe, if it’s okay by you, I could walk you down the aisle.”

A lump forms in my throat. “I’m afraid the aisle is a path across my living room.”

“Sounds perfect.” He swings his arms back and

forth, and then his shoulders slump as he exhales. "Listen, Gracie, I know I haven't been much of a father figure to you, but I'd like to change that. If you'll let me." He reaches into his breast pocket and pulls out the ring Josh had given me. Celia's ring.

I back away. "I can't, Ben. Thank you, though."

"Gracie, I'd like you to have it. I hope you'll give me another chance."

"It's not about having another chance. I'm not vindictive, and I don't hold grudges. Frankly, I don't have the time or patience. But the ring." I shake my head. "It just doesn't feel right. Josh and I will get our own wedding bands."

He nods, tucking the ring back into his pocket.

I suck in another gulp of air, and my lungs feel like two helium balloons. "Ben? Why are you really here?"

He turns, facing me completely. "It dawned on me that life's way too short to be acting like such an asshole, and I'm sorry. You're an amazing young woman, Gracie. I'm sorry it took me this long to tell you." He smiles and sticks out his hand. "Friends?"

Nodding, I place my hand in his and gaze up into his soulful brown eyes. Without thinking, I collapse against his chest, hugging him until I think I may break us both.

I pull back, staring up at him. If he's surprised, he doesn't show it.

"Josh isn't coming, is he?" I ask.

"I don't know." His words are measured.

"Do you…know why?"

"I'm afraid. Maybe. I don't know." He takes a deep breath. "Do you?"

"No."

He studies my face, and suddenly, the light in his

intense eyes dims. He holds me by my upper arms. "He didn't tell you, did he?"

"Tell me what?"

"Christ." He mumbles under his breath as he lets me go. "This is something you should have known before your wedding day. I told him to tell you. But knowing Josh… He probably thinks he's protecting you." He lets out a deep sigh. "Have you, Gracie, have you ever noticed that he's different?"

"Different, how?" My heart races as I dare the question.

"He maybe doesn't fit in like everyone else."

"I guess…" I whisper, stepping closer and bowing my chin like I'm being let in on the meaning of life. "Like when he let those boys beat him up—"

"What boys?"

"At school. You didn't know?"

"I just saw some scratches. He told me he fell running."

"Scratches?" I shake my head. "His face was…pummeled."

"Not when I saw it."

"Well, he took a beating for me. He was protecting me from the school bullies. I've felt awful about it ever since. We saw the boys again at prom, and everyone else was scared, even the teachers, but not Josh. He walked right up to them. It's like he's fearless but passive."

Ben nods.

"Is there something I don't know?"

"There's a lot you don't know, Gracie. A whole hell of a lot. But I don't think it's my place to tell you."

"Ben"—I fight to calm the tremor in my voice—"is he in some kind of danger?"

"You're not. I can promise you that. I would never let that happen."

"You didn't answer my question. Is he in danger?"

"I don't know. I'd sure as hell be a lot happier if I knew where he was, but he hasn't answered my texts all day."

"Or mine." A searing pain shoots through my gut as a panic attack rises up in me. I chew the corner of my lip. "Can you do me a favor?"

"Anything."

"Can you go relieve the Justice of the Peace and pacify my mother somehow?"

"Where are you going?"

I race past him, up the steps, and to the front door. I dodge inside to grab my old beaten sneakers and car keys. I pause to yank the stupid wedding bells off the door.

"Gracie?"

I ignore Mom as I bound down the steps. "Thanks, Ben. Text me if it's an emergency, please."

"He's not at the house, Gracie."

I shake my head as I yank open my car door and toss my cell onto the passenger seat. "Didn't think he would be."

"Where are you going to look? Where did he go?"

I plop myself into the seat and bend my knee so I can reach my foot to pull on my sneaker. My knee bumps the steering wheel. "Ow." I rub my knee as I switch to the other foot and look up at Ben. "The same place I would have gone if I'd had the chance. Away."

He nods. "Be careful, Gracie. Please."

Placing one sneaker-clad foot on the gas, I rev the engine and then throw the car in *reverse*. Backing up, I'm careful to avoid Ol' Sally and the Justice of the Peace's car, and then I slide the gear into *drive* and race away.

Chapter Twenty-One

Josh

"Gracie?" I jump out of my car and rush down the short embankment. I'd recognize her car anywhere, even with the hood collapsed on itself and the tree attached to the front fender. "Gracie?" I try to pry open the driver's side door, but it's too bent to move. "Christ!" I rush to the other side and yank open the passenger door. I climb onto the seat and reach down to unhook her seatbelt. Thankfully, it held.

As carefully as I can, I slide her out of her seat and toward me. Her head rolls backward, and I spot the large bruise swelling on her forehead and blood dripping from a cut. *Damn it.* She needs medical care—*now.* I slip one arm around her waist and do some combination of lift-pull till we're both free of the car. I set her on the ground and squat down next to her. "Gracie? Can you hear me?"

Her eyes are closed, and the swelling is growing by the second. "Gracie?" Still supporting her head, I grab my cell and dial 911. "Hello. Yes. My fiancée's been in an accident. Car accident. We're..." I look around frantically. "I have no idea. Can't you track the phone or something?" I take a deep breath. Losing it now isn't going to help either of us. "Uh, 29!" I remember. "We're on Route 29, heading toward the highway. Yes, thank you."

My hand is shaking as I click off the phone and

quickly press the button for Dad.

"Josh? Where are you?"

"With Gracie. She's been in a car accident."

"Goddamnit." His voice is booming. "That's why she didn't answer her texts."

"What's going on?"

"Nora. I have her at the hospital. She collapsed, and I rushed her here."

"Jesus, Dad!"

"I know. How serious is Gracie?"

"She's not responding. But she's breathing and—" I lean down and place my ear to her soft chest. "—Her heartbeat is strong."

"She needs to be here for Nora."

"I know. The ambulance is on its way—"

"Josh." He takes a long pause. "There's no time for an ambulance. By the time they arrive and try to revive her… Jesus, I can't believe I'm saying this. Can you, can you help her?" His voice sounds desperate.

"What?"

"You heard me."

"But all these years you've said—"

"I know what I've said," he snaps. "But I also know there are things in life that just don't make sense. This is one of them. You need to help her and bring her to her mother so she can say goodbye. It's the least we owe that girl."

My hand cramps from squeezing the phone so hard. "I can't." My words are a whisper.

"Josh, listen to me. What happened with that boy in the hospital all those years ago, that wasn't your fault. You were so young. You tried."

"He was eight. No one is meant to die at eight."

"He was."

There are scuffling and muted beeping sounds in the background.

"Josh. The truth is, I don't know what you can do and not do. And after all this time, I realize there are some things in life we just can't understand. Some people who just don't fit. I don't know how, but you cured me of my cancer. We both know it. Try to help her, Josh. We have to try. Eighteen years you've been waiting for this. *You have to try.*"

I swallow the lump in my aching throat.

"I have to go answer some questions the doctor has."

"Yes."

"And, Josh? Good luck."

The phone goes dead.

I glance down at Gracie. Her normally bright eyes are closed, and her soft cheek is red and rubbed raw. But it's the bruise on her head I'm most worried about.

"Gracie?" I check my watch. It's been only a few minutes since I called that ambulance, and in a rural town like this, even finding us on the highway could take more time than Nora has.

I close my eyes, trying to remember a lifetime of learning. I don't heal someone; I facilitate their own healing. We all have the power to heal ourselves; we simply have to be given the option. And…I take a deep breath…a person can only be healed if they haven't completed their purpose on earth.

Healing's not anything magical. It's just a matter of energy. We're all energy, and we need to tap into it to facilitate healing.

I hover my hands above her—one above her bruised head and one above her abdomen. If I were to do traditional energy work, it would take several hour-long sessions. But I don't have that time, and I shouldn't need it. Closing my eyes, I—

Crap. I pull my hands away, shaking my head. This is such horseshit. Maybe Dad is right. Maybe they're all right. Maybe I am crazy.

Crazy enough to try.

"Come on, Gracie…" I whisper her name. A sudden bolt of adrenaline shoots through me from core to fingertips. "I want to help you. I know you're meant to wake up and see your mom one last time, but I can't do it without you."

I pull her higher into my arms, cradling her. "Gracie, I'm a healer. That's my gift. That's what I never told you. That, and well, a whole hell of a lot more. But the truth is, I don't know if I believe it myself. If I believe in myself. I doubt it every second of every day, and there's so much more to tell you. I'll explain that and a whole lot of other crap when you wake up. I promise." I hover my hands over her head and abdomen again and breathe deeply.

"Gracie"—I speak slowly as I feel the heat under my hands—"the truth is, I don't know who I am. I thought I did, but once, when I was young, I volunteered at a children's hospital so I could help the sick kids…" My words trail off, but I take a deep breath, determined to get through this.

"I spent a lot of time there, and there was this one little boy, Evan. He was only eight years old and had battled cancer since he was five. He wanted to become a fireman. Had the helmet, and he wore it to cover his bald head." My gut feels like someone has plunged a knife into it, but I go on. "Every time I walked into his room, he'd greet me with a 'Howdy Pardner' and use two hands like guns to shoot at me.

"His parents had to work days, so I pretty much camped out in his room. Played cards together, read stories, I even brought in some car parts, like pieces of an old eight-track, and we fixed them together. He became like a kid brother to me."

My soul aches, and the heat under my palms has begun to burn. Careful of her injuries, I place my hands on her. "He asked me what I wanted to be when I grew up, and I told him I wanted to help people get better. He thought I meant I wanted to become a doctor, and I should have left it at that, but I told him I wanted to be a healer. That I *was* a healer."

I exhale through parted lips. "So, I tried to heal him. I placed my hands on his back and waited, but the feeling I'm supposed to get never came. We tried again and again, but nothing. I didn't have the balls to tell him. So when his parents showed up that night, he told them I had healed him."

I choke back the lump in my throat. "The look in their eyes. It was pure disappointment…in me. They had trusted me to be their son's friend, and I gave him false hope. I was whisked away from Evan, and I never saw him again. He died soon after, right before his ninth birthday." I remove my hands from her.

"The thing is, I never want to be responsible for disappointing anyone like that, ever again. And more than anything, I never want to disappoint you."

My gaze lands on her bruised and battered face. She is so beautiful, but even without the injuries, she looks exhausted. She works so hard. She's done everything she could to keep Nora alive. My father's right. She needs to wake up and see her mother one last time.

The very least I owe her is everything I am.

“So let’s try, Gracie. Please. Both of us. You need to wake up and see Nora.” I lean forward and gently place my lips on hers.

She moans and stirs. “Josh?”

“I’m here.” I lean down close.

“Wait.” She puts two hands behind her and tries to push herself into a sitting position.

“No, don’t move. I’ll carry you. We have to get you to the hospital to see your mother.” Scooping her into my arms, I move toward my car.

“Is she…?”

“I don’t know.” A rock under my feet makes me trip and throws me off balance, but I right myself and hold her as tight as I dare.

“Careful.” She shakes her head, trying to focus. “The baby. Is the baby okay?”

“Baby?” I stop short. “What baby?”

“Josh.” She looks up at me and stares into my eyes. “I don’t know how it happened, but I’m pregnant.”

Chapter Twenty-Two

Ben

"Hi, Nora." I walk into her tiny hospital room. "It's Ben. Josh's father. Again. The nurse tells me you're not awake right now. But not sleeping either. If it's okay by you, I'd still like to join you. Have a conversation until the kids get here. And they will get here. So you just hang on, okay?"

The ventilator helps her breathe slowly and steadily. Taking a black leather and chrome chair from beneath the window, I pull it up next to her bed and sit. I lean forward and hold her hand. It's an odd moment, so filled with urgency, and yet, sitting here, there is nothing more I can do. The rest is up to Nora and Josh, but despite it all, I am filled with peace.

"Nice turban." I chuckle to myself as I release her hand.

We sit quietly for a moment.

"Nora, I bet you're wondering what the hell is going on."

The ventilator makes a deep but airy sound with every inhale of oxygen.

"Me too, frankly." I run my hand through my hair. "I think…I think you deserve an explanation of some kind. Especially now. So, I guess I'll just start at the beginning." I take a deep breath and let it go. "Our kids, Nora. I don't know if you know, but they're not like other kids. They're special."

I watch the steady rhythm of her breath.

"I guess you've always known that Gracie was special—I mean—" Shaking my head, I think of her and what she does in a day. "She is an incredible young woman. But the thing you don't know, that Gracie doesn't even know, is that Josh is special, too. In a different way. Yes, he's an amazing young man, but he, uh…he has a condition, Nora. A mental condition. His mom had it, too. Only I didn't know it then."

I feel like I'm betraying Josh, but I'm compelled to go on.

"You wouldn't know it from looking at him or even talking to him. That's what's tricky. Mental illness is a beast. You may never know how much the person sitting right next to you is suffering. Josh has a mental condition called Delusional Disorder. It's odd in someone so young. Usually, people begin to show symptoms around midlife. But for him, it's been here his whole existence. To be exact, he has something called Grandiose Delusional Disorder." I chuckle. Finally being able to share this with someone releases a drop of the stress I've been carrying for the past eighteen years. "He thinks he is special. He thinks, well, he thinks that he is chosen. He doesn't think he's the Second Coming or anything, but he believes that he and his mate—a person with a birthmark that's opposite his—will have a baby that will change the world. Together, they'll give birth to the next Christ or Buddha or maybe Dalai Lama."

I chuckle again nervously. I've never had to explain this to anyone before. In that sense, I'm grateful she's not conscious.

"As if that wasn't enough…" I clear my throat and

go on. “The thing is, Josh believes that when they do give birth to the chosen one, he and his mate will have to give up their…well, their lives. It has to do with energy. Because their energy is a perfect match for the other, those two sides form a single perfect energy and allow the savior baby to be born.”

“Have I lost you yet?” I shake my head. “Well, his mom, Celia, like I said, I didn’t know it at the time—and maybe I should have—also suffered from Delusional Disorder. But for her, it was different. All along, I thought she just believed in an alternative spirituality—auras and chakras and energies. But what she believed was what Josh believes—that they are regular people chosen to do something incredible.”

I take a deep breath and let it out slowly. “The thing is, Celia didn’t die in childbirth like I tell everyone. She committed suicide when Josh was only a baby.”

My chest is so heavy I have to slump my shoulders forward to stay upright.

“Her delusion told her that she would die once her marked child was born. And I’ll be damned—he is marked. But so am I. I tried to explain that to her. I tried to stop her, but she couldn’t face the idea of being mentally ill. She was more terrified of being locked away in some padded room than she was scared of death. She made me promise that I would do the same for Josh. That I would never try to change him and would never have him locked away somewhere. And then, when the time came for Josh’s energy to pass, that I would just let him go.” I take a deep, trembling breath. “When I found her unconscious with the bottle of pills, I panicked—I did all the things I promised I never would—ambulances and hospitals and doctors—but in the end, she got her wish.”

I swallow hard.

"She did rouse for a moment, almost at the very end. I was with her, holding her, and she looked into my eyes. Do you know what she said? Nothing profound like you might expect. Not even one last, 'I love you.' All she said was, 'Let me go.' All that mattered to her was fulfilling her destiny."

A tear forms in the corner of my eye, and I wipe it away.

"So I let her go. There was nothing else I could do. But now there's Josh. And he loves Gracie. And they want to get married—and he says she's marked. And the thing is, Nora, I'm terrified of what he might do in the name of fate."

I lean back in the chair, listening to the ventilator helping Nora breathe, and glance at the clock on the wall. "Come on, Josh," I mutter.

My thoughts are racing, so I keep talking just to keep busy.

"Nora, you remember being young and in love, don't you?" My mind rushes to thoughts of Celia. "I loved Celia the moment I saw her walking across the campus lawn carrying a sign that was three times as big as she was. Of course I wasn't a student. I was a hell of a lot older than she was. I was there working on the library shelving—but I knew. The second I saw her, I knew. I'll bet Nathaniel loved you like that."

Her ventilator keeps pumping its steady flow of oxygen.

I glance up at Nora. "I haven't even told you the craziest part yet. The craziest part in all of this is that sometimes, well, sometimes Nora, I believe him. Josh. You understand that one, don't you? You know what it's like to be a single parent. How terrified you are most of the time, although you can never show it—but how you believe in your kids so much, well, maybe you start to believe the delusions, too."

A robin outside her window grabs my attention, and I turn to it and then back to Nora. "There were these signs, you know? Little things, really. Like that time when he was just two years old and he held a withered dandelion in his tiny, sweaty palm. He closed his fist around it, and when he opened his hand, the dandelion was a full, bright yellow flower again."

My jaw is so tight I rub it with the fingertips of both hands. "Did I misjudge the dandelion? Maybe it wasn't withered after all? Was it just Celia's voice in my head? Or the unrelenting guilt I felt, *feel*, toward her because I *couldn't save her*? Maybe. Or maybe it was something else."

I watch Nora's heart monitor, but it's consistent.

"I think… I think he's a healer, Nora. Does that sound crazy? Christ. Probably does. But he has this…gift. And I think it feeds his delusion."

I get up and cross to the window, staring out. There's a tiny pond with a water fountain.

"Have you ever taken Gracie fishing?" I ask without turning to Nora. "I tried it once with Josh. Packed us up early on a Saturday, crammed our truck with bait and tackle. When we arrived at the pond, and I baited the hook for him, his eyes grew wide as his mother's, and his face turned green.

" 'Why would you kill something that's alive?' he asked. Probably every other little boy asks the same question, but the way he said it, with genuine interest, made me take pause. Was there a reason we were killing something living? For sport?"

Chuckling, I lean my forearms onto the ledge of the window. "Oh, Nora, it's all so funny now. But then." I shake my head. "I knew he wasn't going to kill a worm, let alone a fish. He's too kind. But here's the weird part. I tried anyway. I'd bait the hook with a worm"—I mime the actions with my words—"and then he'd remove the worm from the hook, hold it until it was wiggling in his palm, and then toss it into the grass behind us. Eventually, he demanded we leave and wouldn't talk to me the rest of the day. That was my last attempt at fishing, and that's why fixing cars became our thing."

Turning around, I lean back against the windowsill and cross my arms. "Everything is explainable, you know? The dandelion wasn't really withered. Worms regenerate. Everything could be dismissed except…"

I drop my crossed arms and stare at Nora's petite features. She doesn't much look like Gracie, or I don't know. Maybe she does. It's just that I've made poor Gracie out to be Celia's twin.

"Except my cancer. One day, Josh told me he had met a healer in the town where we were living, and that man invited us back to his reservation. We spent a summer there. While Josh studied with him, I underwent all kinds of alternate healings—most were led by Josh. When the summer was over, my cancer was gone. Did Josh help heal me?"

Nora's face seems even more peaceful. They must have released a dose of morphine.

"Christ, I wish I knew. I wish I knew anything. The only thing that I do know is that Josh thinks he's found his mate in Gracie, and they're getting married. And once they get married, I won't have a say anymore. What little control I have now will be gone. If she realizes what's going on with him and decides to have him locked away—she can. And that's not my biggest fear. My biggest fear, the thing that keeps me up night after night, is what if he follows in the footsteps of Celia? What if he takes the delusion too far and…"

Without thinking, I slam my palm against my forehead.

"There's no way to win this one, Nora. No way at all."

Taking a deep breath, I rush to her side and sit next to her. Careful not to jostle her, I take her hand. "Do you understand what all of this means?"

I squeeze her hand too tight, and she grimaces. I release my grip.

"No matter what happens, Nora, our children suffer."

I release a long, pent-up sigh.

"And that's only if we're really, really lucky."

Chapter Twenty-Three

Nora

It's natural to wonder what death will be like. I think everyone does, and when you have a terminal disease, I suppose you wonder even more. But I never imagined this.

Death is balance.

They tell us things. They tell us about bright lights and meeting our God, about life flashing before our eyes, about tunnels and visions. But what they don't tell us is the clarity that comes moments before you go. Those things we call memories are stored in our own personal keepsake chest in our minds. And it seems at the end, that chest opens up not to recall but to relive—to *re-feel*—those memories, bathing us in a wash of comfort.

I feel my mother lifting me into the air and then dunking my toes into the warm water of our local community pool. I feel Nathaniel's breath just before he kisses me and the love in his kiss. I feel Gracie growing in my womb and the happiness I knew. Memory after memory explodes in my body, sending little zaps of soothing energy all over. It's as if every cell is a box made to hold a different memory, and suddenly, they all burst free. All things return to the sea, I suppose. We started in a warm bath in the womb, and that warm bath is our last earthly feeling as well.

And then, all the secrets of the universe are revealed.

It's the ultimate, "Ah-ha! Moment." I understand why Nathaniel died and why Gracie's life has been plagued with hard work and sorrow. I understand she belongs with Josh, and I understand what they create together will change the world. I've always known my Gracie was destined for greatness. I see it all so clearly, I would swear I'm living it. Who knows, maybe I am.

Strangely, I feel included now—not separated as one human about to leave her bodily form. I feel more a part of everything than ever. I feel my energy melding with the energy of the grass and trees, of the butterflies and wild horses. Maybe that's why so many people believe in reincarnation. I wish I could explain it to them. It's not that we come back as something else. It's that we *always were* a part of that something else, and our life force, our soul, our energy, returns to the earth to give life to something new and beautiful. That's our destiny. Our fate.

We need to protect our earth and all living creatures on it because we are the earth, and every living being is us.

Huh. Thoughts, random pearls come to me, things I wish I could shout from the rooftops. I toss my head, mouthing the words, but only the smallest sound ekes out. I can't tell anyone what I now know. It's for me only. And that's okay. Because someday Gracie and all the people she loves will know it, too.

"Hang on, Nora." It's Ben. He must have seen me struggle to speak. He's a good man. He'll be a good father to Gracie. I'm glad he's here.

"Once"—I don't know why I start babbling, but I do. I don't know if I'm actually speaking, but I feel Ben take my hand and sense him leaning over me—"Nate took me out on a stand-up paddleboard on a lake." I squeeze Ben's hand, and he squeezes back. "I tried to balance but fell underwater. I couldn't see or hear, but it was okay." I suck in a deep breath. My lungs are so heavy. Filled with water. But it's okay.

"Don't try to speak, Nora."

As soon as he says it, a young nurse comes into the room. She switches off the ventilator and moves my bed to an upright position. As I exhale, she slides the tube from my throat. It doesn't hurt. In fact, it feels like freedom. Finally. She nods to me and Ben, and then leaves quickly. I take a breath on my own and do my best to speak.

"Balance. Underwater—balance." I take another deep breath. It's no longer painful, just bothersome. I'm tired of being here. "One reality…becomes another. Better. And it's okay. Tell Gracie."

"Yes." He sits on my bed next to me, holding my hand firmly. "Rest, Nora."

I'm not tired as a human is tired. Instead, I feel whole for the first time ever. The fear so many have, I wish I could alleviate that for them. Dying doesn't mean the end. It means completion. You don't lose yourself. You gain everything you were ever meant to be. I understand, and I'm okay with it. It will be nice to be part of infinity and to be free of the confines of a human body and the fears of the human mind.

But to do it, you have to let go, of course.

Sight is the first human sense we lose. Probably because it was the one we relied on the most. What if someone is blind? What do they lose first? It seems that's not for me to know.

My only wish is to hear Gracie's voice once more

before I go. Before hearing leaves me, too. I'll fight to stay in the prison of my mind just to hear her once more. Her soft tone and strong delivery. Like all of her—soft and caring, but so strong and capable.

No wonder Josh found her.

No wonder she is chosen.

Will I be with Nathaniel again? I will, for in our completeness, we'll not only be with each other, we'll be one another. There's no longer a place where he ends and I begin. There never was. I wish I knew that then. I wish every time I'd yelled, I'd kissed him instead.

"She's slipping." Ben's speaking to someone.

"Is she in pain?" Gracie's voice is softer than usual, but there's acceptance in it. Good girl, Gracie. It's time to stop fighting for me.

"No," Ben answers. "How are you?"

"I'm fine. Must have hit my head harder than I thought, though, since I'm still marrying this one even though he left me waiting at the altar."

"Gracie." Josh's voice is filled with apology.

"Josh. Let's not. Please. You're here now, and that's all that matters."

Gracie understands.

"Are we ready to start?" It's a voice I don't recognize.

"Yes, thank you, Reverend."

Reverend? They're getting married. Here. With me. Oh, Gracie.

"Dearly beloved, we are gathered here to join this man, Joshua Benjamin Cadman to this woman, Gracie Jean Jackson…"

The voice floats away.

"I do." It's Josh. He loves her.

"I do." It's her. She loves him.

"…Pronounce you husband and wife."

The words come and go, but she's married now. She's not alone. She won't be alone ever again. I smile. "I love you, Gracie."

"Mom?" She sits next to me and places her warm hand on my head. She adjusts my turban one last time. I fight to lift my hand to reach out and stroke her hair in response like I always do, but I can't. She understands.

Death is balance.

My time is done, and hers is just beginning.

Chapter Twenty-Four

Gracie

"It's beautiful here. How come I never knew about this place?" We're in a small clearing on the bank of a pond I've never been to before. The air is humid and the forest around us is eerily still. The calm before the storm. I turn to Ben standing a few feet from Josh and me. "How did you?"

Ben steps closer to us, clutching the urn. It was nice of him to carry it for me. I'm shaking so badly, I was afraid I'd drop it. Josh is carrying a large shopping bag in one hand, and the other is wrapped around my waist, helping to support me.

Ben shrugs. "I stumbled on it one day."

"I've lived here my whole life." I shake my head.

"It's hidden, Gracie." Josh tightens his arm around me in a supportive move. I smile at them both.

"You ready?" Ben glances at the sky and then holds the urn out toward me.

I look at the urn in his hands. I know I'm supposed to take it, but doing so feels finite. "Should I be?"

He smiles at me in the most paternal way. It's a smile that makes me understand I'll never have to be alone again.

"No matter how much time I had to prep, it's still so hard to fathom. I keep thinking she'll be home in a couple of days."

"Yes." Josh pulls me closer.

"Gracie." Ben clears his throat. "You don't have to do this. You can keep her ashes."

"No, no." I shake my head, taking the urn from him. "She would have wanted this. She loved the water. She and my father were going to vacation at a beach when they had the accident."

He nods and rests his hand on mine. "Gracie, before…I was speaking to her in her room. She wanted you to know something."

I look up at him, and my heart races but quiets simultaneously, all so I can hear better.

"She wanted you to know that one reality becomes another. And it's okay." He squeezes my hand before letting go.

I nod. "Thank you." She's okay. I look up at Ben and Josh and wipe away the slickness forming on my upper lip. The humidity is intensifying. Any moment, the sky will open. "I know this will sound crazy, but I figure you two can handle a little crazy."

They exchange a look, but I go on anyway.

"I dreamt about her last night."

"That's not crazy." Josh furrows his brow.

"It wasn't a dream—it was like I was living it with her."

"Is that why you were moaning in your sleep?"

"Maybe so. We were sitting on our front steps, and we had coffee together. Like we did before she got sick. She loved coffee; the stronger, the better. Sometimes, we'd have espressos at bedtime. It would be eleven at night, and we were both dog-tired, but she wouldn't serve them until she peeled lemon rinds for us and twisted them in just the right way." I smile. "And we'd drink all that caffeine just so we could stay up later into the night to watch the world go to sleep. She loved the world." I suck in another huge gulp. "And last night, she served the coffee. She took care of me like when I was a kid. And she sat with me and told me everything was okay. She was happy."

"That sounds perfectly normal." Ben nods.

"Yes, but when I woke up, I tasted the espresso. The thing is, I don't think it was a dream. I don't know if she came to me or I went to her, but…"

Tiny raindrops bounce off the pond. Ben shuffles his feet. It's time. I take a deep breath just the way she taught me to when I was a child and I had to do something I didn't want to—like take a test or get a shot. I step away from Josh, and being mindful of the tree roots and dips in the earth, I move toward the water.

Josh follows behind me, and in my peripheral vision, I see Ben take Josh by the forearm and hold him back. I'm at the water's edge, alone. Squatting down, I unscrew the top of the urn. Although I don't want to, I glance inside. It's like I'm peeking between closed fingers at a horror movie. But this time, the horror is behind us.

I reach in with my fingers and loosen the top of the plastic bag inside the urn. Careful to keep the bag from slipping, I turn the urn over, and her ashes scatter on the pond. They pool together near the bank of the river, floating on the surface.

"Goodbye, Mom. I love you."

Standing, I turn. Josh and Ben are right there.

"Gracie"—Ben steps closer—"it's okay to cry."

"Thank you." I smile at him. "But tears won't bring her back."

“No,” he agrees, “I suppose that’s true.”

“Gracie?” Josh holds out the bag he’s been carrying. “I thought you might want this.”

A gentle drizzle starts as I reach into the bag and pull out an old-fashioned bell and mallet. “What’s this?”

Josh gives me a half smile. “She did kick it, Gracie. Cancer. She’s kicked it in her own way.”

I place a hand over my mouth, overcome. “She did, right?”

He smiles. “You should ring the bell for her.”

Nodding, I hold the short chain at the top of the bell and lift the mallet. I hit the bell twice.

The soft sound of the *ding* echoes through the heavy air, melting into the drops of rain as they begin falling steadily.

Ben walks past me and takes a large stick from the ground. He squats at the riverbank and carefully pushes Mom’s ashes to the middle of the pond.

Rain falls on the ashes. Droplets bounce upward and sideways—a cacophonic farewell dance for Mom—before they mix into the pond, and Mom dissolves into nothingness.

“I am really sorry, Gracie.” Ben hugs me.

“Thank you.”

He nods. “I’m going to head home and give you two a little space.”

“You don’t have to,” I tell him.

“Yes, I do.” He smiles. “You have a lot to learn about each other. A lot.” He glances at Josh, and then gives his attention back to me. “The rest of this journey, Gracie, it’s yours. You and Josh. I’m…well, I’m done here.”

Before we can say anything, Ben walks up the

embankment to Ol' Sally. He opens the driver's door and then turns to us. "If you need anything, either of you, just tell me. And take a day or two. We'll get Gracie settled in her new job as soon as she's feeling ready."

"Thank you." I smile.

Josh and I stand perfectly still on the embankment as the rain begins to lessen and the humidity grows even more oppressive. As soon as Ol' Sally drives away, I turn to Josh. "Let's go."

"Okay. My house?"

"No." For the first time in I don't know how long, excitement bubbles up inside me.

"Where then?" he asks.

"Anywhere," I tell him. "Let's just get the hell away from here."

Chapter Twenty-Five

Gracie

"Hold on, Gracie." Josh takes me by the hand and turns me toward him, gently. His face is etched in pain. "There's something I need to tell you first."

"Now?" I look up at the sky. It's still gray, but the rain has stopped. The clouds are fat and dark, holding back the weather.

"Yes. It's something you need to know."

"What is it?" I take a deep breath as I gaze at his strong jaw and the slight scruff darkening it.

"It's about me."

"Okayyyy…? What about you?"

He doesn't answer. Just then, the image of Ben telling us that we had a lot to learn about each other flashes before me, and I realize… No. It can't be.

"Josh? Are you…sick? Do you have…cancer?" I whisper the word. Maybe if I don't say it loudly, it can never touch us again.

He exhales. "No, no. Nothing like that."

"What about… Ben?"

"He's fine, too."

"Thank God. Then what? Come on. I think by now you know that you can tell me anything."

"Yes, I do. It's just…this is tough."

A sinking feeling settles in the pit of my stomach, but I ignore it. If he's not sick, then what is it? And why am I feeling so "off?" This is Josh, after all. The man who's stuck by me through everything.

"Josh? Come on. You're scaring me. What is it?"

"There's something I should have told you a long time ago. And I'm sorry that I didn't."

"Okay, now you're flat-out freaking me out. Will you please just tell me?"

"I'm trying, but I'm not sure how to start."

"Start at the beginning. Josh? Please? What is it?"

"Gracie, I'm…I'm not like everyone else."

"Is this one of those 'I'm not like other girls' moments?"

I smile just to lighten the mood, but he doesn't return my smile.

"You're serious? Okay, I'm sorry. Well, you're certainly not like any high school guy I've ever known."

"It's more than that. I'm, uh, different than other people."

"What do you mean, 'different'? Different how?" I cross my arms before my chest.

He keeps his eyes on me. He's probably waiting for me to understand, but I've got nothing.

"I'm sorry, Josh. I know you're telling me something here, but I just lost my mom, and you know I do not play games. Especially cryptic ones."

"No games."

"Then explain, please."

"Okay. It's—well, there are people in life—regular people—who are chosen to do…things."

"What kind of *things*?"

"Make a difference."

"Everyone who's ever lived makes a difference, Josh. They do." I have to believe this for the sake of

Mom's memory.

"Yes, of course. But this is…different. More direct. Think about your history classes. There have been people throughout history who've had the ability to change the world."

"Yes. And?"

He widens his eyes and raises his chin in response.

"You're telling me that you have the ability to change the world? Great. Good for you. I believe it. Go start a non-profit or something when you graduate college."

"It's not quite like that." He stares into my eyes. "And it's not just me."

His words are so soft I'm not certain I've heard them. I push on anyway. "So, what you're telling me is that you're part of a group that'll end global warming or world poverty or something?"

"Not exactly."

"Then what, exactly, is it?"

His brow furrows. "Here's the thing. You know how some people believe in God?"

"Of course."

"But those people have probably never seen God, it's faith. Well, that's what it's like for us."

"Us?"

"Those of us in history that have been…picked…I guess."

"Picked?"

He walks down the embankment to the pond and rests his hands on his head, turning his face upward to face the sky. Then he drops his hands and walks back to me. "Gracie, I'm, uh, *chosen*."

"Excuse me? Chosen?"

"Yes."

"Chosen for what?" I take a step back, but I stay close enough to him to study his eyes, looking for the joke. There isn't one.

Squinting, I try to read his face. "Josh, are you high?"

"No. Never. I drink sometimes, that's it."

"Are you drunk, then?"

He shakes his head.

"Okay. Is this a joke? Because I don't think it's all that funny."

"No joke."

I can't believe I'm doing it, but I look up at the street, hoping Ben's still there in case I need to make a quick getaway. "This, uh…" I take a deep breath. "Are you trying to tell me you're the Second Coming or something?" I twirl the plain silver wedding band on my ring finger. Seems the ring was only one of the surprises Josh had for me.

He looks defeated. "Of course not."

"Then what? What the hell does *chosen* even mean? Wait." A dull ache forms in the back of my throat. "I read all those vampire books in junior high. You're not going to feed me some crap about not being human or something, are you?" I cross my arms, exhausted and frustrated. *This* is how I say goodbye to my mother? "Because I am way too pragmatic for that. Sorry, but I'm not the girl to buy into all that crap."

He cocks his head, staring at me blankly. "I am most certainly human." He takes a breath. "Look, Gracie, I've never had to explain this before, so give me a chance, please. This isn't easy."

I nod.

"There's this belief. It's like the world is this big puzzle, right? And pieces are meant to fit together."

"Okay."

"There has to be balance. Day, night, winter, summer, that sort of thing."

"Still with you."

"Well, there are times when that balance is off. Like now. There are times when the bad outweighs the good. We're in one of those times now. War, poverty, politics, human rights violations, human trafficking, climate change, slavery, genocide—"

I put up my hand. "I get it."

"If we keep going as people, we'll become extinct in a matter of a few centuries. Or less."

The humidity sits on me like a weighted blanket. I reach up and wipe away a bead of sweat that's trickling down my temple. "Josh, please. What are you talking about?"

"Our birthmarks aren't coincidental."

Fear begins bubbling in my gut where excitement had been moments before. Again, I glance up the embankment and toward the road. Ben is long gone, so I need to make a decision here and now: could I outrun Josh if I needed to?

"I've spent my entire life looking for my other half. For you," he explains.

"What happens now that you've found me?" I whisper.

He clamps a hand on the back of his neck. "Promise you won't freak out?"

"Too late. Sorry."

"Okay. Well, I'm told, uh, you and I will…"

My heart is pounding like crazy. "What? What will

we do?"

He stares into my eyes. "Gracie, please, please understand no one ever taught me how to explain this to you."

"What is it, Josh?" My voice is low and breathy. "You're my husband. I'm pregnant with your baby. If you have something to say to me, say it."

"The prophecy is…"

"Prophecy? There's a freaking *prophecy*?"

"Yes. It says well, it says…" He closes his eyes and recites:

"We are all born with a unique destiny.

A blueprint of our lives.

The lucky ones are those who are ignorant of their fate and spend their lives chasing the unknown inevitable.

The unlucky ones are the two who are marked.

One as masculine.

One as feminine.

For they alone can save the world."

"What. The. Fuck." I move away from him as fast as I can and start scrambling up the embankment.

I stumble, and feel him right behind me.

"Gracie, wait, please."

Suddenly, I'm caught—stuck on something. I gasp and flip around to discover that Josh is holding me by my ankle.

"Let me—ugh!" I kick and flail, trying to break free, but he holds me tight. Crawling backward, I fight my way crab-like up the hill.

"This *is* the prophecy, Gracie. Don't you understand? It says that you and I will have a child. And that child is the one who will save the world. I didn't know it was happening at first because you said you couldn't get pregnant. But now I'm even more sure." He lets go of my ankle and drops his head. "Please, Gracie. Please."

The terror inside subsides a bit, so I sink down into the grass and place my hand on my abdomen protectively.

"How? How will our child presumably save the world?" My voice is raspy.

He shrugs.

"Will he or she be some great religious leader?"

"Maybe. I don't know. I just know he'll *do* something."

"Like curing famine or something?"

"Maybe. I'm not told."

"The baby will be a he?"

"That's how he's been described to me."

I nod. "And you think I'm the one you do this with?"

"Yes. It's your birthmark."

"I'm sure lots of people have birthmarks like this."

He shakes his head. "Not this perfect. Not that matches mine so completely."

"My mother has one."

He raises his eyebrows. "She does?"

"Yes. So it's got to be more than that."

"It is. It's how you got pregnant when the doctors said you couldn't. It's the way I feel about you. The way I'm so drawn to you. The way I love you. And my headaches have stopped since I found you."

"What?" Shaking my head, I try to make sense of any of this as I push myself up onto my feet. I wipe my damp palms on my jeans. "Wait, wait, wait. Because I've got an unremarkable birthmark and your headaches have stopped since you've met me, I'm suddenly the Virgin Mary? 'Cause as you're well aware, that ship has sailed."

He stands to meet me. "I already told you it's not like that."

"Then how is it?" I take a bigger step back as anger and frustration wash over me. "Huh, Josh? What's happening here? Are you…are you insane?"

"No." His word is firm. "I mean, maybe. I don't know. Sometimes, I worry I am, and I know Ben worries, but no. I don't think I'm crazy. As long as I stay on my meds, I'm fine."

"Your *meds*? Jesus!" I step away, turning in a full circle, and then come back to face him.

"Gracie, I'm just a person who's aware of my own fate. And yours." He drops his chin and looks up at me.

"W—wait a second. The prophecy. Your meds. You *think* you're not crazy? Josh, I'm really trying here. You've got to do a better job explaining"—I wave my hands before me—"this. Whatever this is."

"I know. I know."

He steps closer, but I move farther up the embankment. From this angle, I'm a few inches taller than him.

"Gracie. We're all destined for something. There was a reason we were put on the earth. For some of us, it has a greater global impact than for others. That's all."

"So how do you know you're chosen? And our child?"

"I was told. I've been groomed. There were signs, I don't know." He turns his back to me and then faces me again.

"Does Ben know about this?"

"Yes. It began with my mother."

"Were your parents in some kind of cult? Is that how they met? Is that how they got this idea?"

"Close. Liberal Arts college." The corner of his mouth turns up slightly.

I glare in response. "You think this is funny?"

"No. And that's not where they got the idea."

"Then where?" I cross my arms before my chest again. My BS meter is at capacity.

"They didn't *get* the idea. It just is." He barks his reply.

"Hey." I step closer to him, matching his caustic tone. I drop my arms to my sides, and my body feels alive with prickly heat. "Don't get snippy with me. You just dropped some bomb about being a *chosen* person and maybe being crazy, and I didn't run screaming. I'd appreciate a chance to process this, please."

"Yes." He nods. "Sorry."

"So what happens now? Now that I'm pregnant, and we've both done our part?"

"Now comes the tough part."

"Tougher than *this*?"

"The next part of the prophecy says we are both supposed to, uh, move on."

"Break up?" Raindrops fall on the pond again as panic begins to rise in me. "You're leaving me?" It feels like there's a weight on my chest, caving it inward. I'm going to be alone. Again.

"Of course not. Never." He steps closer. "When we move on, it means that our energy, when it's combined, will make this perfect little soul who saves the world."

"And…" I hold my breath.

"But to combine our energy, it means we have to release our own."

"Release how?"

"Say goodbye to our lives here and transition to the next phase."

"Die? You mean we have to die?"

"Yes."

"What the hell! You *are* crazy! You had sex with me believing that I was your match, knowing that if I got pregnant, it would kill me? Kill us both?"

"I didn't think you could get pregnant. Or I never would have."

Reaching into my pocket, I grab my phone, open a car app, and text for a driver.

"What are you doing?" His voice is shaky as he nods to my phone.

"Not that it's any of your business, but I'm calling a car and getting the hell out of here."

"Don't do that. I have my car. I can drive you. Do you want to go home and grab some things—"

"Stop," I snap. "I don't want to go anywhere with you ever again. This is nuts. I can't believe I trusted you. I can't believe I *married* you." *FML.*

Turning, I storm up the embankment and begin walking toward the road where the driver can find me.

"Gracie, wait, please." Josh is suddenly beside me.

He grabs me by the arm.

"Let. Me. Go." I yank my arm from him and storm away. "Do not follow me!" I yell over my shoulder as fear pushes me forward. "And stay the hell away from me. You—you are crazy!"

Frantically, I break out into a run heading toward the intersection, and I don't stop until I wave down my driver. The car slows, and I open the back door. "Go, go, please," I tell my driver before I'm even completely in the car.

As our car pulls away, I turn back to see Josh standing at the side of the road, looking almost as heartbroken as I feel.

Chapter Twenty-Six

Gracie

I'm alone.

Completely alone. I have no job. No father or mother. No boyfriend. Even though I'm technically married, no husband. No partner. No family of any type, and at this rate, probably no chance to graduate high school.

Pulling my boring white covers up over my head, I inhale my own smell. Ugh, I stink. But it's not my usual cumin-laced scent of hard work and stress. This is a combination of sadness and despair.

Why did this happen? It's not that I blame Josh. Really. The more I lie here and think about it, the more I realize he's sick. He can't help what he is. But I do blame Ben. He should have—

"Gracie?"

There's a man's voice at the door. Followed by a loud knock.

"Gracie, please. Please let me talk to you." It's not just any man's voice, it's Ben.

"Go away," I mumble from my bed. I'm not moving. I'm savoring every moment of being here. Who knows how long I'll have a bed to sleep in? There's no way I can pay the mortgage without a job, and then what becomes of me? Despite everything, I'm technically still a minor. A chill washes through me as he knocks again, even louder this time.

"Gracie, please. Please. I'm not going away. I'll stay here at your door until you answer. I want to make sure you're okay. Please let me talk to you and explain everything."

"Make sure I'm okay? Explain everything?" I kick back the covers, lurch out of bed, storm across the scratched wood of my bedroom floor, and march to the door. I yank open the front door and glare at Ben. "What the hell do you want? What could you possibly *explain*?" My stomach rumbles. It's the freaking soundtrack of my life.

"Gracie, may I come in?" He's dressed in fresh jeans and a T-shirt with a plaid shirt thrown over. He smells clean, and when he lifts his arm to hold the door open, all I want to do is fall against his chest.

But not this time.

"You fucked me over."

"Gracie. Please, can I come in to talk about it?" His voice is measured and calm.

"Before all of this, Ben, I never believed in holding grudges or staying angry at people. But now…now that I have this extra time on my hands, I've been lying in bed thinking. And I've decided I'm going to fill all that extra time with hatred. I am going to become an angry, bitter person who holds you, Ben Cadman, personally responsible for my entire fucked-up life."

"Gracie." His voice is soft and laced with pain. "I understand. Truly. And I get that you're blaming me. I would, too. So, go ahead. Dump it all on me. I've got wide shoulders. I can take it."

Despite everything, the smallest smile starts at the corner of my mouth.

“Please, can I come in?” His eyes are so kind and gentle.

Nodding, I step aside, and he walks in. My stomach rumbles again.

He glances at my belly. “When was the last time you ate?”

“I don’t know.” It’s the truth. “I didn’t eat much before spreading Mom’s ashes because I was sad—and then…except for some stale crackers and old yogurts, I guess it’s been a couple of days.”

“Gracie. You have to eat. Please. Throw on a sweatshirt, and let me take you out for a burger. We can talk there.”

Every fiber of my being wants to scream, *No!* But my stomach decides to take charge of my mind. Besides, it’s not just me I need to think about. “Give me a sec.”

His shoulders visibly drop. Leaving him in the living room, I go to my bedroom to change into a pair of jeans and a T-shirt. Despite the fact that something is definitely happening in my belly, I yank at the waistband of my jeans to keep them from falling. Yeah, a meal would be good. I glance in the mirror and am horrified by the circles under my eyes and hollows beneath my cheekbones. I look like death.

And I would know.

When I walk back into the living room, I find him in the kitchen, opening and closing cabinets.

“Let me guess, you’re going to call Child Services because I don’t have enough food in my house, and I’m pregnant and underage?”

“Actually, I was seeing what I could do to fix these. So your house isn’t falling apart around you.”

“Doesn’t matter.” I shrug. “I can’t pay the mortgage

anymore, anyway."

He opens the front door and nods to me. "Come on. Hop in the truck, and let's grab a meal."

I want to protest and say I'll drive my own car because at the rate I'm going, I fully expect Ben to sell me to some pimp outside of town. But my car is still a wreck, and deep in my gut, I know he'd never do that. So instead, I lock up the house and climb into Ol' Sally. The step up into the truck makes me woozy. I flop onto my seat and hold my head in my hands as he climbs in.

"Gracie, I know this is a stupid question, but are you okay?"

I lean back and stare out his windshield.

All the normal answers pop into my head. *Of course, I'm fine. It's nothing, thanks for asking.* But instead of any of those, I turn to him and say, "I honestly don't know."

He nods and starts the truck.

****

We pull into a diner on the outskirts of town. I appreciate that he's taken me away from any place and anyone I may know.

He cuts the engine and turns to me. "Okay to go in and have a bite?"

My growling stomach answers for me.

Nodding, he jumps down and walks around Ol' Sally to get my door for me. We walk into the diner, side by side, and for the first time in days, I don't feel so alone.

As we slide into opposite sides of a booth, the smell of the restaurant overtakes me, and my stomach begins to howl.

Ben raises his eyebrows in response and flags down

the waitress.

"Two cheeseburger platters—medium-well, with extra fries, please." He turns to me. "Seltzer?"

"Please." I nod.

She finishes scribbling our order in her notepad and is about to leave when he reaches out and touches her arm. Then he drops his hand, looks up at her, and smiles. I swear, she blushes.

"Could we have a rush on them, please? My daughter and I are both famished."

Daughter.

Despite the warm feeling in my belly, I shift uncomfortably in my seat. No man has ever called me his daughter before—and the thing is, I kind of like it.

The waitress glances at me, and her stern expression softens. Suddenly, despite her harsh Emo makeup, she looks ten years younger.

"Your daughter? Of course." She smiles at me like I'm twelve, even though she's probably only a few years older than me.

With one final smile at Ben, she scurries off, and I level my gaze on him.

"What?" He seems clueless.

Inside, I'm totally freaking out about him calling me his daughter. I liked it way too much, so I need to change the subject.

"Do you always wield that kind of power over women?"

"What power?"

"You know. The kind where they get all flustered and giggly when you're near."

He leans forward and rests his forearms on the table. "Gracie, I hardly think anyone is flustered around me."

"I am," I confide. "But not because I'm crushing on you. It's because I don't know what to think of you."

He sits back. "I know that. That's why I'm here. To try to set things straight."

"Can things be set straight?" I look him in the eyes. "I trusted Josh. And you. I gave up my entire life thinking I was going to be with people who cared for me. People who wanted a life with me as much as I wanted a life with them. And now"—I lean forward and lower my voice—"I find out he believes all of these *things*, and I am, as usual, fucked."

"Gracie"—his voice is low and calm—"you're not fucked. I would never let that happen to you. I told you, that's what I'm here for. To work this out with you."

"What is there to work out?" I search his eyes for the answer.

"How about a job to start?" he asks earnestly. "And a mortgage payment."

"I don't want the house." It isn't until I say it that I realize it's the truth.

"Fine. Then we'll sell the house. You'll get a nest egg for college, and you can move in with Josh and me."

"Are you kidding? You think I'm going to trust either one of you—"

My thought is interrupted by the smiling waitress delivering our food. It smells so good, I forget I'm with Ben, pick up my cheeseburger, and take an enormous bite. I force it down and take another.

"I grabbed someone else's order," she whispers as she winks at Ben. "They ordered the same thing, so they'll just wait for yours. They'll never know the difference. So, um, is there anything else?"

"I don't think so." Ben glances at me and chuckles

as he answers.

I'm sure I look like some wild animal attacking my prey, but I don't care.

"Well, if there is anything, *anything* you need"—she emphasizes her words—"just wave me over, and I'll come running."

I glance up to see she's giving a full-toothed smile to Ben, but he doesn't take the bait.

"I think we're fine," he answers. "Thank you very much for your help."

Finally, after an even brighter smile and a hand on Ben's shoulder, she walks away. I take another bite of my cheeseburger. For the past couple of days, I've been lying in my bed thinking about what I would say to Josh and Ben when I saw them. Now here I am, face to face with the enemy, and I've got nothing.

My cheeseburger is almost gone, so I begin to slow my eating. As I pop a fry into my mouth, I glance up at Ben to see he's staring at me.

"What?" I sit back and wash down the burger with my seltzer. The fries are so damned good I pop another and another. I think if this were my last supper, I'd be okay with it.

"I want to talk, Gracie."

"So? Talk." I keep my eyes on him.

"I don't know where to begin. I've been dreading this day since Josh began having his delusions. That's what his beliefs are called, medically. Delusions. I knew someday he'd fall in love, and this would all come out."

"Is that why you didn't like me before?" I nod to the door like it was yesterday.

"I've always liked you, Gracie," he continues. "I just had a hard time with it all. I knew that one day he'd want to get married, and that person—you—would have complete control of him." He drops his chin and looks up at me. "I was afraid that when his delusions got grander, well, you'd lock him away somewhere."

"You think I would do that?" I whisper. "You really don't know me at all."

"It's not you. Gracie, you have to understand. I've spent eighteen years worrying about him and stressing over his illness. Making sure he takes his meds daily. Making sure he doesn't do anything to harm himself."

"I do understand. It was four years for me, but I think I know exactly how you feel," I answer as my anger begins to dissipate.

He nods. "Yes, I guess you, more than anyone else, would understand."

"But, Ben, what I don't understand is, why didn't anyone tell me all this before?"

"I just assumed he would."

"He didn't." I shake my head. "Not until the other day when we spread my mother's ashes. And truthfully, I'm pretty freaked out about it all." I place my hands on my belly. "I'm carrying his child, Ben." I take a deep breath and ask the question I've been wondering for the past couple of days. "Will the child be…like Josh, too?"

"I don't know."

He smiles sadly, and I nod.

"Thank you for telling me the truth."

"Gracie, I never wanted to lie. Not to you and not to anyone. I don't believe in lying."

"For someone who doesn't believe in it, you sure do a lot of it."

"What do you mean?"

I stare at my plate. "You just told that waitress I was

your daughter." My words are meek.

"Aren't you?"

He reaches his hand across the table, waiting for mine. I glance up to see he's looking me straight in the eyes. For the first time, maybe ever, my eyes feel prickly. I think of Josh and Ben. Of my lost job and my late mother. Of my father, whom I've never met. Of my high school that I may never finish, and this baby that will be here long before I'm ready for him. Suddenly, tears start flowing, and they just won't stop.

"Hey, hey." Ben comforts me as he slides out of his side of the booth and comes to mine. He puts an arm around me and pulls me close.

I blubber into his chest.

"Gracie, honey, I know it hurts like hell now, but I promise everything will work out."

"How?" I'm crying so hard I can barely get a word out. "How do you know?"

"Because everything always works out for Gracie Girl, doesn't it?"

I know that voice. Lifting my head off Ben's shoulder, I wipe my snot on a paper napkin and turn toward the person standing by our table.

"Louise?" My vision is blurry, but it's definitely her. She's holding a pot of steaming coffee. "You're working here?" My spirits rise as I imagine her happy and set in her new job.

"No one else would hire me," she says coldly. "Imagine that? No one wants a middle-aged mom of three sick boys who needs to make good money with more time off than on. So I'm stuck working here, and most of the time, it's the late shift. The boys stay with my neighbor, who plops them in front of her television all night. They can't even get their homework finished because the TV is so damned loud."

"I—I'm sorry, Louise." My cheeks heat with embarrassment—both because she saw me cry and mostly because it's my fault she's miserable.

"Oh well." She sighs. "So my boys won't get an education. My kids won't be the ones who break out of this Godforsaken cycle. Maybe their kids will."

"Louise."

"Hello." Ben interrupts our conversation. "I'm Ben. Gracie's dad. Could you please tell me what's going on here?"

"Her dad?" The expression on Louise's face is smug and angry. "So you didn't just get a handsome husband, Gracie. You got yourself a new daddy, too."

"Louise, please." I hear myself pleading with her, so I turn to Ben. "Louise and I worked together at the Shakes 'n' Slaw."

"We didn't work together. Gracie was my manager," she corrects.

"Fine. I was one of the managers. When I found out about the cameras, I called the police before I spoke with Louise. I cost her the best job she had."

She leans over our table. Her voice is low, and her words are tipped with venom. "You cost me *everything*, Gracie. Every ounce of hope I'd ever had. And if I didn't need this job so desperately, I'd tell you—and every other customer in this damned place—exactly what I think of you."

"That's enough." Ben's voice is a low growl.

Louise straightens up and steps back so quickly it seems like he's just slapped her across the face.

"Gracie did what she was legally obligated to do,"

he explains. "She had no choice. And she saved you from years of potential nightmares and embarrassment."

"It was my decision to make."

"No, it certainly was not. You just told me you weren't management. Gracie was. It was her responsibility, and she did what she had to do. You think keeping a convenient job is worth your self-respect? You think you don't care about being filmed? That Jerry is just going to keep those videos to himself? You're not as smart as you seem. What happens when those boys of yours are old enough to be on the internet? Do you want them finding videos of their mom?"

"No…" She looks calm.

"Of course not. You should be thanking Gracie, not yelling at her. Now, I think it's best if you leave her be. If you have something to say to her, you can say it to me." Ben pulls me tighter to him.

Louise bites the corner of her lip and nods before scurrying off to the next table. As she pours their coffee, she glances at me out of the corner of her eye.

"You did the right thing," Ben whispers.

"Maybe." I watch Louise walk from table to table, chatting it up. "But she's still miserable."

"You're not in charge of someone else's happiness, Gracie."

"Her dream was always to make jewelry." I watch Louise work as I speak. "She makes these pretty cuffs and earrings and necklaces all out of wood…"

"Really?" He sounds impressed.

"And here she is. Pouring coffee for twelve hours a day, knowing that her sons will never have a chance. For anything." I turn back to Ben. "Why is life so hard?"

"I wish I knew, Gracie. I really wish I knew. You

ready?"

I nod, and he helps me out of the booth. Together, we leave the restaurant.

As we sit side by side in Ol' Sally, I speak softly. "Do you think Josh…well, that any of it is real?" I stare out the front window.

He turns to me, and I meet his gaze. "There are so many things in the world that we don't understand. All I know for sure is that everything happens for a reason, and every person you meet is in your life for a reason."

"You believe that?"

"Yes." He nods. "Gracie, honey, I can't tell you what to do about Josh. You're pretty much a grown-up. But I will tell you that no matter what you decide, you have to let me help you. You need to finish high school and get a college education."

"It's a little late for college," I counter.

"No. Community college is a viable option."

"That's what Mom used to tell me."

"Then listen to her. To both of us. You also need money. A good job where you're not on your feet while you're pregnant. And then you'll need help when the baby comes. Please let me be that person who helps you."

"What about Josh?" I whisper.

Ben exhales loudly. "Josh is an incredible man. He's smart and capable, and I know he would do anything for you. But he also needs care. He needs someone who listens without arguing with him. Someone who makes sure he stays on his meds. Someone who understands that he believes all of this."

I nod.

"I'm certain you could be that person, Gracie. Look

at the way you took care of Nora. The thing is, do you want to live the rest of your life around illness?"

Before I can answer, he goes on.

"Remember, the toughest part of all of this is about to come. He's convinced that the day his child is born, he'll pass away. You both will."

"I know. We'll be passing our energy to the baby." I take a deep breath and wrap my arms around myself. "Ben? How did I heal so quickly after my accident? How did your cancer disappear?"

"I don't know the answer to that. I wish I did. Gracie"—he shifts in his seat—"the thing I've never told anyone, well, except Nora at the end, is what I'm most scared of. I'm terrified that he'll try to hurt himself—or you—just to fulfill the prophecy of his fate." He rests a hand on the wheel and sits back. "When it comes to Josh, Gracie, I'm afraid it's a decision only you can make."

"But, do you think…any of it can be true? That he's a healer? That he's here to find his mate and make a child who will save the world?"

Ben takes a deep breath and releases a long sigh. "Not to be coy here, but like I said, that's a decision only you can make."

I nod as he starts the car, and we drive away.

When we reach my house, I thank Ben for dinner and jump out of Ol' Sally. I climb the few front steps, slip my key into the lock, and without turning back to look at Ben, I step inside.

Standing there in the cold, quiet house, I sense death all around me. The scariest part is, it's not just my mother's death I sense. It's my death as well.

It feels like the walls are closing in on me, so I fight to take a deep breath. Glancing around at all the wood paneling and heavy wood furniture, I begin to panic… It's like I'm in my very own coffin.

And truthfully, that may be exactly where I am.

Chapter Twenty-Seven

Josh

"Gracie?" I peer in through the kitchen window, but she's not there. She must have snuck back off to her bedroom.

Crap. I resume my pacing around the perimeter of her house like I have done every damned day for the past three days. Ever since that day we said goodbye to Nora and sprinkled her ashes.

Since that moment, I have spent almost every moment of every day here—sitting on the steps or walking the grounds—hell, I've even slept in my car—all in the hopes that she'll talk to me and let me explain.

I know she's awake because I saw her in her bedroom window, looking out. Dad dropped her off less than an hour ago now, and I've been waiting for her to answer even just one of my texts or a single knock on the door.

The hell with this. I can't lose my chance at winning Gracie back. Jogging up the front steps, I lift my hand to knock—

The door opens.

"Hey, Josh."

"Gracie. Hi."

We stand there staring at one another. I want to say a million things to her, but instead, I reach out and pull her tight to my chest.

She falls against me willingly.

"Gracie," I murmur into her hair. "I've missed you. So, so much."

"I've missed you, too," she says, and then she peels herself off my chest and looks up at me. "Let's sit for a minute and talk." Her eyes are glistening, and her voice is soft.

I take her by the hand and move her toward the couch, but she shakes her head.

"No. I can't stay in this house any longer. Let's sit on the steps, please."

We make our way out onto the tiny concrete front steps of her house and sit shoulder to shoulder. This is the place where our relationship began, and it feels so freaking good to be this close to her again.

"Gracie—"

"Wait. Please." She turns to look at me. "I have some things I want to ask you. First, why did you wait so long to tell me?"

"When you told me you couldn't get pregnant, I thought you couldn't be the one. Despite your birthmark and the feelings I had for you. So I saved you from the rest of it. I meant to protect you, I swear. Not to alienate you."

"Don't ever keep anything that important from me again."

"Okay." I nod in agreement. At least she's talking about our future.

"Next, I know what you told me. That you are chosen, and I guess, in a way, so am I…?"

She looks up at me with those beautiful eyes.

"Yes. You have been chosen, too."

She nods. "And you're telling me we both die when

this baby is born, and Ben raises him? And then, when our son is old enough, he goes on to save the world?"

"Yes."

As she processes this, I notice that she didn't ask me what I *think* happens—she asks what *will* happen. It's a small distinction, but for someone who's been told he's crazy for most of his life, it's a big one.

"Will the world be different then? After our child saves it? I've never thought that a world that allows so much pain and suffering would be worth saving. But my mother always believed it was. She believed the good far outweighed the bad."

"She was right."

"Maybe. Will it be different?"

"I hope so."

"Me too."

Tentatively, I reach out and take her hand. She turns our hands over, interlacing her fingers in mine.

"Gracie, this idea of our destiny. Of our fate. It's a lot to process. I know that. If you need time…"

"No." She shakes her head. "No, I don't need time. You believe it, and that's all I need to know. I love you. I would love you if you had cancer or took a job where you were away from me for months at a time. The practical side of me says that if what you say is true, then there's nothing we can do anyway. We might as well spend our last moments on earth together."

My heart races from adrenaline. "And the impractical?"

"The impractical side of me says that I believe in fate, too."

"You do?"

She nods. "I do believe we were meant to find one

another. I believe you came to my school at the time I needed someone most."

"Yeah." I reach out with my free hand and tuck a stray hair behind her ear.

She closes her eyes and lets out a small murmur. "Mmm…that feels good."

Sliding my hand down, I rest it on her cheek. "And I think you found me just at the time I was beginning to doubt everything. Doubt myself."

"And now?"

I pull her tight to my side and lean down to kiss her on top of her head. "And now, I know exactly who I am and where I belong."

She pulls away and turns to face me. Her brows knit together, and a serious expression hardens her face. "But here's the thing, Josh. Whatever we're facing, we're not facing it without a fight."

"What do you mean?"

"I mean, whatever time we have left, we are going to make the most of it."

"You mean, like travel the world?"

She shakes her head. "No. I mean the opposite. I'll explain, but to start, you need to promise me you'll stay on your meds. I don't know all of the details yet, but I know Ben believes in them, and I trust him. Do you agree?"

"Yeah. Of course." I smile at her. "And in return, you're going to graduate high school."

She bites the inside of her cheek. "That's the part of all of this that's really going to need a miracle."

"Bio?"

"Yup. All my other grades are there. It's just damned Gibbons. He failed my paper, so all I have left is the end-of-year exam. I'll need a ninety-five to get a D in the class. That's the only way I can graduate."

"We have…" I glance at my watch. "A few days left to prep for the exam. Go grab your book."

"Now?" She smiles, and her eyes search mine.

"When you're not guaranteed tomorrow—"

"—All you have is today. I get it." She stands and looks down at me, smiling.

I catch her hand and hold her there. "What did you mean about a fight? That we're not facing our future without a fight. What fight?"

"I have no intention of losing you, Josh. Or making Ben raise another baby on his own. We're just beginning our lives together, and we're going to say, 'screw you' to a fate that wants to take it all away."

My stomach flips. *How? How can I tell my life's calling to fuck off?*

She sits next to me again. "I'm not saying you won't fulfill your part of the prophecy. You and I, we're making that child we're supposed to make. I just think we both need to fight to stay here with him. You have to promise me that you won't do anything to yourself. You can't hurt yourself because you think that's the fulfillment of your prophecy. The world needs you, Josh. Not just your child."

"Gracie"—my voice is soft—"are you messing with me? Are you patronizing me because you think I'm…crazy?"

She shakes her head. "No, Josh, no. Look, there are so many things in this world I can't explain. Why good people get sick. Why people do evil things to one another. What happens to our energy when we die. But one thing I do know—intimately—is illness. Maybe I can't understand your prophecy, so what? What I do know is that you're not sick."

Those are the kindest words anyone has ever spoken to me. I'm so overcome, all I can do is reach out and pull her to me. "Thank you, Gracie," I mumble as I hold her tight.

"Yes." She pulls back and looks into my eyes. "But we can't give up. This won't be easy, but we have to fight. Both of us. Fight like hell to change our fate."

"Us against fate?" I ask.

She smiles. "Us against fate."

Then she leans forward and kisses me.

Chapter Twenty-Eight

Gracie

Five Years Later

"Where should I drop this, Gracie?" Ben's hovering between the kitchen and living room, holding a package that was just delivered.

"In the dining room would be great, thanks." I know I look like I'm standing at the kitchen sink, handwashing dishes, but what I'm really doing is staring out the picture window, watching Evie. I can't pull my gaze away from her. She's in a safe, gated area of the beach, just off the house. Her arms are out to her sides, and she's spinning in circles in the sand. Celia's diamond glimmers on the chain around her neck.

"She's going to lose that diamond one day, Ben. When we moved to the beach, I told you we should pack that away."

"Nah." He walks up to me and looks over my shoulder and out the window at Evie. "Doesn't she get dizzy?"

"Nope. She's such a stinker." I grin at her. Out of the corner of my eye I glance at him and shake my head.

"What?"

"What, what? Look at her." I motion with my shoulder since my hands are elbow-deep in sudsy water. "She looks more and more like you every day."

"You think so?" He scrubs his beard.

"Aside from the beard and the gray hair, yes." I chuckle. "It's not just her skin color. It's her curly black hair, the deep brown eyes, the high cheekbones. It's like Josh and I weren't even involved."

"Seems only fair since Josh got so much of Celia." He shakes his head, smiling.

"I suppose so." I finish scrubbing the stubborn prep dishes from dinner, thinking about how much has changed and how fast. It was just a few years ago, four actually—when Evie was born—that Ben bought this house.

He steps away from me and inhales deeply. "Is that chicken pot pie I smell?"

"In your dreams." I nod to the oven. "It's tofu pot pie, and you know it. Why is it around six p.m. every night you forget we're all vegetarians? The pot pie will be done in twenty. By the way, you get to scrub the baking dish tonight. And no letting it soak overnight and leaving it for me till morning. It's only taken me a few years of living in the same house, but I've caught on to your ways."

"I was going to teach Evie how to rebuild a carburetor tonight."

I keep my hands submerged as I turn toward him. "Ben. Evie can't have a late night. School starts tomorrow. And besides that, she is the only child going into preschool who knows how to fix a flat and change a car battery." I rinse the last dish and place it in the dish rack. Then I grab the towel from the stove and dry my hands.

He shrugs. "Good. Now she'll know how to rebuild a carburetor, too." He claps his hands together. "We're moving onto bodywork soon."

I nod, swallowing hard. "You miss him, huh."

"Yes."

"Me too."

"I know." He claps his hands together again and rubs them like he's trying to start a fire. "Come on. Open your package, Gracie."

"What's the rush? I ordered paper goods because with the cabinetry installations you have coming up over the next few weeks, I'm not going to have any ti—" I walk over to his beautiful handmade table. "Ben." I clamp my hands on my hips. "How many times have I told you not to put anything but dishes on this gorgeous table? Think of all your hard work."

"You said it was just some paper goods. How could that damage anything?"

"Still." I lift the box to move it to the counter, but it's heavier than I expect. "Wait." I peek out the window to make sure Evie's fine, and I catch her trying to open the gate. "Hang on a minute, Ben." I walk to the door and push it open.

"She okay?" His voice is strong and concerned.

"She's fine. Evie?" I call out. "Move away from the gate, honey, please. I've asked you not to touch that. You can't leave the gate or the beach."

She turns and runs to the back porch and picks up her plastic pony. I exhale.

"I was just out there. There's no one around," Ben assures me.

"I know." I shake off the odd feeling I have and turn to Ben. "It's just, we're close to the brush, and the woods are right there…" I take a deep breath and exhale, releasing my stress. "Anyway, back to the box. Did you order something?"

He shrugs. “It’s the end of summer. I might have added a thing or two.”

“What did you buy her now?” I grab a short knife from the butcher block and puncture the packing tape.

“Careful.” Ben stands next to me. “You don’t know what’s in there.”

“Apparently, I don’t.” Zipping the knife carefully, I open the box, use both hands to remove the packing material, and then pull out the contents. “Notebooks, pens and…” I dig around and find a few folders and a pencil pouch. I place them on the table. “Ben, it’s very sweet, but you just took her school shopping last week. She’s set. Remember those cute folders with the puppies on them? They’re already packed in her backpack and waiting on the peg over there.” I nod to the coat rack where we hang our jackets and bags.

“It’s not for her.”

He raises his eyebrows in a way that reminds me of Josh. I sigh.

“Ben, I don’t understand. We run your business online. You know that. Software and spreadsheets. We don’t need the old-school supplies.” I glance at the notebooks and pens again. “Wait, this isn’t some elderly thing setting in, is it?” I tease. “Want me to go over your website with you again or explain this newfangled thing we call the internet?”

He chuckles. “No, thanks. I’m fifty-eight. Not a hundred and eight. And this isn’t for the business, Gracie. It’s for you.”

“Why would I need this?”

“For college.”

“What?” I look up at him.

“It’s been a few years since you graduated high

school."

"I barely graduated."

"But you did. Against all odds."

"Ben, I don't need to go to school. We have a great business. I'm busy."

"Yes, but you deserve to do something for yourself."

"I do plenty for myself." Moving to the oven, I open the door and check the pie. Then I close it quickly to keep the heat in.

"No, you don't. You run the business. You mother Evie. You keep me on track. And think of all the years you took care of your sick mother. You're a caretaker, Gracie. Go to school. Become a nurse or a doctor."

"A doctor?" I chortle.

"Why not?"

"Did you forget my D in bio?"

"That's nothing. Your mother was dying. You were working more than any adult I know. Cut yourself some slack. It's a miracle you passed."

A miracle. Thanks to Josh and our late-night study sessions.

"Thanks, Ben." I turn my back to the oven, and the heat warms my legs. Crossing my arms, I stare at him. "My job is to raise her. You know that." I move my head to glance out the window and turn back to Ben.

"I do. And I understand that you're doing it in a way to honor Josh's beliefs. And it's one of the many things I admire about you, Gracie." He takes a deep breath and lets it go as he walks over, closer to me. "Listen, I don't know what we have out there. Maybe she will do something great to save the world. I don't know. But I do know what you've got up here"—he taps the side of my head—"and in here." He taps my heart. "Make a life,

Gracie. I understand what being lonely is like. She's going to need her mom for whatever she has coming."

I freeze, gripping the counter behind me. I lower my chin and raise my gaze to meet Ben's. "You don't think, there's no way she'll…"

He takes me by the shoulders and looks me straight in the eyes. "Despite everything, the one thing I can promise you is that the buck stops with her. We'll make sure of it."

I nod.

He releases me and goes to dig through his old canvas bag on a peg near the door. It hangs next to Evie's overly stuffed backpack. He pulls out a pamphlet and brings it to me. "Start at a community college. I spoke to the admissions director yesterday, and she said you can still enroll. Live your life. We can afford the tuition for this and med school if you decide you want to go that way. I'll watch Evie whenever I can."

"You already do too much, Ben." I twirl my wedding band. "Evie and I, we're not your—"

"Don't you dare say family." He scowls as he speaks.

I take a step back. "I was going to say responsibility."

"Of course you are. If you two aren't my responsibility, then what's my purpose?"

My heart aches for him.

He shakes his head. "Gracie. We're a family. And I love you. You're my daughter. You know that."

I nod, fighting the now familiar ache in my throat.

"Good. Now, enough with all this corny, cringy stuff. Could we please set an extra couple of plates? Louise and the boys are going to join us."

"Louise and the boys?" I can't fight my smile. "Are you two becoming a thing?"

"It's only business, Gracie. You know that."

"But you get along so well, and you're both lonely…"

"We work together, that's all. She does some of the most beautiful wood finish work I have ever seen."

"I'm just saying that—"

"How about we serve up some of that tofu casserole I like to pretend is chicken?" He cuts me off.

I try to hide my smirk. Obviously, I've touched on something.

"Don't know what I did to be surrounded by vegetarians," he mumbles good-naturedly as he walks to the kitchen door. "You know," he adds, "if we don't have enough casserole, they can have some of mine. Or, better yet, I'll order a pizza—"

"Nice try, Ben. We're keeping your cholesterol down. There's plenty of casserole for everyone."

He smiles at me as he opens the kitchen door and bounds down the porch steps. The door closes behind him.

I walk to the door and push it open to see them better. There's Evie, spinning again, but when she spots him, she stops, and her whole being lights up. Her arms go high into the air, and she runs straight for him, her hair flowing in the breeze behind her.

"Ahhh!" he yells as he turns around and runs through the gate and away from her.

She laughs and chases him at full speed. They get a good distance down the beach and near the water, and then he turns and crouches low. He squat-walks with both of his hands, reaching for her like he's a robot crab trying to catch her. It's a game they play often. She spins on her heels, giggling, and runs from him, but he's quick. He grabs her by her small waist and swings her around and around, up and down, like she's the beautiful festoon on a carousel horse. In her little blue dress, she looks like a bluebird of happiness flying up and down. And her grandfather is there to make sure she never falls.

Ben lets her down onto the sand and then turns away. She runs at him. "Grandpa!" She squeals, jumping onto his back.

My breath hitches. I wish Josh could see this. A warmth floods over me, starting in my belly and rushing outward, through my arms and legs, before finally gathering at my heart.

Ben hoists her up onto his shoulders and carries her across the beach. They walk toward me, but suddenly, I can't get to them fast enough and rush out onto the beach to meet them.

"Hi, Mommy," she says as she leans down, hugging Ben.

Celia's ring tangles in his curly salt-and-pepper hair, and her dress bunches around his shoulders. He reaches up and dusts her bare feet with his hands.

"All right, little weasel." He lifts her up off his shoulders and flies her high into the sky. Then, gently, he places her down.

It's a move they've done a million times before, but tonight…

She links her little hand in mine. "Mommy! I did seventeen twirls. Did you see me?"

She gazes up at me with giant eyes, and that's when I see him. Deep in there. It doesn't matter that the eye color is Ben's. Josh is in there.

“Mommy?” She wiggles her nose, scratching it, and then turns to Ben. “Grandpa? Why is Mommy weird?”

Ben looks over at me, and I can see concern etched in his brows. There have been so many years of worry stored deep in those grooves.

But he doesn’t need to worry. I’m fine. Really fine. A wave of gratitude passes over me, and then my cheeks flush hot, and my jaw aches. My nose burns, and my breath quickens. I know this feeling now—I know what it’s like to cry—but today is different. Today, my eyes feel like they’re trying to escape from my head, so I shut them tight and will them to stay in.

Evie scrunches up her face and then smiles. “Watch me, Mommy!” Breaking free from me, she holds her arms to the sides and spins and spins again.

Ben stands by me, not making a sound. The moment is too special.

Our silence is interrupted by a car door slamming.

“That’s Louise,” Ben announces. He won’t admit it, but I hear the lilt in his voice. “Let me just go see if she needs a hand.”

“She doesn’t need to be cramped in the guest house with the boys,” I call after him. “Why don’t you ask her if she’d like to stay over in the main house? We have plenty of room.”

“Not going to happen, Gracie,” he answers.

Chuckling, I go back into the kitchen and slide the casserole out of the oven while Evie plays with her toy horse on the porch.

Suddenly, that weird feeling I’ve been fighting subsides, and my body feels like it’s wrapped in a pure silk cocoon.

But I know this feeling… I’ve felt this way before,

and there's only one person who's responsible.

"Josh?"

I spin around, and he's standing in front of me, smiling.

"You weren't supposed to be home for another two months!"

I throw my arms around his neck, and he holds me tight.

"I missed you too much," he whispers into my ear.

"I missed you, too."

"Daddy!" Gracie squeals as she comes running into the kitchen.

"Be careful of the hot oven!" I warn as she runs at Josh full tilt and jumps onto his back.

He spins her around, and she wedges herself between us. It's all so good I hold on extra tight.

"Josh," I whisper as I come up for air, "are you…" I'm careful how I ask this. "Are you supposed to be home?"

He smiles. "Yes. I'm doing okay. Better than okay. My doctors said I'm doing really well."

"So, how long are you home?" My heart races as I wait for his answer.

"Two days. I have some more work to do before I'm ready to come home for good."

Nodding, I turn to Evie. "Evie, please go wash your hands for dinner."

"Okay, Mommy!" She runs off for the bathroom, leaving me alone with Josh.

"Josh." My heart is heavy, and a flood of words come out before I can stop them. "I never wanted you to go. Not to that place or anywhere. You have to know that. Neither did Ben. I was sure we would all be fine together. But when you started telling Evie that she could do…*things*…things that were different from other people—that she had abilities, well, we had to protect her."

"I know that. I know how hard you fought to keep me home. It was my choice. I needed some help."

I take his hand and place it on my heart. "It's us against fate, Josh. We didn't die when Evie was born. The prophecy was wrong."

"The prophecy *was* wrong," he agrees. "Gracie, all I want is to be with you and to be a good dad to Evie. And as long as I stay on my meds—"

"Hello?" We're interrupted by Louise's voice.

I pull myself away from Josh and smile at him. Then I turn to the door. "Hi, Louise."

Just then, the boys, Bo, Dillion, and Dalton—who aren't really boys anymore—rush in behind her with Evie in tow. She claps with delight.

"Dinner is almost ready," I tell them. "Boys, why don't you go play with Evie on the beach for a few minutes? Do you mind watching her for me?"

"We've got it, Gracie," Bo mumbles. They take Evie by the hand and run out as quickly as they came in.

"Just stay out of the water and away from the brush and woods!" I call out, then I turn to Josh and smile again.

Louise clears her throat. "Gracie Girl, I'm gonna go see if Ben needs help bringing our bags into the guest house." She's beaming at us. "I'll let him know Josh is home."

"Okay, Louise, thanks."

She stops short in the kitchen doorway. "Speak of the devil."

"Josh?" Ben rushes into the kitchen and embraces his son.

Suddenly, I'm sniffling again. I close my eyes, and when I open them, one hot, giant tear falls down my cheek, and then another and another.

I'm crying.

"Gracie?" Josh leaves his dad and walks up to me. He pulls me into his arms. "Are you okay?"

I nod. Looking into his gorgeous eyes, all of my tension falls away. "I'm more than okay. For once, I don't know if I dare say it, but I think, well, I think everything is perfect."

No sooner do I say it…

"Gracie! Josh!" Bo, Dillion, and Dalton come running back into the house. All three are wheezing and out of breath.

"What is it?" That nagging feeling in my gut feels like it leaked into my bloodstream. My heart is pounding, and fear has taken over. "Where's Evie?"

"She went into the brush, and we lost her."

"Why the hell did you let her go in there?" I hear Louise ask, but I'm already gone, out of the house, rushing toward the woods.

Josh and Ben rush after me, passing me on the beach. Within a minute, the three of us are in the brush, looking for Evie.

"Evie?" I call out as loudly as I can.

The men echo me, and soon Louise and her boys are there, too. All of us dig through the thick brush and the dense marsh. Ben runs off into the woods.

My heart is pounding in my ears. I can't hear anything but the sound of it and my racing breath. Fear and doubt, which came rushing into me as fast as a bullet, are now at war for control of my brain. But no matter which one wins, I'm screwed.

Then the thought pops up. The one I refuse to let myself think except in the middle of the darkest nights, when I wake alone, drenched in sweat but shivering:

What if the prophecy wasn't wrong? What if Evie can't live because we didn't die?

"*Evie!*" I howl as we continue to canvas the beach.

I don't dare turn my head, but I hear Louise on her cell giving directions to the police.

"Hurry!" is the last word I catch, but no matter how fast the emergency workers come, it won't be fast enough.

They're not just battling time. They're fighting against fate.

And right now, in the blackest regions of my soul, my deepest fear rears its horrifying head. I am terrified that even love can't conquer fate.

Fate always wins.

"Evie? Evie?" I call out through my aching throat.

Our small group continues to spread out to cover more ground, and I know by now Ben must be deep in the woods. But how will he know which direction to turn?

"*Evie!*" The low brush near the wood catches me. I trip and fall forward, bracing myself with my hands. "Oh, ow." I stand and look at them. The thorns and branches have left my hands bloody and scratched, but who cares right now? "Evie!" I choke out.

"Gracie! Josh!"

I whip my head toward the woods, and there is Ben, walking out, carrying Evie in his arms.

Her little body is limp. She's not moving.

"*No!*" I scream as I rush toward them. I hold out my arms, and Ben slides her into mine. My bloodied hands are staining her dress and legs.

"She was at the base of a tree," he tells me. "Just lying there."

"Evie?" I call to her, shaking her slightly. "Evie, baby? You need to wake up for me. Please."

"I'll flag down the ambulance!" Louise yells as she and the boys run off toward the house.

Josh places a hand on my shoulder.

I whip around to face him. "Can't you do anything?" I plead. The doctors warned us not to play into Josh's fantasies, but right now, I have no choice.

"Gracie"—his voice is soft—"we need to get her to a doctor."

"There's no time!" Suddenly, a long-repressed memory comes barreling forth. "That day of the accident. My accident. How did I come back?" I'm speaking so fast that my words are tripping on my tongue. "I—I know you think you're not a healer because of what happened to the little boy in the hospital—"

"You heard me?"

"Yes. You helped me, Josh. And you helped Ben when he had cancer. Can't you help Evie, too?" Desperate, I hold her out to him.

"Gracie." It's Ben. He steps up so he's standing shoulder to shoulder with Josh. "We can't do this, you know that. Let's get Evie to the hospital."

I snap my head around toward him. "What I know, Ben, is that you have spent your life protecting your child. Now it's my time to protect mine." I look from Ben to Josh. "Josh," I plead. "You can do this. Whatever is going on with her, bring her back to us. We dodged fate before. We can do it again. Please. It's us against fate, right?"

He focuses his dark eyes on Evie, and then closes them. After a breath, he reaches out toward her and—

"Mommy?"

"Evie?"

Her eyes open, and she smiles a bright, beautiful smile at me before Josh ever had the chance to touch her.

"Oh my God, Evie." I roll her toward me, against my body, and hold her as tightly as I dare.

Tears stream down my face as Josh holds us both.

"Evie, don't ever do that again," I whisper.

She wiggles in my arms, and I lessen my grasp, giving her some space.

She looks up at me. "Don't cry, Mommy." With one chubby little hand, she wipes away my tears. "Everything will be okay."

I slide her around onto my hip so I can look at her. "Why did you leave, Evie? I tell you over and over not to go into the brush, and especially not to go into the woods."

"I had to help."

My breath catches. "Help what?"

I glance at Josh, and his brow is furrowed. Ben steps closer to us.

"Evie? Help what?"

"There was a bunny. He needed my help."

"What kind of help?" I hold my breath and glance at Ben.

"He was tired. Too tired. He was going to die, so I helped him."

"How?" The word feels like an ice cube in my mouth.

"Like this." She closes her eyes and holds out her hands.

"You sent him good thoughts?" I ask, trying desperately to make this anything other than what it actually is.

"No, silly." She opens her eyes and smiles, and her cheeks puff up.

"Then how?" Josh asks the question I don't dare.

Holding my breath, I tuck my hair behind my ear. Evie frowns as she notices the scrapes on my palm.

"The same way I can help Mommy."

Before I can pull my hand away, she reaches out, takes one of my injured hands, and turns it palm up. I know that I should drop my hand, but I can't. I have to know.

Evie lays her soft hand on my palm. Then she closes her eyes. When she opens them, my palm is still dirty and bloody, but the scrapes have been healed.

"See?" She shrugs.

"How long have you known you could do that?" Josh asks.

"I don't know." She smiles at him again.

"Evie, you have to promise you'll listen to us. You can't go wandering off, no matter who needs help, okay?" Josh's voice is stern and paternal.

"Okay."

"And what you did for Mommy, you need to keep that our little secret. Do you understand?"

"Why?" Her face scrunches up into a scowl.

"Because it's one of the many things that make you so special, and we don't want other people to feel bad because they can't do it." He explains it in a way she understands.

“Okay. I’m glad you’re home, Daddy.”

She reaches out to him, and we slide her from my arms to his. He holds her tight.

“I’m glad I’m home, too.”

“And…” Did I truly just witness this? All of it? What the hell is happening? Have Ben and I been wrong? All this time…? “Evie, I think maybe Daddy…if he wants to…maybe he should be staying home with us now, for good.” I raise my eyebrows at Josh. “What do you think, Daddy?”

“I think there’s no place I would rather be.”

I smile at him as I rub her back. “Evie? Are you hungry?”

“Yes!” she squeals.

I turn to Josh and mouth, *I’m sorry.* But really, how can I even begin to apologize for this?

Josh just shakes his head. *It’s okay*, he mouths back.

“Okay.” I nod at Josh and Ben, swallowing hard. “So let’s let the medics check her out when they arrive. If she’s good—which I think she is—how about some dinner?”

“Yes!” Evie and Josh speak in unison.

Laughing, they begin to walk away and toward the ambulance that’s just pulled up. Ben and I fall in behind them. Before we reach the driveway, I turn to Ben.

“Ben,” I place a hand on his forearm, stopping him. “Did you see what she did? I mean, did she actually do that?” I search his eyes for the answer.

“I don’t know, Gracie. I’ve never known. I’ve spent my life denying what my eyes saw and my heart believed.”

“What does your heart believe now?” My words are a whisper.

"I believe that we belong together. All of us. Home, together. And that whatever happens, whatever comes our way, we'll handle it together."

"Yes." We begin walking again, but then I stop and turn to him. "I'm sorry about that remark I made. The one about taking care of my child."

"Don't be." He shakes his head. "Believe me, Gracie, I understand."

Nodding, I drop my hand and smile. "Yes, I guess you would."

"Gracie." Ben sighs deeply. "You and I…" He points at Josh and Evie and then looks at me. "We have a long road ahead of us. I'm really glad we're on it together. No one I'd rather face the future with than you."

I smile at him, and he nods. Then Ben joins Louise as I run up to Josh and Evie. Evie is laughing with a young EMT as he checks her vitals.

She reaches out to him, and I hold my breath.

"You like this?" he asks, lifting his stethoscope from his blue shirt and slipping it off his neck. "Here." He places the ear tips into her ears and the chest piece on her heart. She squeals with happiness.

"Hear that?" he asks.

She nods.

"That's your heart. And it says you are perfectly healthy and all set." The EMT smiles at Evie as he takes his stethoscope back. Then he puts up a hand, and she high-fives him. "Just make sure you don't wander off from Mommy and Daddy again. Deal?"

She smiles. "Deal."

"All right. See you, Evie." He continues speaking as she runs up to us. "The fact that you all found her when you did… She's a lucky little girl. So many kids just wander off." He shakes his head and turns to Evie. "I hope you use that good fortune and grow up to change the world, all right, Evie?"

"She will," Josh assures him.

As the emergency personnel leave, I squat down next to Evie and brush her hair from her face, just as Mom used to do for me. Once again, my eyes well with tears.

"Mommy," she tells me. "Don't cry. Everything is okay."

"Everything is okay, Evie." I nod. "And I think everything will get a heck of a lot better. Thanks to you."

She scrunches up her face and then smiles. "Watch me!" She yells as she holds her arms to the sides and spins and spins again.

Ben runs up to her and scoops her up, swinging her up and down like a carousel horse. Josh takes me by the hand, and we stand together, unmoving and not making a sound.

I don't look at him when I speak. "I used to think it was us against fate."

"And now?"

I smile. "Now I think it's all of us. Making our own fate." I turn to Josh, looking up into his dark, smart eyes. "Fate didn't just choose *us*, did it? It chose a generation. And it's about damned time."

"Yes."

Ben swings Evie high and throws her over his shoulder in a practiced move. Giggling, she climbs up onto his shoulders as he balances her. They both fly their arms to the sides like airplanes as he carries her toward the house. We walk after them, hand in hand, lagging behind.

I stop and turn to Josh. “I’m sorry that I ever doubted you.”

“I doubted me, too.”

“I shouldn’t have.”

He reaches out and strokes my cheek gently. It feels so good I close my eyes. “All that matters now is that we teach her what fate has taught us. The most important lesson there is.”

I open my eyes and smile at him. “Love?”

He nods. “If love has the power to change our destiny, then Evie and her generation can change the world through the power of love.”

Without warning, he reaches out and pulls me onto his back. Laughing, I wrap my arms around his neck, and he lifts me higher into a piggy-back. Evie looks back at us and laughs. She taps Ben on the head, and he turns to us, too.

“Whatdaya say we catch them?” Josh asks.

“Okay,” I agree, grinning.

“Well then, hold on,” he tells me. “This is going to be quite a ride.”

“Don’t I know it,” I whisper.

Together, we take off across the beach, running after Evie and Ben.

A word about the author…

Cathrine Goldstein is a many-time bestselling author and award-winning playwright (including a win by Broadway World, Chicago for Best Streaming Play). Her poetry, short stories, and blog posts have been widely published, and her work has been featured on CNN, HLN; AOL; Jane Radio; and many additional television and radio shows.

A wife, mom, vegetarian, worm farmer, and tree hugger, Cathrine is also a speaker, a wellness coach, and a long-time yoga instructor/studio manager.

For more information, please visit: MyDharmicJourney.com and @mydharmicjourney. You can also find her at: CathrineGoldstein.com

Thank you for purchasing
this publication of The Wild Rose Press, Inc.

For questions or more information
contact us at
info@thewildrosepress.com.

The Wild Rose Press, Inc.
www.thewildrosepress.com

www.ingramcontent.com/pod-product-compliance
Lightning Source LLC
Chambersburg PA
CBHW072100020726
47501CB00003B/658

* 9 7 8 1 5 0 9 2 5 7 9 4 2 *